The
Deadman's
Curve

The
Deadman's
Curve

TAVORRIS ROBINSON

iUniverse, Inc.
Bloomington

THE DEADMAN'S CURVE

iUniverse books may be ordered through booksellers or by contacting:

iUniverse
1663 Liberty Drive
Bloomington, IN 47403
www.iuniverse.com
1-800-Authors (1-800-288-4677)

ISBN: 978-1-4620-4338-5 (sc)
ISBN: 978-1-4620-4339-2 (ebk)

Printed in the United States of America

iUniverse rev. date: 08/04/2011

"For every hustler suffering from ambition."

The Dead Man's Curve;

1. Treacherous curve of Interstate 90 near downtown Cleveland, OH. Infamous for being lethal if taken too fast.
2. The point in a plan or procedure where overall success of failure is dependent on the outcome.
3. A life or death gauntlet

CHAPTER 1

"Just doing my thing trying to get in where I fit in you know . . ."

-Chris

Staring out the window into the thunderous clouds and rain soaked streets he could only feel a certain familiarity with the vibe of the night. The beading drops running down the window pane reminded him of that fateful night in the early 90's that seemed to change everything. It was strange how what was so many years ago seemed like it was just yesterday.

"I don't know where that boys at!" Bird could hear Laura saying to Tyco as he entered the front door soaked in rain water. Of course that was before anyone knew of "Bird". Back then he was Lil' Chris, just a kid in the hood like any other trying to find and define himself, though Bird would be the nickname that many would come to know and respect, although few would ever learn the origin of it.

"Sorry I was with Ant." he replied, removing his rain drench garments. "What's up Tyco?

Laura jumped in before the two could begin a dialogue. "You almost made us late for the movies! And you know mama gone get on both us if you don't have that homework done before she gets home!"

"I know L, I'm sorry!" he responded with a slight smile. "I did the homework before I left though."

Laura being the loving sister she was always forgave him with just that smile. Six years older than him, she was the prototypical older sibling—always getting good grades and staying involved in something. She had just turned nineteen and started college. With their mother working twelve to fifteen hours a day she was more of a mother figure for him than a sister, but there was no sibling rivalry. Chris appreciated everything that she did for him and really tried his best to not let her down in any way. Standing 5' 5" with a strikingly beautiful smile and quick wit she was a magnet for attention from the opposite sex, which likely is what drew Tyco to her.

"So what's been going on Lil' Bird?" Tyco asked with a grin.

Chris didn't mind Tyco calling him by the same nickname that his family did. Especially after all he did for Laura. He was family in Bird's eyes. He was a key component in Laura being able to go to school, fronting the money for her tuition and taking care of her needs. Even with the five year age difference he was able to win their mothers blessing, which was nothing short of amazing to Chris. Big Tyco (as he was known in the streets) was a very well known hustler in the city let alone the area. There weren't many movers and shakers his age, and he and Laura seemed to have fused a special bond.

"Just doing my thing trying to get in where I fit in you know . . ." Chris said softly as to not let Laura hear him as she prepared for the two to leave. He knew she would have something to say if she did.

"Get in where you fit in?!" Tyco asked with a concerned tone.

He knew all too well what that meant being a product of the locale himself. Aside from being with Laura he had a taken a liking to Chris. Observing him and the other kids he ran with, Chris always stood out. He was astute for his age and a quick wit like his sister, having just the right balance of book sense and street smarts. He was quiet and observing, never saying too much or too little with just the right amount of edge to him. Tyco knew that all of his attributes would be worthless if Chris got in where he truly didn't fit in and before he even knew it, it'd be too late to get back out. That would not only hurt Laura, he thought, but it would also be a tragic waste of potential.

"Yeah you know . . . just doing what I can do." Chris replied ambiguously looking directly into Tyco's eyes.

He could tell that he was looking for a direct answer but Chris wasn't willing to give that until he knew where Tyco stood on the matter. Would he give the info to Laura who in turn would let their mother know of the possibility that Chris was hiding an unsavory lifestyle? Or would he lend some insight from experience of a world in which he had an abundance of?

"Alright Tyco, I'm ready.", Laura's voice bellowed as she made her way down the stair case rendering a stalemate to Chris and Tyco's mental chess match.

As the two made their way into the car Tyco couldn't shake thoughts of the verbal exchange that he had just had with Chris. Maybe there was more to him than meets the eye. The thoughts overwhelmed him to the point that he couldn't bring himself to pull off.

"Damn baby!" he said to Laura. "I've gotta use the bathroom right quick."

"Ok, well hurry before we don't make it!" she said handing him her keys.

Chris was sitting on the floor in his room counting money in a shoe box when Tyco opened the door. Both were stuck in silence for moment. With Chris sitting on the edge of his bed with what appeared to be two or three hundred dollars in his hand and a couple thousand in the box, an explanation wasn't necessary. Tyco broke the silence.

"Listen here," Tyco said strongly. "I'll be out the way the next couple of hours with your sister at this movie and there's some things I need handled while I'm away." He pulled a large Motorola out of his jacket pocket and tossed it into Chris's hands. He sat there, with his eyes gaping, a little taken aback by what was happening.

"You know Flex right?!" Tyco continued.

"Yeah." Chris attentively responded.

"Well that's my ace. I'll let him know you'll be assisting him for the next couple of hours so he'll hit you and give you details on that phone. Don't answer any number other than a 451 when it rings, you understand!?" Tyco rambled, giving Chris the crash course. "Take these keys", he said as he tossed the set into Chris's lap. "They're to a black Buick parked on Eddy Rd. When he calls go to him. Give him the black bag in the trunk under the spare tire and get your ass back in before your mother gets here! If anyone other than Flex calls that phone, take the battery out and break the phone. You understand!?"

Chris nodded as he made mental note of everything that was said. Before Tyco could say another word he was interrupted by the incessant honking of his cars horn. "Here take this . . ." Tyco said extending his hand to give Chris the .38 revolver that he had tucked in his waistband.

"I've got my own." Chris said blankly.

Looking down on the city streets through the window pane, entranced by his flash back he could still see Tyco's face at that very moment like it happened yesterday.

Tyco was visibly thrown off. It was hard for him to fathom that the mild mannered kid that he had watched had a much more sinister side to him. There was nothing more to say for Tyco. He quickly left the house and sped off down the block, still thinking about what had just transpired.

"Maybe Chris was just acting the roll to impress him?" he thought as he wrestled with the idea of moving forward with his plan to see what the deal with him really was.

Finally after entering the theatre and getting Laura settle Tyco excused himself to the concession stand. He just had to see if there was a more sinister individual underneath that unassuming demeanor. He stepped outside and made the call to Flex, keeping his monologue direct and to the point the managed to make it back inside before the opening scene began, content that he'd have the answer to his question regarding Chris by the end of the film.

Back at home Chris was experiencing a calm anxiety as he typically did when in high stakes situations. He always seemed stoic, almost unshakable in the most intense of moments. That ability would prove to serve him well throughout his life. As he was lacing up his shoes the phone rang.

"Hello?" he answered.

A dry deep voice responded from the other end, "The 72nd pier, thirty minutes." Click

The caller had hung up without question. But Chris was certain that it was Flex by the number and that this was the play. Flex was Tyco's muscle, and a very good one at that. He had a reputation that preceded him, enigmatic with an extremely efficient violent streak, yet smart and deliberate. Chris would keep that in mind in dealing with him as he grabbed his jacket and pistol and headed off into the night.

Everything was just as Tyco described it to him, an older model black Buick parked near the busy intersection. Growing up in the ghetto with friends like Lynx afforded certain luxuries and lessons, learning to drive being one of them. Lynx was Ant's nickname in the streets—he and his cousin Lindsey Saunders aka "Tuffy" were a couple of the wildest juveniles the courts had the displeasure of dealing with and an unlikely friendship that Laura despised.

Once inside the car, Chris quickly pulled away from the busy intersection and around the corner to a dim lit side street. He wanted to make sure that every light on the car was working properly so the police had no reason to even look in his direction with suspicion. Once satisfied everything was good, he was on his way.

The ride was a fairly quick one so Chris arrived with several minutes to spare. He slowly pulled into the lake front pier "Where were the quickest exits?" He thought to himself. As he continued looking a truck with a steely black figure inside masked behind window tint flashed its lights as if to signal him to the far end of the lot. It wasn't the safest spot in the lot in Chris's opinion with one way in one way out but he proceeded anyway. He pulled into a parking spot adjacent to the truck, took the pistol from his waistband then cocked it and placed it in his jacket pocket for easier access.

The figure stepped from the truck with a menacing presence. Standing about 6' 4" with a penitentiary build in all black he approached the Buick.

Chris stepped from the car to address him. As he got closer he could see more of the man's features, the thick beard and dead eyes with the cold stare as he continued his ominous approach. It indeed was Flex.

"What's good?" Chris said extending his hand to shake Flex's.

Flex glanced at his hand and immediately dismissed it. "Your jobs done shorty! Give me the keys to the car, and walk up to St. Clair and catch the bus home and Tyco will get with you." he said dryly to Chris.

Chris paused for a moment, feeling as if he was being shaken down. This wasn't the plan and there was no way he could walk up to St. Clair, catch a bus and still get home before his mother arrived.

"I can't do that!" Chris replied in a relaxed tone although with a lump in his throat as he looked into the abyss of Flex's eyes.

"What the fuck do you mean, you can't do that!" Flex growled as his chest swelled, visibly aggravated by the non-compliance.

It seemed as if this situation was about to turn volatile with a known killer, Chris was thinking as his heart began beat through his chest. Yet he maintained his stance, in that moment prepared for anything as the adrenaline raced through his veins. The two stood there for a moment, in a stare down. Chris had managed to slide his clammy palm inside his jacket undetected or so he thought and was gripping the revolver tightly.

"That's not what I was told to do. So that's not what's going to happen." he said sharply. "I don't have time to go back and forth with you so let's get this done."

He walked quickly to the trunk and opened it with Flex locked in his peripheral. He snatched the bag from the truck and returned. Flex was standing there still, his aggression quelled by Chris's take-charge attitude. Now he was just a willing participant observing the young boys movements. Chris motioned the bag toward Flex with his right arm while his left hand was aiming the barrel of his firearm through his jacket, unsure of the response his actions would gain.

Flex glanced Chris over before taking the bag. His trained eye had noticed the pistol in his pocket from the moment he stepped from the car. Flex snatched the bag from Chris's hand and told Chris to get back home and wait for Tyco to return. Chris hopped back into the black vehicle and rode off. As he got out of sight of Flex's truck he finally exhaled. The whole transaction which may have lasted five minutes seemed like an eternity, and he felt as if he had held his breathe the whole time.

Chris made it back home and had gotten settled long before his mother reached home. After their usual small talk about school and the likes, she was off to eat, bathe and go to bed as usual. Her job at a local cleaning company kept her near exhaustion with constant late hours and dreadful early mornings. Chris was downstairs on the couch when Laura and Tyco got back. Not much was said between the two then and there aside from a nod in completion of the job and Chris slyly handing the keys back to Tyco while Laura had her back turned.

Chris didn't know what to think. Had he botched the trial run by complicating things and not going along with Flex's demands? It wasn't until he received a call from Tyco about a week later that the journey would truly begin.

That same child-like grin came to Bird's face as he stared out the window pane, his thoughts trapped in a season captured by time, reminiscing on the moment he found that the whole confrontation with Flex was staged. Tyco had wanted to see how he would react, a test of sorts. Needless to say he passed it with flying colors. Unbeknownst to him at that time this small segment in his life would alter the course of his future.

Bird paused, his moments of remembrance partially disrupted by the sound of the tumbler in his locks twisting, and heels entering in. Taking another sip from his glass he dismissed it and continued to stare out the window into the past.

The next year or so after that fateful phone call from Tyco, Chris spent mirroring Flex. In being around him Chris was given the rare glimpse into the mind of what some in the medical field would call a psychotic, but Chris would come to understand and respect the method behind the madness immensely after learning the story of the man.

Flex was originally from New Orleans, an orphan from birth. Spending years in and out of foster care made him naturally emotionally displaced. Never knowing where home may be and whom with only added reclusiveness to his already introverted personality. That was until he was placed in the home of an elderly woman who went by the name of Ms. Etta. Elderly and widowed she gave him the nurturing and love that he'd desperately craved his whole young life. He began to excel in school although the tribulations of trying to overcome social barriers that he had built up over the years still brought setbacks. In light of everything Ms. Etta's patience and understanding remained constant, that was until her sudden death when he was fifteen. Flex then drifted into despair, running away rather than being placed back into the system. He built the rationale that his intelligence and observing nature would never be able to outshine his beginnings in the world which frustrated him, and as he grew older manifested itself in the form of ever increasingly violent acts. After three years of constant trouble in Louisiana he headed north to Cleveland, seeking his birth fathers remaining family only to see first-hand the tree from which his father fell was withering and dead inside as well. He was convinced that he was cursed from the beginning, which oddly gave him a sense of peace. Flex's philosophy was that there was only one purpose to live by which was survival, and when we can't any longer we die. In his words, "Until then you do the best you can with what you have to work with."

Once rooted in the city it wasn't long before him and Tyco would meet and over time forge an unbreakable bond of loyalty.

Once closer to the action Chris could see the operation for what it was. Flex wasn't only muscle but Tyco's friend and partner. Tyco would later tell Chris that the only reason he decided to make the call was because Flex liked his heart. Given his background disputes came far and few between, usually ending without incident and generally in his favor. To see the young boy stand strong in a way most men couldn't made Flex take a liking to the him, and for the better part of the next year of his life he spent what time he wasn't in school running with Flex. But he was also adamant that Chris attended, no matter what transpired in other areas of his life. In that same year so much had taken place. The most major was Laura getting pregnant by Tyco and giving birth to a son, Shawn Ellis aka Lil Tyco.

With the birth of Shawn everything changed in a blink of an eye, and Tyco's desire to change his lifestyle became ever clearer. Within three months of his birth, Tyco bought a house away from the city and he and Laura got married, quieting whatever argument her mother could foster for taking a hiatus from her education. Then to everyone's surprise Tyco purchased a recently closed Burger King with the vision of having Ms. Clark run the food service business that she had always dreamed of with Laura managing the business. He'd front the money to get the business off the ground and from there expand. This could be the out that he needed. After all the years of hustling he was seemingly near the end and his happy ending. Anxious to bring his dream to reality Big Tyco decided to shift things into high gear and sprint to the finish.

Upon entering high school, he was no longer addressed as Chris Clark, only as Bird. His slender frame had grown and filled out. Staying fresh was a must now with the girl's eyes wandering and choosing. Bird kept his low tapered brush waves flowing with his nightly doo rags and weekly cuts. As one could only expect his interactions and affiliations with Flex afforded him a reputation of his own, his demeanor now well exceeding his years. Once there he had time to reconnect with Lynx and Tuffy and though no love was lost in the hiatus between him and Lynx, Tuffy still held on to some deep seated resentment. It was so strong that Bird could feel it, even though it was never displayed outwardly. Maybe it was because he and Lynx always meshed so tight and Tuffy felt as if he was a third wheel when he was around? Or maybe it was because Flex took to him so strong, it was common knowledge that he idolized Flex's dangerous rep, hence his nickname. But he disregarded it as simple envy, which he got more than his fair share of. Driving to school in one of Tyco's cars didn't help much either, but still he tried to keep as low a profile as possible. Being back with Lynx would prove to be a good thing with Tyco moving faster than ever before and his mother consuming money at an alarming rate with her new entrepreneurial endeavor. The timing was just right for Bird to establish his own team.

CHAPTER 2

"If things go wrong I want you to come here and get this."

-Flex

Lynx and Tuffy would be the perfect foundation. Lynx was his ace and Tuffy would follow him without a shadow of a doubt. Neither were strangers to the streets and the reality was neither had much of a future outside of them either. The plan was simple. Chris would be the point man to the supply, Lynx the mover and Tuffy the muscle. Once the proposal was made Lynx was immediately on board and as anticipated Tuffy followed.

For the first few months things went like clockwork. Big Tyco was grinding hard to replenish what had been spent during the initial euphoria of his grand epiphany. To build a business the right way wasn't cheap and that meant the cocaine would be flowing steadily for him to rebound. In the meanwhile Flex and Bird were busy making sure everything went smoothly in the area of distribution. With a consistent flow, Bird was now also able to buy in on packages for his team. That meant wholesale overhead for Lynx to work. Before long they had a strong network going. Indeed the team was prospering so well that even Tuffy's attitude had shifted into one of contentment. All was well until the pipeline was disrupted.

All of a sudden the well ran dry. It was soon discovered that a few sealed indictments had been served to major players, stopping all business. But Tyco was too close to his goal to stop and a drought might be just what he needed to recover even faster. Through his name he was able to find what appeared to be the next best option, in a Jamaican connect from New York. The islander's were supposed to be the temporary cure until things opened back up. Flex didn't like the idea of dealing with the new comers at such a high volume without any background on them but went against his better judgment, a decision that would change everyone.

The first couple of packages were ok. They were nothing spectacular, as to be expected, but good enough to supply the demand. Within six weeks the quality went through the basement, to the degree that the bottom tier sellers and users both were complaining about the procaine laden product that was coming from Big Tyco's team. But Tyco took it in stride and viewed it solely as part of the game. After talking to Flex he decided to scale back purchasing while he sought out another connect. Instead of the usual eight bricks they scaled back to five in the next order. Bird's team was in dire need to stay afloat and decided to add in another brick for good measure. Seeing as how quality was only getting worse and worse it was only logical to try to get enough to hold them off for a couple of weeks until things got better.

Bird made the drop off and pick up as he had the previous trips and headed back to the safe house.

Flex did his usual inspection and break down and within three hours they were off to work. It wasn't until later that night that the streets had finally gotten the merchandise when the problems arose. Bird's pager was the first to buzz with a call from Lynx.

"What the fuck is going on Birdie!" Lynx said when he answered.

"What the hell are you talking about?!" Bird replied in a half-sleep stupor.

"The shit's not coming back! It's not doing anything!" Lynx said in a muffled tone. Bird instantly came to his senses. It couldn't be what he thought it was. His first reaction was to hang up and call Tyco.

"Tyco just jumped out of bed and went somewhere after his phone rang . . ." a groggy Laura said from the other end of the phone.

"Shit!" Bird thought as he jumped up threw some sweats on and headed out. As soon as he exited the door Flex was turning the corner. "Get in!" he shouted.

Bird quickly hopped in. "You got the word too?!" he asked.

"Yeah." Flex said calmly. Bird had seen him like this enough times to know what was coming next. They sped through the city streets to the freeway in route to the stash house. The ride was quiet and seemed to take forever. Bird knew that it would probably be the last bit of peaceful silence for a while. The ride to the far Mayfield Heights apartments was completely silent aside from the radio.

Contrary to the movies that depict stash houses deep in the heart of the ghetto crawling with thugs, guns and pit bulls the opposite was usually case. The apartment building was located in an upper-middle class suburb with an abundance of shopping plazas which made for traffic to blend into and extra police presence as a deterrent for would-be robbers.

Once off the elevator the two headed towards the apartment door, it swung open with Tyco behind it hurrying them inside and shutting the door behind them. He was livid as he paced the floor back and forth and Flex went into the hidden safe to get the remaining kilo for testing. He quickly returned dropping the tightly wrapped and duct taped package on the island in the eating area. Without hesitation Tyco cut through the covering with a razor, dug in with his pinky and prepared to take a sniff. Out of all the transactions that had gone down it was Bird's first time seeing Tyco snort. He stood there—his usually unflappable façade showing his confusion in the moment.

"WHAT?!" he said as he raised his finger to his nose to take the first toot. "It's only one way to really test this shit nigga!" SNIFF

Bird could hear the sound of feet slowly creeping across the floor in the other room. He reached down the window sill, picked up the .45 Springfield XD, cocked it and placed it back on the sill directly in front of him. Smiling to himself as visions of the moment after Tyco's first toke came racing back into his mind's eye.

"What the FUCK!" he exclaimed pawing his nose like a puppy that sniffed some black pepper. "Them dirty muthafucka's iced us!" he screamed referring to the Miami Ice the islanders gave them instead of cocaine. Flex instantly went into the bedroom and returned with the arsenal that he kept hidden there. Tyco was on the phone instantly with the Dreads being as that he was the only one in direct communication with them thus far. But that would change now and talks would take a drastic change in nature—even more so after the talk between he and Tyco went sour.

Flex immediately began to get his resources together to get a line on the Jamaicans and their operation. In doing so the detailed plot that they had established became exposed. They were plotting to take over the city with their own crew by working their way into the cityscape by wholesaling. Once they got in deep enough they began systematically cutting the cocaine more and more to drive the customers away from their purchasers, ultimately planning to cut everyone off and sell straight to the fiends themselves. Tyco and his crew just happened to be the first—a decision that would prove costly. Flex used the double-cross as training class of sorts for Bird and his cohorts sending them out into the night as gunners, hunting down targeted rivals. It wasn't difficult to turn impressionable ghetto youth into ruthless killers. Living a life of simple survival made the loss of livelihood enough to suppress their feelings and emotions, making the elimination of the Jamaicans a game of necessity for them. It was a game which Tuffy enjoyed every minute of, getting sadistically brutal. With different hustlers around the city getting word of the attempt to starve them, information to the whereabouts of the West Indian faction poured in. It wasn't long before they pulled out of the city and Bird and his crew's reputation swelled to infamy.

It was during then that he met Sheena Jackson, known around as She-She. They were the same age when they met, her the product of a home of addicts and junkies. By all accounts she was a pretty young girl, light-brown caramel skin and slender hippy frame, but the underlying issues bore many demons. Unlike most in her situation who detested their circumstances, she embraced them. Her rough up upbringing and contrasting beauty made her pit-bull in a skirt. Bird's first interaction with her would come via a drug transaction of all things. She was as real as they came, standing by the G-Code closer than most of his male counterparts. Toughened by her circumstances, yet twice as attractive as she was hard, Sheena was a certified go-getter in her own right. She could never see herself as that spoiled trophy chick of some hustler as she easily could have been. She preferred being in the mix—a lover of the grit and grime of the streets, a self proclaimed "Gangsta Bitch".

It only took a couple of encounters before the attraction had grown to be overwhelming. She hustled hard. Eighth here, quarter there, all the while maintaining a sexy femininity. Bird had never seen anything like her—feminine, yet raw and intense. Before long they would begin building a relationship that would last far longer than either anticipated.

"Maybe it was his mind-state at that point in his life", he thought to himself as he sipped from his tumbler. Running with Tyco and Flex, getting his own money coupled with the soured dealings with the Jamaican's and what ensued after had changed him. Not only had he seen what to most was unfathomable, he'd also done it. Partaking in things that are only comprehendible to society through scenes of suspense filled dramas and gangster movies. All this gave Bird an added seriousness and dark mystique to his already calm confident demeanor. Quite possibly that stable sensibility, yet crime filled essence is what drew Sheena into him. Whatever the catalyst was, the two would soon become inseparable.

The game had gotten back on track since the debacle with the West Indians. As promised Tyco had found a replacement supplier, this time one that would take him deeper than ever before. His new plug was straight from Mexico. Quality was no longer an issue, so product usually went as quickly as it came.

In the midst of all the drama Tyco had still managed to bring the restaurant to its inaugural run. Business was very slow though, yet he had managed to get back on his feet financially and still subsidize the losses with his ill-gotten gains just as he had planned. Cleaning his money as he went by funneling it through the restaurant, it appeared as if Tyco might just make it to his happy ending virtually unscathed after all.

But Murphy's Law and fate would prove to be a couple not easily divided.

During the heavily embroiled battles in the streets with the Islanders and from the drought that developed as a result, inner lying cities were forced to utilize U.S. Marshalls, Sheriffs and State Police to bolster their cash strapped police forces. This in itself brought a whole new array of problems for those in the game. Marshalls weren't bound by the imaginary city and county lines, so they were everywhere. The guise of moving freely, hidden from radar by bureaucratic red tape was slowly dissipating as information flowed more smoothly between state, federal and local departments. In the prior four months the indictments which began as a slow trickle suddenly flooded in hitting the city like a tsunami. No one knew just how immersed the city was in crime until news of the stings and raids made press almost weekly, so much so that a new federal building was quickly erected, giving them permanent residence.

Some hustlers fled the city as things tightened up, fearing being named by an informant. Others adapted as Tyco and his team did. He was too close to his goal to stop short. Maybe he should have?" Bird thought to himself, in hind sight. His mood took a sobering swing.

The Mexican connect was a serious coup. Tyco had gotten up the chain of command with his alliance with them, getting a better price and better quality. Only problem was the erratic nature of the shipments, which irritated both he and Flex. Packages were sporadic to say the least not to mention typically in volumes much less than what was anticipated, which couldn't have come at worse time. Now it had become a race against time for Tyco. Undoubtedly his name and picture were clipped to a folder on some agent's desk awaiting its turn, as indictments hit closer and closer to home. He would never divulge to Bird, or the world for that matter, what he was feeling like he did to Flex. But Bird easily recognized the mounting tension and restlessness.

Flex would finally lay everything out for Bird one night at his apartment, keeping it one hundred as he always had done before. He couldn't believe what Flex told him. Tyco was contemplating hijacking the entire next shipment and making his exodus. His nerves were shot. Any echo in his cell or a car that appeared to trail for too many blocks only fueled his paranoia. The rest of the night they discussed the in's and out's of such a move. Flex didn't think it was a smart idea by far, but deep inside wanted to see Tyco make it out as much as he did himself, even if it meant his closest friend in the world might fall. He'd just fall with him.

Seeing an emotionless killer visibly compromised by what was on the horizon and the reality that his demise may have been near gave Bird an eerie feeling that he would never forget. The events that followed would only second the emotion. Flex motioned Bird to follow him towards the master bathroom to the medicine cabinet. As he stood there still deciphering what was happening, Flex twisted a couple of hinges and slid the shelving out revealing a hidden space filled with cash.

"If things go wrong I want you to come here and get this." he told Bird referring to the bundles of cash in the wall.

"Man everything's going to be good." he replied with his charming smile in attempt to lighten the uncomfortable mood. Flex stared unmoved.

"Just do what the fuck I said." he replied matter-of-factly. Bird confirmed with a simple nod of his head. Flex put the shelving back in place and the two walked back downstairs and sat at the island in the kitchen to discuss the plan in further detail.

Two hours later Bird was leaving with a full perspective of what was at hand and the hazards of the move. To rob a connect without being suspected was difficult under typical circumstances, so this endeavor was destined to create a tumultuous situation, if not a total disaster. It had to happen with a certain degree of anonymity and ambiguity. Meaning Flex and Tyco would have to be completely out of the way with absolutely no direct involvement. No witnesses could be left, but the scene had to be an organized mess as not to allude to a professional move. Meaning strategic evidence had to be left, just enough to give the police a lead to a dead-end. The Cartel on the other hand would naturally suspect Tyco and a few select others they had dealt with in the region with capability and enough balls to attempt such a feat. Bird went back and forth in his mind over the best way to make things happen with as few complications as possible. One thing was certain, Tyco was definitely going to go through with it, if not with Bird with someone else and if successful it would be the coup of a lifetime. He pondered all of the outcomes and angles. With Tyco quitting and burning the supplier in the process, he'd be cut off as well. Rather than being left behind the money train he decided to be on it. And with that the decision was made to go through with it.

Bird corralled his team and gave them the rundown of the information pertinent to them about the play. Business would go on as usual as far as the drop and exchange. Then they'd wait until the weekend giving them enough time to round up any other monies from the area before exporting it out. It was then that would be the best time to strike. Considering that beef was almost inevitable, it was the common consensus amongst them to leave no survivors as well. And so the stage was set.

Just as planned business went forth with the next drop. Ironically it was a great batch of work, to Tyco's joy. The quality of the work would make the move all that much more profitable.

The following Saturday the plan was underway. Sheena had been staking out the Mexican's location since trailing them to a freshly renovated two-story house on the city's Westside. Located in an area densely populated with other Hispanic's they blended right in and traffic went relatively unnoticed. Being that it was only three streets from the freeway made it ideal for moving large amounts of merchandise fast.

Bird was a great student of the game who observed everything and internalized it. Sheena was instructed to make the call when the consistent traffic had slowed to a halt. The decreased traffic would be means to draw less attention and a clear sign that most the money had been retrieved and a move was imminent.

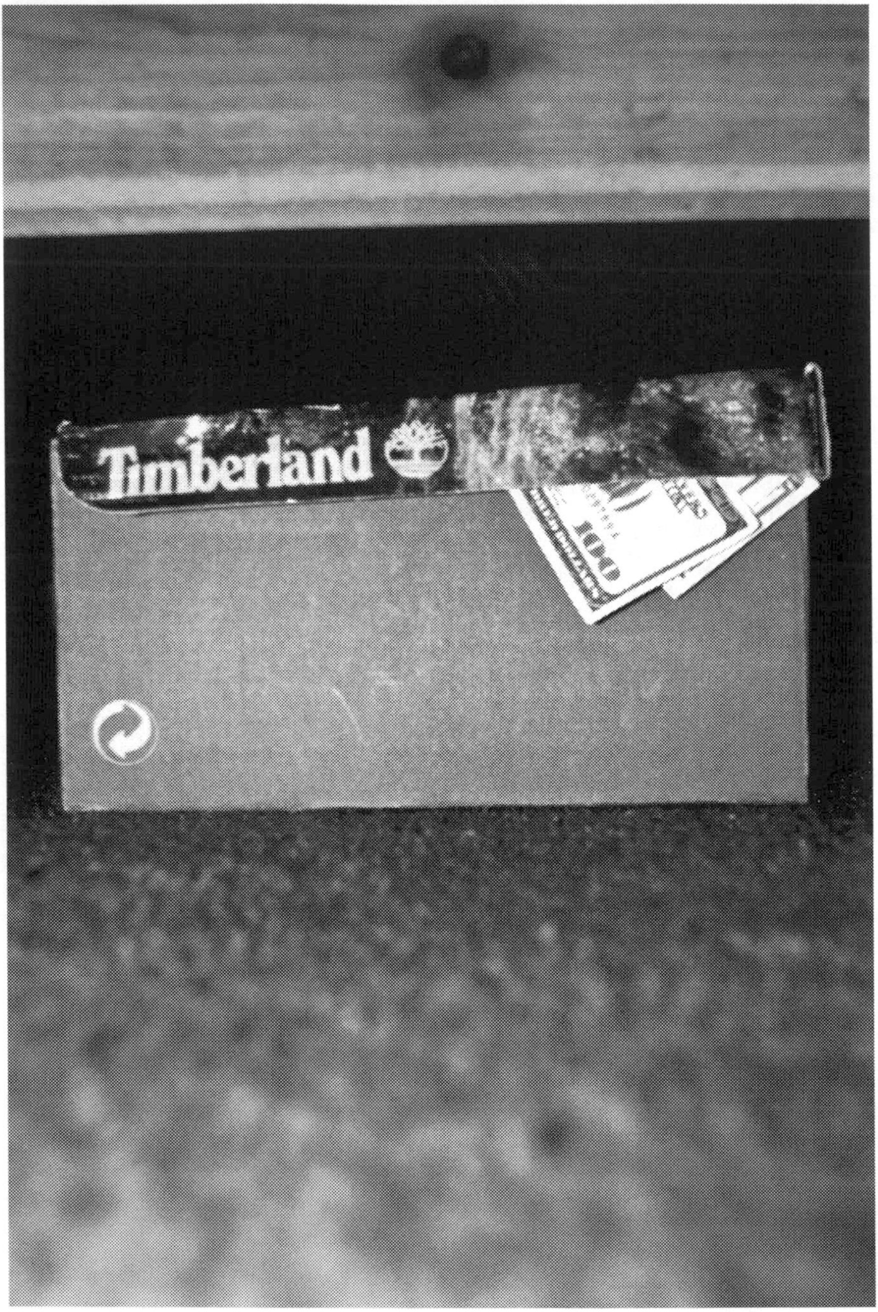
Timberland

CHAPTER 3

"I'ma get what the fuck we got sent here for . . ."

-Tuffy

Everyone was on standby when the call came in to Bird. "Its slowed down baby, I think it's time." she said from the other end. Bird immediately got himself situated and in route. Benji, Birds cousin from Chicago would be wheel-man and backup for this move. He was a few years older than Bird and had come to Cleveland in search of a less troublesome existence, and was his last remaining tie to his fathers' side of the family. But he also was one of the most solid and reliable people Bird knew.

Like clockwork the black Yukon pulled up and Bird hopped in. A text came through, "Eddy Rd". He instructed Benji to head there where a flash of the high beams prompted Lynx and Tuffy to exit their vehicle and get in the truck. As they all headed to the freeway Bird sent confirmation to Sheena, "20 minutes".

The trip was quiet as everyone mentally prepared for what was to take place. Everyone but Tuffy, rapping to himself while talking shit in between, seemingly amped to do the deed before them. Before long the truck was exiting the off ramp and everyone began gathering themselves. Again Bird sent Sheena a text, "Go". She knew that this meant to meet them around the corner from her location, which she was doing as the truck slowly backed into the yard of an empty brick house with a Smythe Cramer sign in the front yard. The house was almost directly behind the target which would make for inconspicuous entry.

"So far so good." Bird thought to himself at that moment. "Maybe all the reluctance was for nothing?"

The quartet quieted evacuated the truck—dressed in all black and masked they each took turns sliding through a small gap in the fence that separated the two yards behind the garage.

The group of youngsters moved like a swat unit, converging quietly on the back of the house, covering the rear and side exits. The trap was set, now all that was left was to wait for someone to exit, snatch them up and re-enter with the element of surprise.

After an hour of patience, Tuffy decided that enough was enough. He whispered over to Bird as they knelt hidden under the camouflage of darkness and foliage.

"I'm going in soon! Tuffy said in an agitated tone. We can't wait forever nigga!

Bird knew that to some degree he was right, but not at the moment. "Slow down nigga! He scolded. "We'll be in there soon enough . . ." Just as the two began to drift into a spirited debate the door creaked open and slender figure began to emerge out of the darkness. Luckily Lynx was undistracted by the two and moved in from the backside of the house followed by Benji.

Before the door could lock closed Lynx had the barrel of his Ruger to the man's temple, arm around his neck in a choke hold. In an instant Bird and Tuffy snapped out of their riff and back into reality, rushing in to cover Lynx as he forced the man back in the entryway. Music could be heard playing loudly as they made they their way up the dark stairwell. Lynx made sure to apply just enough pressure with his choke hold that there could be no yelling to forewarn the others in the house. Bird's skin was tingling as his instincts took him over knowing the moment that they reach the landing and were in clear view of the kitchen bullets would likely begin to fly. In an instant they stormed through the door off of the kitchen. To Birds surprise they indeed had caught them off guard, as they were sitting at a table in a small nook of the kitchen eating.

Before they could react Tuffy rushed over, striking the man closest to him square over the eye with the butt of his pistol before yanking him from his seat and throwing him to the floor. Benji followed him up with is MAC-10 subduing the other simply by instructing him to the floor while covering Tuffy as he zip-tied both and stuffed their mouths.

"Clear the upstairs after that." Bird said to Tuffy and Benji. "You check the basement," he motioned at Lynx. "And I'll search down here."

Bird was in think tank mode while quickly perusing the lower level of the house. Reaching living room closet it was evident that they had impeccable timing, finding that some of the money was already bagged up and probably awaiting transport. The fact that there was no rental car there yet struck him as odd. He took it as a sign that someone was likely headed there. In Bird's mind the clock was running on getting in and out and the quicker the better. So far not a shot had to be fired and their identities hadn't been compromised.

"Let's grab this shit and get the fuck outta here!" Bird yelled to the others as he grabbed one of the three duffle bags and threw it over his shoulder. As he made his way back to the kitchen . . . "POP" . . . "POP" . . . two shots went off. Gun drawn Bird ran into the kitchen, only to see one of the corralled men shot twice in the head, Tuffy standing over him straddled, gun still smoking.

"Why the fuck did you do that!?" Bird screamed enraged.

"These muthafucka's won't tell where the fuckin' work at!" Tuffy yelled back simply. "I'ma get what the fuck we got sent here for nigga, by any means!"

The race to get out of the house was now in the red zone. Not only had shots been fired, but there would no doubt be another visitor soon to pick the money up.

"You fuckin' trippin', the money's already on the floor . . . . fuck the dope!" Bird said clinching the pistol tightly in his hand.

"Who the fuck you yelling at!?" Tuffy gritted his teeth, his body tensing.

Before the moment could reach critical Lynx grabbed Tuffy by the shoulder and pulled him with away. "Ain't no time for that shit y'all on! Let's check the upstairs and get the fuck out of here!" Lynx said as the two headed up the stairs off the kitchen.

Bird was absolutely livid standing in the kitchen with Benji and the two remaining hostages, one of which was begging profusely for his life, the other cursing them. Before he could gather his thoughts to speak all hell broke loose.

Shots rang out from what seemed like every room upstairs. Bird and Benji took cover as Lynx came backpedaling down the stairs off the kitchen returning fire. Tuffy managed to make it down the stairs that led to the living room, diving behind the loveseat before returning fire back.

What likely was fifteen seconds seemed like twenty minutes as the shots subsided. Bird made his way over to Lynx who was also holed up behind the wall adjacent to the kitchen now.

"How many people up there?!" Bird asked.

"Just one!" Lynx exclaimed. "He was waiting on us when we hit the door!"

With more goons or police likely in route the red zone had become the dead zone, being that the arrival of either before they departed would make an unscathed escape unlikely. Survival and freedom were both dangerously in jeopardy.

The Mexican voice upstairs yelled out, "You all going to die!" in a thick accent.

Bird went over to the corner of the wall closest to the kitchen door. Glancing around the corner he saw Benji, held up in the corner of the nook trying to avoid being struck by the random shots, while the two hostages were feverishly attempting to undo their trappings.

"We gotta get that bread and get the fuck out of here! Cover me . . ." he said to Lynx as he darted into the living room.

The cease fire was by no means caused by a lack of ammo, as the moment he was in sight of the stairwell near the closet shots again began raining down from upstairs. With cover fire from himself and Lynx, he was able to recover the duffle bag and make it back to the cover of the wall, but not before noticing Tuffy peering from behind the couch as he made his way back, his gun clutched in his palm yet silent. In that split second time almost stood still, the expression on his face glaring with anticipation as if he was waiting to see Bird's body riddled with the bullets raining down from above.

In that very moment it was if time slowed to a crawl and Tuffy's contempt radiated out through his eyes and enraged Bird to his core. But it would have to wait to be addressed as the priority was to safely get away with the botched heist.

"Let's go!" He told Lynx as he reached the safety of the wall. He responded with a nod of his head, before heading opposite of Bird to lay cover for Tuffy to escape his foxhole behind the couch. Bird was still furious inside as he duck-walked back to the doorway of the kitchen, only to see that one of the Mexicans had managed to partially free himself and was attempting to free his cohort. Bird exorcised his fury unloading on the two rapidly, until the bodies collapsed, life slowly escaping them. The firing from the stairwell subsided with a slew of profanities in Spanish after Bird's slaughter of the two men.

"Let's go NOW!" He screamed again. Everyone was ready at attention now—all except for Benji who was slumped in the corner. In the midst of all the chaos Bird hadn't noticed that he'd been hit.

"Aw Shit!" He cried as he ran over to his fallen comrade as the other two scampered out of the door. "Get up!"

Benji gathered himself to his feet at the request. "It's my shoulder Birdie . . . shits pretty bad . . ." He slowly spoke in obvious pain. Bird barely had an opportunity to wrap Benji's good arm around his shoulder before he heard the screech of car tires outside.

"Fuck!" Bird yelled. "Police always show up fast when you don't want them to!" He thought to himself. For a brief moment fear and the reality of plausible outcomes fought to gain their way into the front of Bird's mind yet he managed to quell his doubts and focus on the escape.

Quickly they made their way to the exit at the landing of the small staircase at the side door. No sooner than Bird stepped out of the doorway a bullet flew past his face. Instinctively he returned fire; two shots, while staying low and dragging Benji with him to the cover of the adjacent house.

This wasn't the police, firing first wasn't their style and after return fire they'd quickly have unloaded their weapons. They were the Mexicans reinforcements!

Bird knew he had to move fast, with the police he could stall and be strategic, as they were limited by the laws. With the Hispanic muscle it was pure guerilla tactics. The flurry of bullets recommenced as Bird began dragging Benji through the underbrush toward the garage. Down to his last couple of shot, Bird knew it was only a matter of time before they would be hit if they couldn't return cover fire. As he fired his last shot, a shadowy figure emerged from behind the garage directly in his path and fired what seemed like a hundred shots continuously. It was Lynx, he had come back!

"Come on B!" He yelled as he emptied the semi-automatic MAC 10. The sudden rush of adrenaline seemed to energize both Bird and Benji as he they got their footing and jogged to the getaway vehicles. As they did they could hear the gun battle take a different twist as the police flocked to the house. Bird had never been so happy to hear sirens in his life. Tuffy was already inside with Sheena as they ran up. "What the fuck?" A breathless Bird exclaimed. "Why you in there? She's taking the guns remember!?"

"Man we might as well leave the guns in that hot ass truck and all bounce together nigga!" Tuffy replied.

"Ain't enough room you dumb fuck and Benji's hit . . ." Bird said.

"No time to argue B! Get in! Let Ben take the truck!" Lynx said as he hopped in.

"Man fuck y'all, I ain't leaving him here!" Bird said as he made his way to the truck and pushed Benji into the back. Sheena sped out of the driveway headed south and Bird quickly went north, still seething from all that had just happened. Disbelief would be an understatement in describing what consumed his thoughts.

"How could Lynx leave him hanging, and even though he came back, how could he divert from the plan with Tuffy?! He pondered. "Even still how could Sheena?! And Tuffy . . . ." Bird had made up his mind that he was as good as dead, as his inner rage grew.

Remain cool he thought to himself as Benji writhed in pain behind him. "Think . . . think . . ." he thought to himself. He needed to get to a hood hospital quickly, that way a random shooting could be easily explained away, but first he would have to make it there in a stolen truck full of guns out of an area that had just bore witness to something reminiscent of a Hype Williams film.

Benji had lost a lot of blood by the time they reached the hospital and was drifting back and forth from consciousness. Bird talked to him the whole ride, giving him the play by play of their statement for the authorities hoping he'd retain it in his state.

Miraculously they made it safely and Ben survived, actually managing to retain the story that Bird had relayed to him. It was rather comforting finally being able to exhale as the ordeal had seemed to draw to a close. It wasn't until watching the news from the hospital waiting area and hearing the broadcaster interrupt himself with breaking news of it all that reality again struck him squarely.

"*Authorities have three individuals in custody, in what appears to have been a botched drug deal that turned a local neighborhood into an all out warzone . . . .*" The news anchor announced.

"Fuck!" Bird grunted under his breath. It was all bad now with the direct connection to Tyco being inevitable with the apprehension of Lynx, Tuffy and Sheena.

So many times during periods of retrospect Bird would be brought back to this moment. It seemed like the slip up of the getaway completely altered the future.

At that moment knowing that Benji was ok gave him a little clearer mind, enough that he could begin to sort things out. With him safe in care Bird immediately turned his attention to ditching the getaway ride and alerting Tyco. Walking through the hospital to the truck he methodically plotted out his next move one after the other like a grand-master of chess would. First order of business was to reach Tyco or Flex.

Once back in the truck Bird drove to a safer more low-key side street where he could gather himself. Searching for a cell phone he realized that in switching the plan, his partners in crime had damned themselves. Although they had thrown most the weaponry in, they had forgotten to take their personal belongings. That meant no cell phones and no identification in the event of a stop, which also equated to probable cause to search the vehicle.

Taking a visual inventory of the tools used in the caper to make sure everything got properly disposed of—Bird realized that one was absent. "During all the confusion Lynx must have forgotten to throw the gun that he had used to save Bird into the truck like Tuffy had." He thought to himself. Whatever the case, things had taken a toll for the worst that no one had anticipated.

Bird grabbed his cell and feverishly attempted to contact Tyco, "*the voicemail box is full at this time and cannot accept messages.*" Then Flex, "*this phone has a voicemail box that has not been setup, goodbye.*" In Bird's mind he knew something was wrong then, but kept telling himself otherwise.

In the meanwhile he made his way to the scrap yard owned by one of Tyco's old buddies named Virgil. An ex-hustler turned scrap man after his bid, he knew the game. He and Tyco went way back, so he'd take the truck, scrap it out, and crush it with the contents in it with no questions.

With that taken care of Bird knew he had to get out of plain sight to see and hear everything that was going on. By late morning he'd taken care of the necessary business and gotten home. It felt strange sitting still, the pace of his life usually being so hectic that his bed felt alien to him. With a restless mind, sleeping was nearly impossible. He had been so consumed with the darker side of his life lately that he'd almost completely forgotten that graduation was only ten days away until Laura had called expressing her excitement. Running with friends he had long given up any attempt at a typical education, often pushed it to the rear of his mind, but Tyco and Flex always insisted that he go. As their conversation ended, her inquiry into Tyco's whereabouts brought Bird's mind back to his dilemma. It also brought to mind the fact that he'd neglected to inspect the duffle bag he'd taken from the heist.

After fifteen minutes of counting the rubber band bundled stacks, he totaled the take. One hundred seventy-five thousand dollars. "One hundred seventy-five thousand dollars, for a million dollars worth of fucking trouble!" He kept thinking to himself. After splitting the money between them the whole thing was pointless and that was even if things had went smoothly. Taking into consideration all that was going on now it was an exercise in futility.

With no line of communication to anyone, letting the smoke clear seemed to be the most sensible approach. He only could hope that his senior partners had chosen to do the same.

The days following were tumultuous as things continued to unravel and the depth of damage slowly came to be realized. Two days had passed and still no word or sign of Tyco or Flex, and Sheena, Lynx and Tuffy all had a host of charges against them in connection with the robbery and slayings and were being held over without bond.

Aside from Benji, who was still recovering, Bird was a lone wolf and the streets were chattering with different adaptations of what happened and why. Paranoia struck him hard and heavy as he ran through every plausible outcome in his mind. On top of everything else he had been dodging calls from Sheena and Lynx.

"To communicate with them could possible implicate him in what happened, and with all of them in lock-up there'd be no one to help any of their situations." He rationalized. There was no one to trust with transferring information. He decided until their release Bird would have to fade to black for a while or at least until he could find a great attorney to sort things out.

CHAPTER 4

"Well when he does you be sure to tell him to catch up with us before we catch up with him, alrighty?"

-Detective Blake

Still staring through his reflection in the pane, seemingly backwards through time, Bird's head dropped and a tear gently formed as his memory came to events that he had long repressed. It was a Monday, four days before graduation when he learned the definition of Murphy's Law. Bird was still playing the background, sifting through different lawyers when everything changed instantly.

Worried about Tyco, Laura had been staying over for help with caring for Shawn and also to be close to the area in hopes some word would turn up. That day a soul piercing scream came from the front door, followed by uncontrollable crying. Bird hurried to the door only to see Laura being consoled by what he instantly recognized as a homicide detective. He slumped against the wall, his back sliding down it as his legs gave way to shock. The commotion from becoming a bastard woke Shawn who was asleep on the couch. Seeing his mother and uncle in such distress he instinctively began crying while racing over to her. Bird watched almost entranced, his nephew hugging Laura's leg tightly, beckoning her to pick him up to comfort him. It seemed surreal, like a scene befitting a movie.

Bird finally got himself together and coerced Laura to take herself and the baby to their mother's room while he gathered information on what happened.

"So what happened?" Bird said as he approached the Detectives at the door.

"Are you related to the deceased?" The larger of the two responded back instantaneously.

"Yeah, I am." He replied aggravated by what seemed to be a senseless question.

The other detective opened the leather carrier he held and began rambling off the details.

"Approximately five days ago dispatch sent officers to the scene of a reported burning vehicle in the east bound lane of Interstate ninety at Dead Man's Curve" he stated. "Some type of incendiary had been used, presumably kerosene making the fire to hot to be extinguished. After it burned itself out the body was found and they later identified the deceased as Tyco Ellis."

Bird could only stand there, stone as the words came from the detectives mouth. In his heart he had known all along that something wasn't right. It wasn't like Tyco to go cold for so long, not even returning a call. He just never anticipated retribution would be so swift.

Seems Tyco's paranoia was justified all the way around. It was obvious as the questioning progressed that there was quite a bit of information on the individuals involved in the team. Too much for a recently begun homicide investigation.

"Do you know the whereabouts of this man?" the lead detective asked in a patronizing tone as he presented him a picture of Flex.

"Nah, I haven't seen him in a while either." Bird replied looking the officer squarely in the face.

"Well listen here Bird," the secondary detective began before being cut off by his partner.

"We have reason to believe that the man in this photo is responsible for the victims slaying." he said. "They were last seen together on the Turnpike less than 10 hours before the coroners estimated time of death.

In that moment it took all the restraint Bird could muster to not dispel the two's theory that Flex had murdered Tyco. Still he remained at ease and simply played along. "That's wild." he said with mock surprise. "I don't know where he could be though. I'm sure he'll turn up sooner or later."

"Well when he does you be sure to tell him to catch up with us before we catch up with him, alrighty? I mean, he is a convicted violent criminal wanted for questioning in a homicide and presumed to be armed and dangerous. Anything can happen, you know?" The second officer said, clearly aggravated by the "cat and mouse" exchange between Bird and his superior.

"Of course it can officer." Bird said blankly. "Someone could get killed."

"That's detective, Detective Blake!" he snarled. Bird flashed his infamous smile and gave a taunting thumbs up to the two while ushering them to the door and closing it closely as they exited.

No sooner than the tumbler on the lock clicked Bird's mind instantly went into analyzing what had just taken place. Tyco was dead. Flex was missing. The involvement of the police and their investigation. Things were getting more and more complicated as time went on. Once the word got to the streets that Flex killed Tyco, as the police would surely put it, the story would grow and spread like wild fire. It was safe to assume that any vultures that had been circling would surely land to feast now. There was only one thing to do.

"Get to Flex's place and see if the stash is still there!" he thought. That would be the telltale of his whereabouts, though knowing Flex and his affinity for Tyco, it was safe to assume he was dead too.

In the midst of his thoughts he had let Laura slip from the front of his mind. There was no telling the range of emotions she was experiencing at the moment. But there was no time for tears just yet. Business had to be handled and Bird was in desperate need for closure in the situation. Without it he couldn't plot out his next move accurately. He went to the door of the room where she was, with full intention of opening it and letting her know he would be stepping out for a moment but the sorrow in her crying permeated the door. It was so stark that it nearly pierced his soul, stealing any words that he considered uttering. With the baby fast asleep in the adjoining room, Bird simply left without word. With so many inquiries of his destination and location due to be headed towards those closest to him this was probably best.

Every move had to be closely calculated now. It was safe to say that the law's investigation would shift to Bird with the death of Big Tyco. And with word of that the streets would undoubtedly be watching too, lurking in hopes that he'd lead them to the jackpot of Tyco's ill gotten gains. That in conjunction with his crew being locked up indefinitely being public knowledge, would surely make him and his family targets. He was all alone on this mission, but oddly there was a since of solace in the solitude of only having to watch out for himself, something that he'd rarely done. Before leaving the house Bird went to the closet and grabbed his gun. Exiting the door was like opening a portal to the unknown. Pulling his hoody up, he was off into the night.

Bird decided that taking his car would probably be a bad move, instead opting to take Laura's. Checking his rear early and often he managed to notice that as expected he had a police tail on him. At first inclination he thought to attempt to lose the tail, but after a few more lights passed Bird figured they were attempting to be incognito. Exposing them would likely back them off and send them back to the drawing board. Purposely, he turned on to a main street with dense traffic. With the bright lights of the city combined with the glow of headlights Bird could clearly see the faces of his stalking lawmen. Just as he thought, Detective Blake and another officer, and from the highly animated body language of Blake during their interaction he concluded the other officer was lower ranking.

While waiting for the light he jotted down the license plate which looked like a civilian plate.

To say things were getting more and more interesting would have been the understatement of a lifetime. As the light changed Bird sped off, losing the trail in a sea of automobiles roughly ten car lengths, before hanging a right on a dim lit street, racing halfway down before pulling over and parking the car. Bird raced to get out the car, grabbing the disposable camera Laura was planning to use for his graduation ceremony, he positioned himself in hopes to capture a crystal clear image of his trailer speeding past.

Just as he anticipated the unmarked vehicle came racing down the street about a minute behind him. As the car came past Bird's camera flashed, catching Det. Blake looking squarely into its lenses. Hesitating after the flash the vehicle quickly sped off down the dark street. Bird jumped back into the running vehicle resting assured that this would be that last of them for the night at least. The hidden gift in what just played out was that with the police following the jackers were unlikely to be on him either, and with that he made his way to Flex's.

"Why didn't they stop me and harass me?" he questioned. "Then, speeding off after being exposed . . . could it be this wasn't a department sanctioned stake-out?!" Bird was certain that the answer was held in the license plate, which he'd investigate in the morning after getting the photos developed. But now it was time to unearth other answers as he parked the car half a block off from Flex's place and made his way inside.

Once inside he methodically made his way around the apartment. It was obvious that no one had been there in weeks, clothes were still hung, and dishes were in the sink. Bird swept through each room, making sure that there were no unexpected occupants laying in waiting before heading to the stash. Once in the bathroom, he slipped on latex gloves and began just as Flex had instructed him. Just as he thought, the money was still there. Flex hadn't come back and Bird knew just what that meant as well. He was gone. Everyone was gone. In the stillness of the empty apartment, away from the world he finally succumb to his emotions, breaking down in tears. For all that he had done and seen, and though the outcome was highly inevitable for the life they all lived, the reality of it was all too unreal. In the blink of an eye he was the last man standing, yet was barely a man himself. The tears flowed torrentially down his face, drying at the collar of his shirt. He made no effort to move, no effort to stop or slow his emotional meltdown. It was much too needed and long overdue like rain in the Sahara. And just as rain in the Sahara, when they dried it would be as if they never fell, and back to the real world and what was on the horizon.

He gathered himself to his feet and dusted his jeans off with his hands. There was too much money to just stuff in his pockets so he ran to the bedroom closet and grabbed an old shoe box and stuffed it with the rubber banded stacks of cash. With the shoebox in a bag he casually made his was from the building and back to the car, peering out of the corners of his eyes to make sure that no one was observing him too closely as he left the scene.

Once back home, he doubled the block twice before parking to make sure there wasn't anyone staking the place out. To his surprise there wasn't. He quickly made his way into the house as his mother sat in the living room, quiet.

"Hey ma." He softly said trying to make his way to his room quickly.

"Hey nothing!" she exclaimed. "Where the hell you been boy! Don't you know what's going on around here!?"

"Yeah, I just had to get a little air that's all." he replied.

"You see what happens when you doing the wrong thing, huh!? Now look at your sister . . . I told her . . ." she continued on.

Bird paused for a moment. Taken aback by the brashness of the tone his mother was taking in the matter, he couldn't bear another word that was coming from her mouth. Instead he stood there in disbelief. This was the same woman whom owed her economic freedom to "the wrong things", the same woman whom was a large contributing factor in the whole matter whether she knew it or not. It was in this moment that the great separation was birthed between him and his family and sculpted a portion of his mind in moving forward. The realization that glory was fleeting and the "what have you done for me lately" rule would always apply to those a hustler dealt with, no matter how close the personal relationship was.

Not caring to delve any further into the conversation, he ran to his room locked the door and settled in, intent on tallying his cash reserve.

In his haste to be move quickly stuffing the shoe box most of the rubber bands had broken, partly due to the dry rot caused by the bathroom moisture. Bird hated counting this much loose cash. It took Bird well into the night as he'd waited until everyone was fast asleep to avoid any chance of disruptions. With the chaos of things that wasn't until at least 2 a.m. The thumbs usually began to tighten and cramp in upwards of twenty thousand which only made for miscounts and recounts. It ended up half an hour to count the eighty-two thousand dollars. He stuffed the money into the duffle bag with the money from the heist and stuffed it into a hidden space behind a square of loose drywall in his closet, and attempted to finally lie down and rest which was no short order to say the least. His mind wandered from situation to situation as he laid there in the dark room, illuminated only by the street lights that glowed outside. So much had gone on in just the past twelve hours alone that his mind could barely settle. Tyco dead. Flex dead. His closest friends held in custody and a seemingly rogue cop hot at his heels. All the while his nephew was a bastard, his sister a widow and his mother's livelihood now subject to the reality of true urban economics without a financial backer. There were so many things to manage and so little time to make decisions on all of them. All Bird did know for fact was that with his stash included he had over a quarter of a million dollars tucked away and a million dollars worth of issues to solve. First priority was his crew, he thought to himself. If he had to fend it alone he'd make it work but if his team was together he was certain they could weather the storm. Maybe it was his deep down longing that maybe this nightmare of a day was just that and hoped that a night's sleep would render things anew. With his restless mind comforted by the game plan for the following day he abruptly drifted off into a deep sleep—the sudden blankness covering him being a feeling he would never forget.

The disappointment of waking to the same reality the next day was just as unforgettable. School functions and graduation preparations were taking place the next few days. Bird couldn't help but think that while he was preparing for a pivotal moment in his young life his sister was preparing services, marking the ending of life for the man whom had become his brother. Tyco and Flex were his biggest supporters in his educating himself and using his intellect to merge the concrete grind with the boardroom hustle. He'd never envisioned the day coming and them not being there, or his love Sheena for that matter.

Bird had managed to procure different attorneys for each of them using a member in each of their family's as a go between. The fees were ridiculous. Being that officers were injured in the shootout and subsequent may lay, no attorney wanted to touch the case without added incentive.

Thirty thousand dollars was spent on their collective representatives just to retain them. Or at least that was what the various family members of his friends that he had chosen to be the buffer told him. Many of them had no income themselves let alone had dealt with so much money before. He hated going to Tuffy's mother, Ms. Tami, on he and Lynx's behalves but had no choice. Lynx's mother was too far strung out so his shady Aunt won by default. She'd likely make some unnecessary additions to the bills but anonymity in the situation was priceless and her gap was an expense he had no choice but to accept.

Bird hadn't so much as had spoken to anyone but Sheena since they had been caught and that was only twice or so. Messages were sent to Lynx, whether or not he had gotten them was debatable, as he never responded. A feeling was slowly growing in Bird's gut that his partners as a whole weren't happy by him keeping his distance while being in possession of the spoils of their collective deed. "Would everyone hold true?" is the question that had taking residence in the front of his mind and grew as the days went by. He reminded himself that whatever the case was, all he could do was maintain and make his next move better than the last.

The funeral for Tyco was set for the coming Saturday, the day after graduation undoubtedly putting a somber mood on Bird's moment.

That Friday as Bird awoke it was a strange feeling in the air, as if there was a vibration that was causing unease inside him. "It's just the nerves", he kept telling himself as he picked through the breakfast his mother had prepared. Bird couldn't remember the last time she was home to cook, usually working long hours from dusk until dawn. That coupled with everyone's seemingly sense of disregard for what would be taking place less than twenty-four hours managed to quell him.

CHAPTER 5

"We want immediate transferral to the county!"

-Langdon

After breakfast the day was a blur. In the blink of an eye Bird was at graduation in the procession line headed to the stage to begin the commencement ceremony. His classmate and fellow hustler Joe Calloway, aka Joe Money, came close and leaned over to him speaking into his ear.

"Yo Birdie, I just wanted to say it's fucked up about Tyco man . . ." he said extending his hand to grip Birds. "The streets talking crazy . . . I'm damn sure goin' to show and pay my respects. If it's anything I can do just holla . . ."

Bird gripped his hand their shoulders meeting with a pat on the back. "Fa sho, I appreciate the love bruh . . ." he replied. He'd known Joe Money since they were in grade school, and knew that he was one of the few honest and true guys from their generation. As cold as the streets were Bird wondered how Money even flourished amongst the vultures and constantly circling of the buzzards, being a different breed. Joe Money was a finesse hustler with a natural knack for getting to the money and stacking it, yet he had no gorilla in him at all. Though it hardened Bird he had learned a certain appreciation for the necessity of putting in work from Flex. It wasn't done from love of bullshit and conflict yet out of fear of potentially being on the other end of the gun. But he liked Money and on the couple of occasions he'd gotten wind of potential plots against his counterpart he diffused them without word. As he walked back to his place in line with an innocent grin on his face from a comment he received from a female, Bird's eyes followed him, unconsciously wondering how long Honest Joe would survive before the evils of the lives they led captured his soul like Tyco and Flex.

His thoughts were broken by one of the faculty prompting him to proceed in line. The long walk down the aisle was a reverberating memory. It seemed as if he was moving in slow motion and all eyes were on him, yet he was so mentally detached in the moment that he was oblivious to them at the same time.

Once seated, Bird surveyed the room, seeking the whereabouts of his family. He eyed the crowd twice over before locating them with balloons near the rear of the auditorium. After acknowledging them with a smile Bird again zoned out, staring into the sea of people while daydreaming as segment after segment of the program ensued. Again he was brought to from the clapping of the audience. It was finally time to end the ceremony with the symbolic transition of the tassel. The smiles on the faces surrounding his were infectious with the hope that the transition to a better future was on the horizon.

Bird looked back to the seating area where his family was their faces glowing with pride back at him. In the midst of the tumultuous lives of those growing up and living in the environment that they did, this was a reason to truly celebrate and feel a sense of completeness. Bird had unknowingly taken Laura's disposable camera again. Taking it from his pocket, he thought a picture of the onlookers' from his perspective would make for a memorable shot. As his eyes panned through the lens what he saw further behind his family quickly turned his smile into a look of disbelief.

It was Detective Blake.

The moment their eyes met it was as if two natural enemies in the wild were within striking distance of each other. Neither broke stare nor blinked—so engaged in their glare, that Bird missed the tossing of the caps. Out of his peripheral he could see other plain-clothes officers moving around the audience as they began to let out. He knew where things were headed as it developed and immediately decided Blake wouldn't get the satisfaction of putting cuffs on him in this setting.

Bird quickly moved into the crowd disappearing from Det. Blake's line of sight flowing with the crowd into the atrium before disrobing and doubling back into the auditorium and escaping through one of the fire exits inside.

His temper flared as he made his way down St. Clair to his hood, taking the "cuts" to remain inconspicuous. He stationed himself in the backyard adjacent from his apartment. The police had a car stationed in front. All around him from block to block he could hear the sound of the Interceptor engines zipping back and forth. Bird deliberated what could be the cause for so much backup to come and get him. He'd lapsed in his responsibility in taking the information from the picture that he had gotten of Det. Blake trailing him earlier in the week and doing his homework on him. In that thought Bird quickly decided he needed the pictures for his defense and falling into custody with them would only mean they would come up missing.

He quickly made a call then pulled the battery from his cell and stuffed it and the disposable camera from his pocket into an empty Doritos bag in the yard, before he kicked loose a lattice adorning the back of the house—

creating a gap just big enough for him to stick the bag inside within arm's reach.

There was no way around being taken into custody he concluded as he heard the sound of the ghetto bird circling, yet the attempt at embarrassing him only made him want to return the favor.

Through sheer craftiness Bird managed to make his way further down the block hopping fences in his slacks and square toes while dodging the eye in the sky, only to emerge in the backyard of a house of fiends. A few dollars later Bird was slumped in the backseat of a tattered and bruised late 90's Cadillac, with the driver following his every direction. As he got within walking distance of the district police station Bird motioned him to pull over. With an astonished look on his face the junkie reluctantly followed his orders dropping him off in front of a corner store. Nonchalantly Bird went inside and bought himself a bag of snacks and walked down the block and into the precinct.

"Hi my names, Christopher Clark" he said with a mouth full of Flaming Hots. "I heard you all were looking for me or something???

The officer behind the glass paused for a moment with the exact same expression the addict had on his face ten minutes earlier.

"One second son." he said trying to maintain his composure.

After speaking a few words into the phone two more officers appeared from behind a large door and ordered Bird to place his hands on the top if his head. Within minutes he was processed and placed in a room to await questioning, still eating the snacks he'd coerced the officers to allow him to keep.

Bird had just opened the ginger ale he'd bought when a furious Det. Blake busted in the door.

"So you think you're a smart lil' fucker huh?!" he asked rhetorically.

Bird sat speechless, staring at the detective blankly. He knew that for an elaborate attempt to serve an arrest warrant, as Det. Blake had no doubt orchestrated, he had to get his superiors involved and approval. What better way would it be to extract an irrational emotional response from the cop than to embarrass him in turn in front of his superiors? To spend tax payers' dollars to hunt down an eighteen year old that turned himself in would definitely ruffle a few feathers.

"Oh! You're not going to talk huh you lil' bastard?!" he said growing increasingly agitated opening a folder. "Well your lil' crew told us all we need to know about you "Lil' Birdie! That plan was all yours genius. Now your ass is done. Luckily you graduated today . . . now the state won't have to pay for you to get a GED."

Still Bird sat staunchly, staring in the officers reddening face, unaffected by his words. "I'd like to call my attorney." Bird said matter-of-factly, twisting the cap off of the bottle and taking another sip.

Detective Blake had reached his boiling point, leaping from his seat and yoking Bird from his chair by his dress collar causing him to spill his drink all over himself, knocking chairs over in the process screaming, "You're going to tell me everything you little black motherfucker!!" at the top of his lungs. Just as the commotion began his phone call prior to stashing his phone paid off, as the attorney he called was entering the interrogation room escorted by the precincts Captain just as Bird instructed.

"What the hell is going on in here!" the lawyer exclaimed. The Captain stood there in shock. Detective Blake's face was priceless.

"Captain I . . . I . . ." the detective stuttered.

"Out of here NOW!" the Captain shouted, before beginning to apologize vehemently as he quickly exited behind the officer

"We want immediate transferral to the county!" the lawyer lashed out, closely behind the Captain as he walked out.

Bird knew that he'd have to spend a few nights in jail due to the seriousness of the situation when he turned himself in. He also knew that if one of his friends turned he'd likely end up a co-defendant with the amount of information any of them could offer. But the trap was set, and the unsuspecting Blake fell right into it. With the pictures he would at least be able to mount a harassment defense to distract a jury if it came down to it. But the things he said concerned Bird deeply. Thoughts of who the leak could be plagued him all night. Once he made bail Monday he'd figure out his next move. The only silver lining to getting arrested if there was one was that his attorney could now see exactly what he was being charged with. And give him a chance to catch word through the "jail grapevine" as to what really was going on. After a barrage of threats from Bird's chosen counsel the Captain fulfilled his request.

Other than the facility, being in the county jail didn't bother Bird very much. He was certain to come across some characters he had dealt with and obtain the information he was looking for. As word traveled that Big Tyco and Flex's protégé was on the pod a curvaceous female C.O. made her way to him.

Her sex appeal could hardly go unnoticed with the attention of her co-workers and inmate's alike, glued to her as she approached him. Bird quickly sized her up. She was older, early to mid thirties' maybe, with a near flawless complexion. Her frame was something to be coveted—unreasonably thick with proportions so extreme, it was as if the Devil himself had sculpted them to inspire lustful cravings. Though the possibility that she had children was likely, her demeanor was not that of a "baby mama". With a sly flash of her inviting smile as she reached him, he struggled to read her name tag. His eyes wrestling between focusing on the words or her body.

In the softest of tones she introduced herself, "Hi, Chris is it? I'm Officer Williams." No sooner than she had given him her name she immediately began expressing her condolences on Tyco's death, explaining how her older brother was an old friend of his. With a little more conversation she explained how Tyco had given him a large sum of money so he could get back on his feet without going back to the streets, after he had gotten home from prison. She also expressed how much that meant to her and her family.

As they conversed she offered insight into his current situation, confirming that the things Detective Blake stated weren't fabricated though she couldn't specify exactly who gave in. But as word would have it, all of their accounts of the event seemed to be corroborating.

Bird stood before her with a blank expression on his face for a moment as he digested what she had just told him. Needless to say he was more than shocked at the development, but his mind quickly snapped back into gear. He decided to make the most of his opportunity and do some reconnaissance.

"So what's the deal with this Detective Blake dude?" Bird asked.

"Man . . . ." She replied with a pause. "Half the nigga's that got knocked in the last month he caught! He's like a super cop or some shit . . . . getting awards left and right." glancing around to make sure no one was within earshot. "The Governor just invited him to some dinner. That was until you just made him look bad with that stunt you pulled. After what you did I know he's hot on your ass, if he already wasn't!"

Bird's face remained stoic. "Well I haven't done anything wrong, so I'm not worried. I know what I'm doing." he said.

"Yeah ok. I really hope so hunny." she said with a sly smirk, as she turned to walk away.

"So no first name?" Bird said smiling back, enjoying her exit. "The badge says N. Williams, what's the N stand for?

"Maybe if we cross paths when I don't have the badge on you'll get a chance to find out." She flirted back without turning her head as she switched away.

Bird retreated to his bunk. There was nothing more to find out for him. His situation seemed to only be getting progressively worse as the days passed by. He thought that Blake was a run of the mill cop looking for a raise and extra vacation time, not a crime fighter hell bent on actually catching criminals or people with a complexion that he felt was criminal.

He lay still for hours, thinking through his every move, his every option and the possible outcome of each and reflecting on the things that had brought him there. "What was his mother and L's take on things?" He wondered. Then it dawned on him that he would miss Tyco's funeral completely which only infuriated and frustrated him even more. Just as his mind settled and was about to shutdown the very same female C.O. escorted a small Latino man into his cell.

Not in the mood for pleasantries, Bird kept quiet and listened to the inmate's interaction with the guard to see what he could decipher from the conversation. Other than the thick Spanish accent there wasn't much he could pick up. That was until he heard her say, "You won't be here long Mr. Hernandez, the FED's will be taking you into custody by morning", she said while helping him get situated in the cell.

"Si." he said plainly in response.

Bird's mind reeled with curiosity. "What the hell could this lil' Mexican guy have done that would make the FED's transfer him on the weekend?" He sat up in his bunk and watched the young Latinos every move, in between sharing chance glances with Officer Williams.

Bird could tell that he could sense him watching and wanted to see his reaction. "Would he be intimidated? Frightful even or maybe aggressive?" Bird pondered. But the man gave no reaction at all, moving around as nonchalantly as he had with the guard. The moment she left Bird broke the silence of his glare, "So . . . . . you wouldn't mind biting her chalupa either, huh!?

The two immediately burst into laughter at the remark.

"So what's your name fam?" Bird inquired.

"Carlos, but my compadres call me Los." he said still hesitant to engage in conversation.

Bird soon had made Carlos warm up to him and from there the two talked nonstop for at least two hours, sharing tales of women to encounters with the law. Carlos wasn't the usual cell-mate. Bird could recognize his pedigree from the moment they spoke. He was well kept with a neatly trimmed mustache lending maturity to his youthful face. He also had a sort of aristocratic arrogance in his demeanor that only money afforded. Bird had managed to get his whole rundown for the most part yet the burning question still remained, and he figured now was as good a time as any to ask.

"So what the fuck did you do bruh?" Bird asked directly. There was a moment of silent deliberation before Los spoke.

"Well . . . I didn't DO anything. It's what your government suspects me of doing that has me here." He answered. "My Uncle has businesses throughout the country. Recently there were some trust issues and he decided to cash out of certain regions. I merely was transporting a little revenue that's all. Just a simple misunderstanding." he said with a chuckle.

Though he spoke ambiguously Bird was able to read between the lines and decipher what Los was saying. His explanation alluded to the fact that he was wealthy, yet far from corporate.

"So what type of numbers we talking Los?" He asked.

"Eh . . . . Two . . . Three . . . give or take." He casually replied.

"Hundred thousand?!" Bird asked.

"Million." Carlos said simply.

It was Birds fortune that Los couldn't see the reaction when he stated the numbers. Not one to be easily impressed, his interest immediately peaked.

"Damn good numbers there! But shit . . . the FED's are going to be on some bullshit. What type of time you facing??" He asked.

"Time?" Los responded puzzled. "No . . . No . . . time. It's not illegal to have money . . . I'm not American. They will send me home. You will see." he said laughing as he rolled over in his bunk.

Bird lay, confused by his response yet intrigued by the entire conversation as a whole. Before thoughts of his personal situations seeped back into his mind he dozed off, the interaction with Carlos serving as a welcomed distraction from his turmoil.

The next morning the FED's beat the rooster to the punch. A corrections officer loudly introduced himself to the cell.

"Rise and shine homez!" a large redneck screamed. "Your rides here . . ." Within moments Carlos was up and on his feet.

"Parajos!" Carlos screamed waking Bird from his sleep. "You ever make it to Mexico look me up."

"Mexico's a big country." Bird replied in a half sleep daze.

"Juarez." he said as he was ushered out. "Better yet Las Cruces."

"Las Cruces." Bird recited to himself as he dozed back asleep.

Monday came soon enough and Bird was herded down to holding until he was next on the docket. His young attorney was pushing the clock as he arrived right as Bird's case was called. Being escorted out into the court room he looked out into the benches to see his family. But there was only one familiar face in the crowded pews, Laura. She forced a pained smile to her face as their eyes met. Before he could deliberate on the reason that his mother wasn't there he was called to stand before the Judge to answer to the charges.

His mind wandered as the Judge spoke. "She isn't here." He kept thinking to himself, "How could she just not show at a moment like this, when he needed her most." Luckily the motion made by his attorney for bail was accepted, though set at two hundred and fifty thousand dollars.

"Bird, I only have ten thousand, I didn't expect it to be so high!" a frantic Laura hurried to say as they ushered him back away. Bird only nodded back, still in a daze. Luckily courtrooms were crawling with opportunists of the legal slave trade and a bail bondsmen's crony overheard Laura's plight. After a half hour the two made concessions for the bond to be paid.

As he met with his attorney for the first time since being at the precinct after the hearing, he learned the seriousness of the charges he was facing

Manslaughter, kidnapping and a host of other charges. "Evidence couldn't be produced to get a murder conviction" his lawyer explained. "They say that they have multiple defendant testimonies from individuals involved that warrant these charges but we'll see about that during open disclosure. If so you might want to consider a plea deal. We can push for no more than fifteen"

Bird sat there virtually in awe by what he was hearing. For the law to even know enough to press the type of charges they named had him shaken to his core. Though he had done many things that only grown men do he was still just a kid barely fresh out of high school, caught up living a life that came easy and was even easier to get lost in. That's where Bird found himself in the moment, experiencing a wild array of emotions tearing through him like a meteor through the atmosphere, burning hotter and hotter until it disintegrates. But it was also in the most adverse situations that his mind went into overdrive and found solutions.

"Fuck it." he said instinctively, cutting his attorney off mid-sentence. He hadn't been paying attention anyway. "Detective Blake. I want to file an assault charge on Detective Blake."

"What!?" exclaimed his attorney. "Listen, I truly wouldn't advise going at the police in your situation, son. He's a highly decorated officer and well known throughout the law enforcement community, and in your current . . . ."

Again Bird cut him off. "I'm not your son, you're what, nine years older than me maybe!? And I'm paying you." he said, staring firmly in the attorneys eyes, visibly disgusted by his admission of weakness. "If you're not up for this I'll find another attorney who is."

The lawyer paused and composed himself.

"Well I guess it's your life to play craps with." he said. "I'll get the papers filed immediately. That will be another fee you know?"

"The first fees weren't an issue and neither will the new ones be." Bird said strongly.

Before long he was released on bond, right into the waiting arms of his sister.

"You ok Birdie?" she said as she welled from emotion.

"I'm cool L." he said quietly. "Where's Ma?

Laura paused. Bird could see that something was wrong in her face. "She didn't want to come." she said slowly. "she said that she wants you out the house."

Bird was floored as his premonitions came true.

Laura sensing his dismay quickly tried to soften the blow. "You know people have been telling her all types of shit Bird and she's just tripping right now . . . that damned Detective Blake keeps popping up with questions and stories . . ."

"Fuck it L.", he said again cutting her off in the exact same tone as he'd used on the lawyer. "It is what it is right now."

It was silent as the two made it to the car and got in. Laura stared at the young man that was almost as much her baby as their mother's. As she put the key in the ignition, she was in disbelief at the transformation in him that seemed to happen overnight. Bird could feel Laura's discomfort in his coldness. In his heart she was the last person that he wanted to displace so he quickly lightened the subject, "I'll make sure you get the money back from the bond L", he said softly. "Are you okay though?"

His change in tone did just that. "I know you will Birdie, I'm okay." She replied. But he knew that she wasn't and that hard times lay ahead in dealing with the daily struggles single mothers face. But he would be there when she needed him as she always had been for him. The change in him had begun several years ago when he and Tyco first dealt and now he was entering into a new stage of his evolution. Now all that he knew and felt had converged, love and compassion giving way to reality and strife. Now was his time to claim the crown or renounce it.

The moment he got home Bird went straight to his room to gather his belongings. His mother wasn't there. "Maybe it was best at that time or maybe it was for the worst", Bird pondered as he reflected on his childhood as he casually sipped from his glass.

Maybe if she were home to say "Don't leave." history would have been rewritten. But glancing around the loft he stood in he wasn't sure if he would have liked to have it any other way.

Within an hour Bird had stuffed trash bags with his belongings, gotten his hidden fortune from the wall and made his way to the door. Laura turned to him just as he was hitting the door, their eyes meeting momentarily for what seemed like an eternity. Her's saying she wished she could have things the way they were, her little brother, her family. His, that things could never be the same—that at that moment the boy she was looking at had a heart void of any love other than what was reserved for her.

"Just be careful." she said solemnly.

He agreed with a simple nod, tossing a stack of money on the couch where Laura sat before exiting off into the night. The uncertainty of what lay ahead covered his mind in a veil of mystery, Bird being one to rarely move without a clear path, knew that this was one that had to be made. Only time would tell his outcome, but regardless of his fate it was his to choose. As the door closed behind him so did the option of returning.

CHAPTER 6

"So this will be cool, right?"

-Jasmine

The hurdle that first night leaving was finding somewhere to stay. He tossed his belongings in the trunk of his car and rode for hours thinking, wrestling with the voices of self doubt. Needless to say, with all the things going on in his life it seemed to be all going downhill but Bird knew that there had to be a way. For him, getting settled somewhere alone with his thoughts was crucial. Racking his brain, he recalled a girl he used to talk to that was a little older than him who worked at an Embassy Hotel, roughly twenty minutes outside of the city. Reaching for his phone he remembered he'd left it hidden in the brush under the house. He'd have to get it first thing in the morning. With no chance to call before arriving Bird could only hope that she was still employed there and working that night.

After a while Bird pulled up into a parking space outside the Embassy Suites. It was a nice hotel and far enough outside of the city that he could notice any trail, yet calm enough were suspicious activity wouldn't go unnoticed either.

Duffle bag over his shoulder, Bird walked through the sliding doors and headed towards the check in desk. There were two women at the counter, an older white woman and a young black one, roughly twenty-four or five. She was average looking yet had an inviting tone. Bird figured that he'd fair better with her and so he made his way to her end, the white woman eying him nosily.

"Welcome to the Embassy Suites, how can I help you" she asked.

"Hi, my names Chris, actually I'm looking for an employee here . . ." Bird said uncertainly. "Her names Layla?"

"Layla . . . Layla . . ." repeated the clerk trying to recall. "Oh, Layla Thompson, she transferred to the downtown Cleveland hotel. Is there anything I can do for you?"

Bird smiled. "Maybe." he said leaning on the counter and softening his tone while the woman on the other end was preoccupied with another matter. "I was supposed to pay Layla to book me a room here for a few weeks but I guess she spent me. Can you make something happen? I'll take care of you."

The slender clerk glanced up from the computer monitor over her glasses. "Boy, what you need a room for . . . a graduation party or something?! You can't even be old enough to book a room!"

He thought fast. "Hell naw, I ain't trying to party!" he said. "I'm just trying to relax a couple weeks before I go out of town to school."

"Couple of weeks!!" she exclaimed. "You know how much that's going to cost sweetie?! Even with a discount!"

Bird knew what it would take for her to take him seriously. He reached in his pocket and pulled from it five neatly rubber-banded stacks of fifty dollar bills. "So you'll do it?" he whispered across to her.

As soon as she glanced up her eyes met his hand perched on the counter palming the stacks of cash. She looked at it long enough to get a rough estimate in her mind of how much it was.

"Let me see what I can do . . ." she whispered back smiling at Bird. "Give me your last name Chris."

He gave her the necessary information and within moments she had a price. "It's like twelve hundred with my discount after the fees and taxes!" she said.

Bird knew that the price was probably inflated before giving her a few more dollars but didn't care. Without pausing he handed her one of the rubber banded stacks and counted out ten fifties from another. "That should cover it right?" he asked as he handed her the money.

"Yeah, that'll do." She replied trying to mask her exhilaration at the few hundred dollar tip.

Bird's mind had been so consumed with securing shelter he hadn't even taken the time to look the young lady over, let alone get her name. As she gave Bird his key she brought that fact to light by fumbling the keycard to the floor then slowly bending over to pick it up.

"Ok Chris your all set." she said handing him his keycard. "Don't party too hard please!"

"I'll make sure I invite you!" Bird laughed.

"How are going to invite me and you don't even know my name?" she said flirtasciously twisting her glossed lips.

"How could I not know, Jasmine Bueller customer service specialist." He replied reciting her I.D. badge information to her.

She laughed aloud, impressed by Bird's attention to detail.

"So which way do I go to get to my room?" he inquired.

"I'll be punching out in a minute, I'll show you if you can wait?" She replied seductively.

Bird had been so inundated with the matters of his life that he hadn't thought about pussy in the slightest for over a week, but the tone of the young lady standing across the counter from him struck a carnal nerve inside him.

"I'm not in a hurry", he answered smiling. "I'm sure you're worth waiting for."

Speechless, she glanced back over her shoulder with a salacious look in her eyes as she gathered her things. Fifteen minutes later the two were on the elevator ride to the sixth floor, flirting along the way. It always amazed him how people became so enamored in status and money. The green paper could spark a fire within people that brought the lowest parts of their nature to the surface. He'd long learned that it and fear were two of life's strongest motivators.

His time around Tyco gave him the most bird's eye view of this contrast in character.

Big Tyco, the hustler, always shining and never without had a steady flow of women chasing him. But he knew that it wasn't real, and from Bird's unobstructed view even he could see it, another lesson he was fortunate enough to learn. It was the thrill of the danger that baited them in. The notion that if they stood close enough to the Sun that it's radiating heat would warm them too. That if allowed to stand with it at their back it would cast a glorious glow around them for the world to bask in as well. Whether it was the money, the perception of it or actual attraction was all debatable but the reality and outcome wasn't. There was nothing unattractive about winning—even the very façade of it was beautiful to the unsuspecting eye. And the power it possessed to make an unwilling soul willing was unreal.

With thoughts of how far she would go in his head Bird moved a step closer to her as they rode up in the elevator alone. Now that his mind was on her he could see she was a fairly attractive girl, roughly five foot seven and one hundred forty-five pounds with an athletic build. Her glasses accentuated the subtle features of her face and coupled with her full lips, gave her a seductive look.

"They let you wear clothes this tight to work?" Bird asked as he slid his index finger into the back of her slacks at the top of her ass, giving them a gentle tug.

"Oh so you just gonna touch on me like that!?" she said sharply in a mock tone of disapproval.

"Yeah." He replied plainly looking her square in the face. "Did you like it?"

"Whatever!" She exclaimed turning away trying to maintain her look of seriousness. "Your room's this way." she said stepping from the elevator quickly after it arrived at the sixth floor.

Bird walked behind her amused at her attitude, wondering how long it would be before she dropped the charades and let her true self out. Ultimately it didn't matter to him whether she complied or not, whether he spent his night entertaining himself with her or alone made no difference. Yet the cat and mouse act was somewhat entertaining at the moment.

Once at the room she took the liberty of escorting him all the way inside. Bird walked in and tossed his duffle bag under the desk in the corner. He pulled back the curtains and observed for a moment the view which overlooked the freeway.

"So this will be cool, right?" She asked.

Bird had gotten so entranced he'd almost forgotten his company completely. "Uh . . . yeah . . . this'll do. Thanks again." he said never turning around to face her.

He expected to hear the clicking of the cylinders the electronic lock initiating shortly after that, but after a minute of silence the voice spoke again, only now it was directly behind him so close that he could feel her breathe as she exhaled before speaking.

"And what made you think it was cool to just touch my ass like that in the elevator?" She asked softly. "What if I just grabbed your dick like that?"

Bird smiled to himself as the inevitable came to fruition. Unbeknownst to him at that moment scenes such as this would almost become commonplace over the years, reenacted more times than he could count.

"It's only one way to find that out right?" he said calmly as her hands reached around him and found their way inside his pants. "Just like I'm wondering what those lips would feel like wrapped around it . . ."

Bird must have used the proper phrasing because no sooner than he had finished his sentence Jasmine had shed any reserve she had and was aggressively testing her gag-reflex. Bird felt his mind slowly relaxing and tensions ease as she repeatedly took the length of him beyond her throat, stopping occasionally to change techniques and to catch her breath. He watched her closely with no intention to return the favor.

After thirty minutes of two-play, Bird stood between her spread eagle legs at the edge of the bed as he rolled the condom down, poised to exorcise his built up anxieties on the wetness of her walls.

As Bird pushed into her tightness, a wanton expression of pleasure overtook them—her gasping at the initial rush of the intense sensation. Both of them finding their own personal gratification in each other.

For her it was hope. Hope that there was a distant possibility that her pussy would be good enough to foster something real out of an act of indecency. For that slither of hope she would give her all to him even after just a brief introduction. In her mind the extreme attraction that she was feeling was real, not a delusion created by his ability to blow seven inch pieces of green paper in bulk.

For Bird it was something simpler in premise yet more complex in nature. He found solace solely in the act, her pussy a place to relieve himself. His typical calm and reserved demeanor being nothing more than a byproduct of an uncanny ability to internalize fears and withhold emotions, yet function unaffected. It was his gift as it was also his curse.

After a few rounds Jasmine had to leave much to Bird's delight. He was finally alone and able to relax with his thoughts or at least attempt to. His next few moves were critical and he knew it. As he lay staring at the ceiling he made a vow to himself that he would utilize everything he had to beat the overwhelming odds stacked against him. He closed his eyes in a moment of thought, mumbling the phrase, "God bless me." and "Fuck the world.", in the same breath as he drifted to sleep.

CHAPTER 7

"I owe you big time."

-Dave Greenfield

The next few months blazed by like the summer sun crossing the sky. After leaving the hotel, Bird had managed to find someone with a clear name and work history to rent him an apartment. It was on the deep eastside off the lake, near the Willoughby suburb. He quickly furnished it, turning it into every young man's dream bachelor suite. And Bird went hard in it, treating it just as that. The very thought of the period bringing a smile to his face in the present. His spending habits got so bad that he had to settle himself down before he went broke. But even with enjoying himself modestly came more expenses, and with expenses the money dwindled. With his lawyer not sparing a sapling in sending invoices at every opportunity and his cohorts fee's doing the same, the reality was without hustling there was no way to maintain this life he had come to know.

It was nearing the end of summer and with the trials of his once friends and mate underway and his own looming, he found himself faced with an unsettling decision between his two options. Keep going at the rate he was which ultimately would end with him fading into the masses struggling for survival or head back into the depths of the concrete jungle to harvest more of the forbidden fruits?

As days went by and the question of which path he should take lingered news reached him that his St. Clair peer, Joe Money, was killed in a seemingly random robbery attempt. Even though the two weren't friends by any means the news gnawed at his mind—Bird feeling as if he foresaw Joe's fate that evening at graduation, which only brought his own mortality to mind. Taking his death as a sign, his mind was made up. The game was over.

During the ball of confusion that was Bird's adolescent life he managed to fair well in his studies, earning decent grades. So after careful consideration of his future he decided to pursue higher education, on his terms though. He opted out of going away, instead enrolling at the local community college. He had no clue what he wanted to do but during the first meeting with his counselor came the discussion of the different majors and opportunities that may be available for him.

"You know there are some things in place that could ease the financial burden on you, son." The middle aged white man said slowly with lowly eyes. "Looking at your FAFSA you likely will qualify for a work-study position we have designed to help people like you to handle school expenses, and can actually lead to full time employment if you're lucky."

Bird distinctly remembered being disgusted by the condescending tone of the monologue. He'd never found himself in the position of needing the kindness of anyone, let alone accepting it from an asshole that obviously needed diversity training. As he listened to the man's subconscious diatribe he sat there, flabbergasted at his audacity and that he could be so oblivious to the facts. The fact being that contrary to the financial statement he had in front of him more money had passed through Bird's hands than he could hope to earn in his life. He was awestruck that someone could be so disjointed from his world. After the lengthy explanation that seemed more like a rant, an offended Bird decided to apply for the position anyway.

"Part time, a minimum of thirty-two hours a week at a pay rate of ten fifty . . ." He read from the paper. He'd never held a job and figured the opportunity would be as good as any to create a work history despite his inclination to duct tape and pistol whip the man in front of him. Plus the added income definitely wouldn't hurt.

Birds first semester of school began and a couple of weeks later he was notified that he had the job and began immediately. The job in itself wasn't hard. Help man the administrative desk, file some papers, transport documents to different offices and answer phones. But the people surrounding him made it unbearable. His supervisor didn't know how to communicate with him either, just as the counselor hadn't. Assuming that he was ignorant or unintelligent, they gave him directions for tasks repeatedly and always cut an eye to see what he was working on nearly every moment. "Maybe it was him?" he questioned until another student, a young white guy slightly older than him named Todd, was hired on to perform similar tasks. Bird watched as he was given responsibilities and duties that he himself hadn't been allowed to perform although he had been there a fraction of the time. From that moment Bird knew that he wouldn't last working a regular job, dealing with normal work relationships and people who obviously couldn't relate to him or his culture.

Late one afternoon just as the offices were shutting down a man rushed to the window attempting to make it in time to drop off paperwork. At the time, Bird's Caucasian counterpart was working the desk, as Bird filed papers in a cabinet within earshot.

"Hi, I'd liked to turn this registration in . . ." he said quickly before being stopped short.

"I'm sorry our computers are off." He replied from behind the desk dryly, barely looking up from his screen.

"I really just need to drop these off and I don't have time to come back another day!" the man pleaded.

"I'm sorry, but the windows closed." he said again this time getting up from the desk and sliding the window close.

The man stood there for a moment in disbelief at the audacity of the clerk. Bird was still behind the filing cabinet finishing up things while analyzing the whole situation. The man was obviously not the typical student coming up to the window. He was in his late thirties maybe early forties, well groomed, nicely dressed and from the Mauri alligator shoes he had on it was safe to assume that he wasn't some suburbanite from the area.

Bird went to the window and flagged the man back.

"Sir!" he yelled. The man casually strode back up to the window. "What exactly did you need again? Bird asked.

"I just need to get these papers for registration in. That's ALL." he said in a frustrated tone as he handed Bird the documents.

"Ok. I'll take care of that for you . . ." Bird said looking over the papers. "Ok, I see you dropped a class and are switching to Psychology 103 with Martz, I have that class myself."

"Yeah, I have a little free time to kill and my daughter talked me into taking some classes", he explained. "She would have killed me when she came home if I didn't get these in, so I really appreciate this." he said with a chuckle. "I'm Dave Greenfield, what's your name?"

"It's no problem. I saw old boy being a dickhead anyway." Bird replied before introducing himself. "My name's Chris Clark."

"Ok Chris glad to meet you and thanks again." Dave said walking away. "I owe you big time."

"It's cool. I'll catch you in class." Bird said. He got back to wrapping up his duties so he could head home, putting the chance encounter out of his mind.

It was well into September and Bird was doing well. But the remnants of his near past were not far behind him. His trial would be coming soon. About the third Wednesday of the month he got a much dreaded voicemail from his attorney.

"Hi Chris, this is Langdon your attorney. I really need to get you in the office ASAP! Your trial begins next week and it seems that the other members of this case have all just taken pleas which may be in return for testimony against you." Bird's heart sank.

If they all turned on him there would be almost no way out for him. He didn't even bother calling Langdon back. His mind was so polluted with deciphering the tangled web that he was in, that he couldn't communicate business properly. In his head he had prepared for the noise of the gavel during his own sentencing. From all angles that he had considered the situation, it was the inevitable outcome.

A few days later as he pulled up to the school his phone rang again, the caller I.D. reading Langdon, he figured it was more of the same talk.

"What's up Langdon?" He answered plainly.

"Mr. Clark, you do know that this trial is very important to your freedom, correct?" Langdon chided. "I would appreciate if you return my calls."

"I know . . . I know . . ." Bird replied. "So I guess you called to tell me we got offered a plea too?"

"No actually I'm calling because the representative of Ms. Jackson has informed me, at her request, to notify you that during standard processing something was found." he said.

"Something found?" Bird asked dumbfounded. "Something like what?!"

"Ms. Jackson is pregnant Mr. Clark and she says that you are the father!" Langdon quickly blurted. "I also have been made aware that she's having the child. Now typically in these situations . . ." he continued.

Bird sat on the other end speechless, his ears deaf, his own thoughts blank. He stayed that way for fifteen minutes until Langdon's incessant repeating of his name on the phone snapped him back to reality.

"MR. CLARK!!!" the voice screamed from the handset.

"My bad Langdon, I'm going have to call you back!" he said ending the call abruptly.

The stakes had just gotten so much higher. How could they bring a life into the world in this situation, destined for failure? He knew that Sheena wanted kids some day and was dead set on having her baby, even if it was while she was incarcerated. In her mind it would almost be some cool shit, sort of a having a gangster by birthright.

The clock tower at the school tolled. Bird knew he had to hurry and get himself to class on time regardless. Mr. Martz was known for his pop quizzes, not to mention the last thing he wanted to defile was school, the only positive constant in his life at the time. But even in class Bird was distracted, and obviously not himself, which prompted a familiar face to inquire after the session was over.

"They giving you a hard time over in that office young brother?" Bird heard as a hand grabbed his shoulder. Bird turned slightly to see it was once again Dave Greenfield.

"Oh, what's up Dave?" Bird answered. "Just having a really rough time. Found out I'm gonna be a father and all type of shit. It's a really fucked up situation right now." He replied bluntly.

Dave was thrown off for a second, and then gave Bird his opinion before parting. "Sometimes shit gets that way. No point in dwelling on it. Now you have to make the decision as to what you want to happen and then get a plan to make it happen. You're a smart kid you'll figure it out. Just gotta be a man about it, that's all." He told him.

The wise words only sank in half way. Bird had thrown the proverbial towel in as to his fate.

"Dave don't know the type of shit I'm going through for real," he thought to himself and dismissed the bulk of his advice. But one point that he made rang true with Bird, "Be a man about it." It also meant no more feeling sorry for himself, but that would prove to be easier said than done in his present state.

The following week his trial began. The District Attorney was Michael Deluca. A brash legal mind from a long line of judges, lawyers, and public officials. His grandfather was famed, long-time ex-Congressman/ex-Governor Michael Pescale. It would be Bird's luck that the prosecutor appointed to his case would be a namesake to a nation political legend. On top of it all the November elections were coming up and it was rumored that Deluca's name would appear on the ballot for district Judge. He would surely use the publicity of this trial to spring board himself into a bench seat.

He went in fast and hard at Bird in his opening argument, painting him as a dangerous criminal intellect that was a threat to society.

"Over the course of the trial I will prove to you that Christopher Clark aka Bird goaded his friends into a deadly scheme of robbery and murder!" Deluca screamed at the jurors. Their faces faint, totally enraptured by his compelling theatrics. By the time the Judge adjourned the case Bird was drained. With his life hanging in the balance he felt that all was lost. He exited the courtroom weak and quickly took a seat outside. As his head hung with his face cupped in his hands a friendly voice spoke to him.

"What's going on lil' Chris?"

He looked up slowly, only to see it was none other than Dave Greenfield.

"Dave . . ." Bird said startled. "What are you doing here?!?"

"I'm here meeting my old college buddy for lunch." he replied. "Better question is what are you doing here?!" he asked in turn.

Bird looked at Dave and paused for a second to think but just as he started to explain a figured crept up behind Dave and interrupted.

"Davie Boy!!!" the figure screamed. Dave turned partially, giving Bird a clear view of the man. To his surprise it was D.A. Deluca!

"Hey hey Mikey!! How's it going? You ready already?" Dave said with a huge smile.

"Sure am buddy." The D.A. replied with a smile that turned into a look of shock as he glanced down at Bird.

"This is the young kid I told you about at the college that kept Jessica from getting on my ass." Dave said oblivious to the tension. "Chris this is Mike Deluca. Mike, Chris Clark."

The two were frozen in the awkwardness of the moment but greeted each other with a simple nod at the introduction.

"Hey Dave we really need to be getting out of here." Deluca said with his body perched to begin walking away.

"Ok Mike. Chris hope everything goes well little brother." he said as he began to walk away with Mike. "Remember what I told you."

Bird just nodded still in shock at what had just transpired. Langdon walked out of the courtroom and up to Bird just in enough time to witness the dialogue from afar.

"What the hell was that about?!" he asked Bird

"Man . . . . I don't even know myself." Bird answered still confused.

Making their way from the building, Langdon explained to Bird how he planned to combat Deluca's arguments, telling him that things would be tough and that a plea deal might be the way to go if offered. But his mind was focused on his child and what that would play out like. As they shook hands before going their separate ways, Bird looked up at the entrance to the courthouse at the large copper tone letters. How in the hell could his tenderhearted attorney beat the grandson of the man that the very building hosting the trial was named after? Bird jumped in his car and sped to the freeway heading for home. He turned the music up and cruised down the Shore way, trying his best to not think about anything.

Watching the birds gliding over the lake, he longed to have the same sense of freedom. Not a care in the world other than survival, his home being anywhere his wings could carry him. In the following days all that would be determined though. Over his head hung the possibility that he may never see the illuminated evening sky like he was at the moment for a very long time.

The trial grew increasingly more stressful as the days went on. Knowing that he was getting closer to his day Bird had skipped class for the week, opting to email his work to his professors for reduced credit. He was determined to make the most of what could be his last days outside of police custody.

Bird was taking a female acquaintance to morning-after breakfast when a call came from Langdon.

"I need you to meet me at the Pescale Building immediately!" he said in a fevered pitch. "The D.A. wants to meet and requested your presence specifically."

By the time he and Langdon hung up, Bird had changed his destination to the courthouse dropping his female companion off somewhere along the way. Within thirty minutes he found himself sitting with Langdon outside of the D.A.'s office waiting to be seen. Neither knew what to expect by this sudden move by Deluca. The questions swirling around in his mind stirred the uneasiness in his gut. Finally, he calmed himself with the reaffirmation that there was nothing he could do to change things now. All he could do was make the best decisions possible as they presented themselves. And with those thoughts he closed his eyes, took a deep breath and relaxed.

"D.A. Deluca will see you now." the secretary said cutting Bird's moment of serenity short.

As he and Langdon entered the modern contemporary styled office, Deluca sat signing papers. Without pleasantries he spoke, "Have a seat gentlemen." Bird and Langdon sat there quietly for at least ten minutes as Deluca signed page after page of paperwork. Bird could feel his tension rising at the arrogance of the prosecutor, but knew he had no grounds to be combative so he again quelled the anger brewing within. Just as Langdon was attempting to gain Deluca's attention, he again spoke, never glancing up or removing his Mont Blanc from the legal pad he was jotting in.

"I assume neither of you know exactly why your here, do you?" he said.

"No. We don't but I assume you're going to tell us." Langdon fired back.

Deluca's pen stopped as he reared back in his chair, first giving Langdon a steely stare and then shifting his eyes to Bird.

"Though it would seem that the jury is with me, I've been looking over the case and it seems that other than the testimonies against your client my evidence is all circumstantial." he said. "That along with the fact that Mr. Clark has a spotless record may make it a push to get convictions on the charges, due to their barbaric nature. So I'm willing to offer your client a plea. We'll drop the more violent charges if you enter a guilty plea to the weapons charges."

Bird could hardly contain his excitement at the news. The relief had to be visible on his face until Langdon shot off.

"Well my client and I will think about your proposal and get back with you." he said gathering his things to leave. Bird was speechless as he turned to him with a look of disdain.

"Hmmm . . ." Deluca exclaimed. "Well be sure to get back with me soon. The trial will be in the jury's hands shortly."

Bird was so unnerved inside he could barely sit still. He wanted nothing more at the moment than to wrap his hands around Langdon's throat and watch his life slip away.

"We'll see." he said cockily as he rose from his seat and began to exit. He looked down at Bird who was still frozen in shock as if to beckon him to follow his lead.

"I'd like to speak to Mr. Clark a little further if you don't mind." Deluca inserted. "You have a great afternoon Mr. Langdon."

Langdon shuffled to come back but sensed that his departure was welcomed by both parties in the room so he exited. "I'll be waiting in the lobby." he said again motioning to Bird as he left.

As the door closed D.A. Deluca finally put his pen down and rose up from the plushness of his seat.

"You know Mr. Clark these are very serious charges you're facing right? I very well could have gotten a jury to convict you on most of the counts. And if not for the retaliatory murder of the kid Carl in his mother's driveway in connection to the Calloway case, stealing the media attention from this one I very well may have pursued it further." he said to Bird as he moved about his office. "But it's not my job to enforce the law only to apply it for punishment. Truth be told I don't care who does what or what their vices are unless it impacts my constituents and I HAVE to. There are right ways to do wrong things, kid. Just like there are good friends and bad friends and sometimes it's hard to tell the difference."

Chris sat attentively listening, observing Deluca's mannerisms in his crisply tailored suit and wingtips—his French cuffs hugging his wrists perfectly exposing his Panerai timepiece ever so slightly.

"So this is what's going to happen. I'm going to drop all the heavy felony charges, and give you a twelve month suspended sentence for a felony four assault charge and a heavy fine. After paying the fine you should be able to get the convictions sealed or expunged." He carefully explained.

"In turn you'll drop your lawsuit against the city and Detective Blake. But understand in giving you this I'm also retracting the plea offers to your pals."

Bird sat and deliberated what was in front of him. His thoughts went to his soon to be child.

"What about Sheena Jackson?" Bird asked. "There's a situation there."

"I'm aware of that." Deluca replied as now he practiced his golf swing with a putting iron. "I'll make sure you get temporary custody of the child while she serves a reduced sentence. But that's all I'm willing to do there. She's already had at least three infractions since she's been locked up off these charges."

Bird knew this chance was as good as they got but the last inkling of loyalty to his friends still surfaced. "I need a few days to think?" Bird said.

"Well the case will probably wrap up with the jury next week if you don't take it and election campaigns will be ramping up as well. So . . ." Deluca paused contorting his face, moving his hands as if they were scales weighing the options. "You have until the end of business tomorrow to decide."

Bird nodded in forced agreement to his timeframe and got up to leave.

"From my understanding you're a pretty intelligent kid so I'm giving you this opportunity to save your own life." Deluca said now seated again. "This is the time in life that you learn the value of good friends and bad friends. Either they can get you in trouble or out of it, it's all in how you play your cards. The decision's yours. Choose wisely."

That statement would stick with Bird. Pondering its meaning as he was closing the door behind himself the D.A. called out to him again. He stuck his head back inside the door.

"One more thing kid . . . bit of free legal advice . . . ." he said again signing papers. "Axe that bullshit lawyer you have before he gets your ass reamed!"

Bird shut the door and headed on his way out of the building. The conversation he just had was echoing in his head. For most, the easy alternative would have been to jump at the deal, but even in the midst of confessionals Bird felt responsible for his team. Then there was the question of the fine. "What were the terms on it?" Bird wondered. Walking from the elevator Langdon quickly sprang up from his seat and over to Bird rambling.

"What did he say?" Langdon asked. Before Bird could speak he continued on. "He's scared. We can win this thing! Just trust me."

In his eyes Bird could see what his true intentions were. It wasn't about him by far. It was about a young lawyer scoring a win against a highly touted veteran prosecutor. "So this is how so many people end up fucking themselves in cases—listening to bullshit counsel like this." he thought as they walked.

Bird's mind was twisting and turning with the outcomes and possibilities of his choice, too much so to listen to Langdon's nonsense. The reality of the situation was that his decision would be either adding time to his friends or giving it to himself. In that respect the answer was an obvious but not easy one, even though Bird had a backup plan in mind.

"You're fired Langdon." Bird said with a stone face as he got to his car. "Drop the charges and case on Detective Blake too."

Langdon was furious at the choice, feeling his chance at staking his claim in the legal arena was slipping through his grasp. "So that's it?!" he said. Without answering Bird got into his car and pulled off leaving Langdon at the curb.

The next day Bird made the call to Deluca and the deal was made. The following week the trial was over and Bird was free, at least for the moment. The fine Deluca attached to the bargain was fifty thousand dollars in which Bird had to have paid within the timeframe of his suspended sentence. If not his legal problems would carry even further into the future. The prosecution undoubtedly made the move in relation to the testimonies outlying how much money was involved in the heist. There was no way the system would let a young black man walk completely scot-free with such a large purse. If he wanted to be free it would cost him. Nevertheless, it was cost he would gladly pay.

Although the money was evaporating like fresh dew on an August morning, he felt relieved. With the burden of incarceration behind him he finally ended his leave and returned to school and work.

His first day back in class felt good. With his mind freed, Bird finally felt normal in class, as if the issues in his life were somehow beginning to resemble those of normal people. After an hour and a half of question and answer dialogue amongst the students and the professor in his Psych 103 class he felt his soul easing further. Gathering his things into his backpack Dave's familiar voice greeted him.

"Glad to see you back little brother!" he said smiling extending his hand for a shake. "You get everything straight at the courthouse?"

"What's up Dave . . . yeah things worked out for me." He replied shaking his hand.

"Well that's good. Good for you son." Dave said picking his messenger bag up that was resting on an adjacent chair. "Hope you learned a lesson about good and bad friends, too."

The words immediately caught Bird's full attention, causing him to look up at the straight-face of Dave staring back at him. After a brief moment Dave's steely stare turned into a wide grin. "Told you I owed you big . . . now we're even." he said. Bird sat there speechless as Dave left. His words brought the magnitude of challenges he had just faced in his recent past back to mind. So many things had happened in such a short matter of time and now with the whirlwind of his life behind him he hoped to maintain the calm of his new world, or so he thought. The feeling of peacefulness subsided exceedingly as his day continued.

Things had changed at work tremendously in his absence, and not for the better. As he got back into the swing of things the difference was evident. It wasn't until he was asked about his absence excessively that it became clear what had happened. They had found out about the trial. The energy in the office, his interactions with co-workers, everything was altered. Now he was treated as a criminal amongst them. People disassociated themselves from him and quiet conversations ceased upon his approach. If the powers that be could fire him then they surely would have, instead they seemed to be taking the more convenient approach of ostracizing him until he left voluntarily. They gave further motivation by trimming his hours to the bare minimum.

At the same time, Birds personal life became an issue again when he received a letter from Sheena. In it she had seemed to be remorseful for how things played out and how she wanted things to be, but in his heart he knew that wasn't the She-She he knew. "Maybe she had changed?" he thought to himself. He came to the conclusion to go against his inner voice. There was only one way to find out and with the impending birth of their child, the only option was to give the relationship a try.

The rides to Ohio Reformatory for Women in Marysville seemed longer each time as the grueling winter progressed. A less than ideal place for a mother to bond with an unborn child, it was the situation that they found themselves in. Luckily the institute that she was in had just created a program to provide prenatal care to expecting mothers. The first encounter was awkward for the two to put it mildly. It was the first time they had seen each other since everything went haywire, not to mention they hadn't spoken since the trials. As she entered the visiting room their eyes met, whether the look they engaged in was pure contempt or intense passion could only be speculated. Sheena was especially beautiful pregnant, the soft roundness of her facial features glowing yet the tightness of her dismal prison garbs served as a reminder of reality.

Over the following months it would seem that things with Sheena and he may work out for the best, which helped him block out his workplace grievances. Her conversation and tone, though still sharp, had mellowed. Yet Bird constantly wondered if impending motherhood had contributed to the transformation or if it was just a simple temporary jailhouse change up. The feeling ate at him constantly but he disregarded it, choosing to give her the benefit of the doubt.

Bird submerged himself in his studies and continued to excel. He was remarkable in solving economic problems, creating business ideas that left his marketing classmates in admiration. He was a natural businessman, applying lessons that he had learned maneuvering in the streets to boardroom scenarios. Every set of circumstances in the business realm equated to the streets for him. Even more surprising for him was learning the legal applications of business law. Bird was amazed at what you could do legally and get away with in business. Things that would end your life early on the streets, happened in the business world on the regular, ending in a lawsuit or dissolution of a company. Learning the history of commerce and financial systems, which detailed many of history's great business minds and their rises to power, made it apparent that the goal of every business was purely generating revenue. The only difference was the legality of the industry of choice. No one ever asked where the money came from. That's because no one ever cares. The only care is that you have it.

The things that he was absorbing from school were changing his whole perspective on life and how he operated. The bizarre truth that revealed itself to him was that every person he had ever dealt with in the streets, young and old, had the same or similar understanding of the business of hustling. The concepts and models that Fortune 500 CEO's used were all concepts that street hustlers applied to their daily grinds just by different titles. Instead of buying wholesale and selling retail it was "getting it for the low and selling it for the high". Instead of cutting costs to keep overhead down and profit margins high it was "putting some cut on the work to stretch it". Things like becoming a distributor, creating a network and a distribution chain were getting "the hook" and becoming "the plug".

Throughout history some of the most influential men began from meager means and often infamous acts. Ruthless business tactics and shrewd conduct all facilitated under the pretense that those in their lineage after them wouldn't have to. Their atrocities would afford those that came after them the comfort to exercise morals and make the transition to legitimacy. Many a gangster proceeded lawyers, doctors and even Presidents. Now more than ever before, all Bird could think about was getting rich.

CHAPTER 8

"You ever make it out to D.C. give me a call!"

-Jessica

It was Wednesday, March 13th when Bird got the call notifying him that Sheena had the baby the night before. It was a boy, Jace Clark. Bird could hardly contain himself at the news and the typically private person that he was couldn't wait to tell all that knew, though the list was short. This marked one of the rare occasions he and his mother spoke, a conversation that was rather joyous in nature.

Bird went about his day as usual beaming with the anticipation of seeing his son. While working the department window a cigar slid across the counter.

"Congratulations!" Dave said.

Bird was stunned that he even knew. "Thanks a lot!" he replied. "But how did you know?"

"How about I invite you to dinner with my family this Friday, at my place and I'll answer your questions then?" Dave asked.

Bird's curiosity wouldn't allow him to deny the invitation and opportunity to learn more about the man who seemed to be everywhere all of the time. With that sentiment in mind he gladly accepted.

"That's what up." Bird replied. "I'd be glad to come."

Dave wrote his address and number on a piece of scrap nearby and gave it to Bird. "If you have any trouble finding it just give me a call?" he said as he walked off. "You can reach it off of Woodland."

Bird looked at the scribble on the piece of paper and read 4953 Woodside Lane. He was very familiar with Woodland but couldn't pinpoint the address in his mind. The Woodland that he knew definitely didn't have any "Lanes" on the end of the address. Bird opened up the internet on the computer terminal at the counter and Googled it. The use of Woodland as a landmark to aid Bird's travel was highly misleading. The Woodland Avenue that Dave was referring to was in Beachwood, a wealthy suburb of the city. Bird's interest heightened even more.

That Friday evening as he headed to Dave's house, his car crept slowly down Woodside Lane, trying not to pass his destination. As he struggled to make out the addresses he couldn't help but admire the neighborhood. The yards were all meticulous even with the remnants of the past weeks snow. Dave's house was located at the end of the plush street. As he pulled into the driveway the attached garage opened, exposing the European autos it housed, with Dave standing inside at the entrance to the house.

"I see you found your way here without trouble!" Dave laughed. "Thought the law had got a hold of you again."

"I ain't trying to see them again. Ever!" Bird laughingly replied as their palms met. "It wasn't that hard to find though."

"Come on in and let me introduce you to my family." Dave said.

As he walked through the doorway behind Dave, Bird was immediately highly impressed by his home. The kitchen was fairly large, with an island in the middle where a lovely older woman was prepping food. Dave called out to her to get her attention.

"Hey baby, this is the young boy I was telling you about, Chris." Dave said. "Chris this is my wife, Sherrie."

"Nice to meet you hunny, Dave's been saying a lot of good things about you." she said pleasantly. Bird wondered what her husband could have told her about him with their interaction being somewhat touch and go. Still he played along with it.

"I hope it was all good stuff." Bird said smiling.

"Come on let me give you a tour of the house." Dave interjected.

The dining area was off the kitchen. A large room with a rich cherry wood decor, the table had seating for ten with ample space for the large china cabinet, filled with fine china and other furnishings, meticulously placed around the room. He motioned for Bird to follow him further into the living room. The living room was awesome. The ceiling stretched clear to the roof, creating a large open room with contemporary styling. A sixty-five inch flat screen was perched on the wall a few feet above the fireplace mantle. Sitting on one of the three couches arranged in the room were two teenage girls.

"These are my twin girls, Mira and Maya aka M&M" Dave said smiling. The identical faces frowned back at their father for exposing his pet-name for them, then waved hello to Bird. "Let me show you the rest."

The two proceeded up the staircase off the living room to the second floor, its balcony overlooking the living area like a mezzanine. Upstairs he guided Bird past several bedrooms belonging to his daughters and the guest room. There were countless professional pictures mounted on the walls—the still images capturing various moments in the lives of the Greenfield's. There were pictures of Dave and his clan vacationing in other countries all the way down to vintage black and whites of ascendants at memorable junctures of their lives. At the end of the hallway laid the master suite.

Beyond the door was a huge room with a massive king-size bed sitting in the center of it with large sky lights directly over it and windows on every wall facing the door. Once inside Bird could see that there were two more room entrances inside of the room, one to the left the other to the right. The room to his right had a sliding glass door that led to a walk-in closet and the other, to the left, the entrance to the bathroom. Each room was more impressive than the last, constructed of marble and wood. Bird marveled at Dave's lifestyle, following behind him in a bewildered state wondering why he was there in the first place.

Dave led him back downstairs to the kitchen area, where his wife was now cooking, to a door that Bird had failed to notice opposite the garage entrance. She only glanced over her shoulder as the two moved through with a friendly smile. This door led to a large finished basement with high ceilings. A stocked bar sat at the far end with a pool table nearby. There were a collection of large theatre chairs facing the far end where a motorized screen was mounted to the wall. Behind the bar was a door that Dave again led him into. It was an office, its wood clad theme consistent with most of the house. Dave walked around the desk and plopped down in the chair and offered Bird to do the same.

As he was taking a seat Dave opened the humidor on the desk and swiveled it towards Bird. He had never smoked a cigar that wasn't filled with green shrubs, but took one anyway, carefully watching and assimilating what Dave did with his. As he clipped the tip of the cigar and struck a wooden match to light it, rolling it back and forth between his thumb and index finger while puffing Bird did the same. Dave reared back in the chair and looked Bird over as he took a deep pull on the stogie.

"I'm sure you're curious as to why I even invited you here." Dave said. "Honestly, I was expecting you to ask by now."

"I was playing it by ear." Bird replied plainly.

"That's why I like you son! You remind me of myself a lifetime ago." Dave said laughing. Then he paused for a second, thumping his ashes in the tray on the desk. "So what do you think of the house?"

"The house is crazy!" Bird answered. "Impressive. But of course you already know that."

"You know. I came from a similar place just at a different time." Dave explained. "I'm probably one of the few people that lead a decent life willing to admit that there's no RIGHT way to make it." Bird sat and listened attentively at his monologue, finding little clarity in the ambiguous rhetoric.

"You're a smart kid Chris, what you need to find is how to get where you want to go." Dave said.

In his mind Bird analyzed everything around him in contrast to what Dave was saying. His lifestyle was definitely something Bird desired, though he'd never seen a glimpse of it firsthand until then. It was obvious that Dave had done his homework and had chosen Bird, for what was the question yet to be answered.

"Yeah, I think I'm finding my way to the right path." Bird spoke up.

"Do you regret the things you've done in the past?" Dave asked.

Bird deliberated over the question, replaying key events and actions over in his memory. Even after, remorse was something that had never truly crossed his mind.

"No." he answered with a shrug. "I did whatever I did. It is what it is."

Dave nodded at the response, taking a long pull of the cigar and watching the cinder glow as it released the smoke off the tip. For minutes the two sat there quiet their thoughts swirling around the room like the smoke in the air. Until Bird opted to break the silence.

"So what is it that you do Dave?" he asked with a straight face.

Dave instantly began to explain his executive position with the local postal service and that he made over six figures, his wife, Rebecca, a RN. Bird was now sizing him up. A six figure salary sounded impressive but after taxes and basic living expenses there was no way Dave could maintain his lifestyle, even on the careers he provided alone. "With a little pressure he was sure he'd get to the bottom of things," he thought to himself.

"Sounds good . . . now what is it that you do that nobody knows about." He asked with a blank stare. Again came silence. Dave reached inside the lower drawer of his desk and produced a vacuum sealed pouch.

"It's not always what you do but how you do it." he said, tossing the bag over to Bird.

It was a pound of weed, but after inspecting it closer Bird could see it wasn't just any weed chock full of seeds and sticks sprayed with treatment, but all buds of pungent top grade. The street value of it was probably somewhere in the area of five thousand a pound give or take, he estimated, marijuana not being his field of expertise. The more Bird probed the more Dave slowly began to disclose, giving Bird his whole background by the time the cigars became burnt relics in the ashtray.

He came from a single parent home and was an only child. He learned to hustle in the streets but his grades afforded him the luxury of a partial scholarship to Ohio State University before his environment could get the best of him. Yet and still, partial being the key word, Dave had trouble providing the portion of tuition that he was responsible for. Rather than drop out he went back to what he knew, selling weed, coke and any other illicit substance he could get his hands on. Before long he was the go-to guy on campus for narcotics. That was when he made acquaintances with a youthful Mike DeLuca and Josh Goldman, who would turn out to be two of his best customers and eventually friends.

After using drugs long enough to learn to the business aspects of the trade, the allure of the "quick flip" compelled them to re-evaluate their positions in the drug chain. Over the years Dave's bond of friendship with the duo had solidified as they transitioned from addict acquaintances into potential business partners, proposing to invest with Dave to purchase more product for a small return on the investment.

"They were cool as hell but I didn't trust them Chris. They had heavy habits! I couldn't believe these rich white boy's that had their whole lives mapped out could be dope fiends man . . ." Dave said reminiscing. "But shit, I figured I could use their paper and stack mines and if I got into trouble along the way maybe I'd have some help."

That combined with the fact that they belonged to prominent broods and would likely be taking positions in powerful family businesses and organizations after graduation, made it an easy decision. Dave went on to detail his life to Bird, pulling no punches. He was surprised to find out just how down Dave was, telling him stories of how he put in work as a young man that led to him catching a case and facing time just as Bird had a few years after college. As fate would have it, being friends with them would teach Dave a precious life lesson in the value of having people in powerful places, pulling him from the fire just as he had Bird. Most importantly he had the opportunity to witness the value of lineage and the strength of family, explaining to Bird the concept of Dynastic Wealth.

"You ever wonder why the rich get richer, son?" Dave asked Bird.

"It's simple, money makes money." Bird quickly shot back.

"That's true." Dave conceded. "But it's a little more to it than that . . ."

"In every family there comes along an individual like you and I. Ambitious, determined and relentless." Dave began. "It's those people that lay the groundwork for those that come after them. EVERY family that's wealthy started with a lowly ambitious, determined, relentless hustler. And don't let anyone tell you different. They did dirt just like you and I, they just managed to mask it under the success of those behind them." Bird sat attentively absorbing the game that Dave was giving him. "If you're going to play the game, you have to learn how to play it to win young gun!"

Dave shared tales of how he had learned that Deluca's great-grandfather hailed from a poor family of immigrants and had been muscle for the local Italian mafia, all the while providing his son with the best education that his ill gotten gains could buy. How he used his local influence to keep him out of trouble and guided him into politics, and then using his subsequent position to help other members of the family. He also told him about Josh Goldman, whom Bird hadn't met yet.

His family owned a huge nationwide trucking and warehousing company that was began by his great grandfather and great uncle. They escaped Germany during the beginning of the holocaust with their families and began working shipping yards, struggling as most were, during the time of the Great Depression. But hungering for more and frantic to save their relatives, desperate measures had to be taken. "It was a different era back then." Dave said of his history lesson. "Sometimes trucks went missing and goods got hijacked. Nobody looked too hard and when they did people got hurt." The two managed to save most of their remaining kin through their efforts though, going on to establish their own company and becoming respected businessmen in the national shipping industry.

"Unfortunately for us, being black, our family system's been fucked up since slavery. With the systematic racism of the judicial and economic systems creating overall fucked up values culturally, it didn't get any better. We usually start from behind if we start at all." Dave schooled. Bird was taken aback at his intellect, his incognito behavior lending no clue to his rogue militant character. "So what you have mostly is a bunch of blind young nigga's going down a path backwards in the dark that was crooked from the beginning and leads to a dead end. Chasing cars . . . jewelry . . . hoes, all that shit's nice but worthless."

"So you don't think your kind of being a hypocrite?" Bird questioned. "You sell your shit to the same people you say are the problem."

"Would you stand behind someone in a hole who had no desire to get out or stand on their shoulders to climb out, where you could reach back and help others who wanted to get out?" Dave explained, giving logic behind his reasoning. "There's no moral victory in not exploiting others to benefit others. It only puts you in position to be exploited yourself!"

His rationale provided an unorthodox theory that quelled Birds inquisitive nature. From there Dave went on to give Bird an in-depth synopsis of his way of doing business.

Dave received one to two hundred pound shipments once a month and usually only opened himself up for business for the following two days. He had been in the game so long that only certain individuals in the area that dealt with him did it direct. He had it down to a science like clockwork and though it was a difficult system to maintain, it had served him well for many years. However, the price of anonymity was costly. DeLuca and Goldman were taxing him at every step of the process for their services in addition to the usual return for fronting the entire cost. Staying low key also meant dumping product fast as possible which made for meager profit. In a nutshell they had turned the tables and now were pimping him.

Feeling that he needed to move a little faster towards retirement and exit, he explained how he had taken a liking to another young kid in the streets who turned out unsavvy and wound up getting killed. Turning to his would-be protégés close friend failed to pan out as well, as he was arrested shortly after for a homicide in retaliation to his friend's set-up.

"The dumb muthafucka threw a pound of weed in the kids lap after he shot him!" Dave illustrated. "I couldn't bring myself the type of heat dealing with someone like that brings."

"So what is it you're asking me to do?" Bird said in hopes of cutting to the chase.

"I'm not asking you to do shit." Dave said simply with a smile. "Only letting you know there's a way and an opening. Ya understand? If you do or don't that's fine."

Before Bird could reply there was a knock on the office door. Mrs. Greenfield's cheerful face peered in, "Dinner will be ready soon. You gentlemen can come on up." she said.

"The Queen has spoken!" Dave said, getting up from his seat.

Bird headed out of the door and up the stairs with Dave closely behind him. Once they reached the top Bird appeared from the door to a room now containing a few more new faces. As Dave entered right behind a young female voice shouted out, "Hey Daddy!" Dave's face instantly transformed into a smile from ear to ear. It was his oldest daughter Jessica who had made the trip home from Howard University as a birthday surprise. She ran over gave him a tight hug as Bird stood there stunned, in some measure by Dave's omission of the fact that it was his birthday but mostly by his daughter. Dave turned to Bird after the exchange. "Baby, this is Chris the kid I told you helps me out at the college. Chris this is my daughter, Jessica."

The attraction was evident from the moment the two were introduced as she smiled at him. She had a natural beauty that radiated from her. Standing at 5' 7" with an athletic build Bird found it hard to be discreet with his glances in her direction as she moved about the room, drawing a subtle smirk from Mrs. Greenfield and a giggle from the twins.

As the evening continued on Bird got his chance to have a one on one conversation with her to pick her brain. From it he ascertained that she was in her first year of school studying pre-med and wanted to be a pediatric surgeon. She was only in town for her dad's birthday dinner and would be flying back out in the morning.

Bird watched her lips move as she talked, shifting into a breathtaking smile periodically exposing her dimples. She had her mother's warm eyes that could melt butter with just a glimpse. And an understanding in them that could clear the most cluttered mind. That surely was the product of being raised into a life worlds away from where Bird had been.

Before Bird could gather his thoughts Dave corralled him to formally introduce him to DeLuca, Goldman and others who had just arrived. As hours passed and laughter filled the air, Bird receded to a secluded wall and observed the room. "Dave lived a rich life." He thought to himself. But still he wasn't sure he wanted to drudge up the old parts of him that he had repressed inside to pursue his own.

As that night came to a close and farewells were being exchanged, Bird and Jessica somehow found their way back to each other.

"Hey it was nice to meet you." Bird said extending his hand to shake.

"Was great to meet you too Chris!" she said back, bypassing his hand and giving him a hug.

"Maybe I'll see you again." Bird said.

"That sounds good." She replied with a sly smile. "You ever make it out to D.C. give me a call!"

D.C. hadn't been on Birds list of travel destinations but climbed to the top of the list with the invite from Jessica. "Yeah, I think I'm going to have to make it out that way." he said with his own devilish smile as he put his jacket on.

Dave made his way to the two, throwing his arm around Jessica. From his glazed over eyes he had obviously enjoyed his evening.

"You heading out, huh?" Dave asked.

"Yeah. I've gotta get ready for this drive tomorrow" he replied. But thanks for having me and everything."

"Going to check on that lil' boy!" Dave exclaimed proudly. "Congratulations to you again! Don't forget what I told you either. Break the chain."

Bird smiled uneasily and turned his attention to catch Jessica's reaction to her father's statement. She stood there under her dads arm with a nondescript look that Bird found hard to read. Either she didn't care about the disclosure of his child or was cunningly masking her disinterest in him because of it. Whatever the case, Bird was quickly out of the door and to his car. The seasons were in the changeover phase from winter to spring, bringing surprise snow flurry while everyone was tucked away inside at the function. Bird brushed the snow off of his car. Sitting there as it warmed, he couldn't shake the thoughts of the young lady he had just met. There was a certain unmolested purity that she exuded, a radiance that he had never seen in a female that was his age. Thoughts of her absorbed him until his vehicle was finally ready. After sliding through a stop sign in the fresh mixture of frozen rain at the end of the Greenfields street, he decided to take the streets home, skeptical that road crews hadn't touched the freeway.

The ride was one of solitude. Bird's thoughts had now shifted to his upcoming day and the ride to Marysville with the weather conditions, which merged with his thoughts on being a new father. Riding slowly down the quiet road pass copious dwellings brought the evening and his conversation with Dave back to the forefront of his mind also, interweaving with the latter. Everything that Dave told him only reaffirmed his own ideals and made the utmost of sense riding past homes with foyers and luxury cars in the yards. It was a life full of opportunity and prospects that Bird wished he had been born into. Now after seeing the life he wanted he was determined to bring it to fruition for his newborn son.

CHAPTER 9

"You ain't strike me as the sucker type anyway."

-Double R

The next day Bird was up at the crack of dawn and on his way with clothes and goods for the baby. Shortly after arriving he received his first bit of disheartening news in that he couldn't bring the things he had purchased into the facility as a security measure to keep contraband out. Bird stood at the entrance near the security checkpoint befuddled by the news. It brought the sobering actuality of the situation to the front of his mind again. Still he complied, excited to see his seed in the flesh.

Sheena had given birth at a local hospital and was kept there with the baby for observation then the two were transported back and moved to a special section. Bird was searched and escorted to a wing of the facility that had been converted to a nursery and mothers' dormitory, created with the purpose of helping incarcerated females bond with their nurslings more naturally. Yet and still, with guards everywhere the feeling of being in a prison was unshakeable. He was first taken to the infirmary where Sheena was still in recovery due to some mobility issues. It wasn't until the two were brought together with the baby that his surroundings were relatively non-existent.

Jace was like any other newborn with an array of features still in development but Bird was in heaven at first sight, pointing out the similarities. "He has my nose!" He insisted. "That's crazy!" Sheena smiled at his remarks. For almost an hour the two new parents reveled in the infant, passing the swaddled bundle of joy back and forth between them pointing out which of them contributed to each plausible element of the baby down to his fingernails. It was surreal seeing She-She as a mother and handling a child but her maternal instincts seemed to be in full effect. It wasn't until feeding time that her lowest nature inconspicuously re-arose to the surface.

"Can't wait until I get out this bitch." she said. "My baby gon' have everything! He gon' be the shit!"

"So what are you going to do when they release you?" Bird questioned.

"What the fuck do you mean?! She exclaimed. "We should be alright from the move still?!" Bird nodded in agreement. "Well I'm going to get back to doing my thing when I get out."

Bird wasn't too sure she was catching his drift but decided to leave the conversation for another time as the heightened tones of their voices had begun to draw the watchful eyes of the guard and startling the baby.

"Til' then me and my baby gon' knock this bid out!" she said to herself in a soft whisper as she watched the baby feed from her.

The ignorance of her remark lit Birds mind on fire. He controlled himself the best he could but couldn't hold his objection to her ridiculous statement back.

"This ain't a place for the baby to be." he said. "After a few months he can come home with me."

Maybe that was a wrong thing to say to a woman experiencing the emotional rollercoaster of giving birth. Let alone a woman with Sheena's typical mental state. That combined with the fact she was incarcerated made her lethally combustible.

"What the fuck did you say?!" She erupted causing the baby to cry. She quickly placed him in the clear bassinet nearby.

"You heard what I said!" Bird replied back, his own contained anger brewing.

Sheena turned back to fully address Bird now, a look of insanity in her eyes. "Nigga, how the fuck you figure I'ma let you take my baby!" She yelled. The guards had caught an eye full of the commotion and were now quickly moving in. "I'll fuck you up Bird! Don't fucking play with me nigga!

It took everything in Bird not to lash out back at her, but Sheena had definitely pushed his button. As the guards dragged her out she spewed profanities at him, ranging from "bitches and hoes", to actual death threats. He couldn't believe how she was acting out, all in the defense of raising a child while in confinement. Bird left as quickly as possible after being questioned by the guards supervising the visit. He was so embarrassed that he couldn't get on the highway headed back fast enough. As he rode home he thought about his altercation with Sheena with a clearer mind and began to notice the cycle.

When on the same page the two were dynamic, but with opposing views they were equally explosive. The elements that made her indispensible in drama or beef made her an absolute liability otherwise. She was the epitome of bi-polar—extremely passionate in every aspect of her personality which was comprised of emotional peaks. Just as she could be loving and caring, she also could be evil, vindictive and heartless at the drop of a hat. This fact made the whole concept of raising a child with her especially difficult. She was one of the few people that could trigger a fiery response from him with her behavior and seemed to enjoy doing it. Knowing there would be no definite conclusion or happy medium in the situation Bird came to grips with the fact that the birth of Jace meant there was no avoiding her.

There was no communication from She-She at all the following day but he really didn't expect to after their blowup. As much as he hated taking Jace from her during her time away he knew it was only right. Bird decided that he would speak with Dave on things to get some objective feedback and also to talk to DeLuca directly on getting temporary custody of young Jace as he had promised. But he hadn't talked to Dave since the get together. Knowing he always had a way of finding him, Bird decided to carry-on in his usual manner until he did.

Monday came and Bird's class for the day was cancelled so he went to work early, walking in on inner-office gossip about a suspected drug dealer at the school that campus security was on to. The first person that came to Bird's mind was Dave but he quickly dismissed him as an implausible candidate. Generally being one to stay to himself, Bird delved into the conversation further with his co-workers searching for the identity of the suspect everyone was referring to. The descriptions were scarce, the only implication to trafficking was that multiple individuals had gotten caught with narcotics and fingered the same person as the source, known as "Double R".

Bird's attention heightened at hearing the name. He'd had indirect business dealings with Double R in the past and a couple of personal encounters. He moved mostly throughout the Southside of town, 116th from Buckeye to Miles and all points in between. He knew a little bit of everyone because he never perched in any particular hood. He was a nomadic hustler, roaming like a gypsy both in the city and abroad. It was a talent that made him elusive for jacker's and police alike. It also gave him a vast network of criminals at his disposal, plugging him to the black market. If it was illegal and someone wanted it or wanted to get rid of it he was the man to seek.

Double R was a hustler by nature. His real name was Robbie Roy, and he wasn't even actually from Cleveland as his associates all thought, but New York. He spent most his growing up in a government subsidized housing project in Harlem, which accounted for some of his flamboyant style and swagger. His mother's family consisted of generations of addicts addicted to heroin and alcohol. During the 70's she would continue the trend starting first with snorting cocaine on the party scene and transitioning into crack at the height of the epidemic. A sexy yellow-bone in her prime with a thing for hustlers she caught the eye of a well known half Dominican crack peddler named Rico and soon would give birth to Robbie.

He stayed in and out of trouble with the lack of parental supervision. Although he was a quick thinker he struggled with school, distracted by the desire to get money and respect like his father. His world changed when his father was found slain in a dumpster in Brooklyn when he was just twelve. Consumed with grief and no outlet, Robbie began speeding through life as fast as he could at a suicidal pace. He managed to catch a couple of possession with intent charges and get shot twice within a calendar year of his father's death. His father's parents fearing his demise was eminent as well, coerced Robbie into moving with his father's eldest sister on Cleveland's west side. His aunt lived a normal life, earning a decent wage in her career as a pharmacist. With a sense of normalcy he managed to regain what remained of his adolescence, enjoying the densely populated Hispanic and black neighborhood he lived in. That was until the calm vanished and death returned when he was sixteen with his aunt passing after a short bout with breast cancer, which she'd kept secret.

In her passing his aunt left him a fifty thousand dollar insurance policy, the house and all of the belongings in it. But before her body was cold in the ground his youngest aunt, Maria and her boyfriend John came scouring and scavenging to pillage what they could from him. Finding Robbie could see through them, they scornfully turned to the law for custody of the minor, and control of his inherited assets which a judge granted.

Not only did his aunt and her beau move in but also their two teenage children. Their presence immediately sparked huge altercations in the three bedroom one and a half bathroom house. The stress of both losing his aunt and forced custody was taking its toll on his mind, forcing his inner demons back to resurface and call him back into the streets. Fearing that a relapse in criminal behavior would jeopardize their custody and meal ticket, John physically reprimanded Robbie. But that would only last until a sudden growth spurt left him standing at six feet four inches and weighing two hundred and ten pound, making him more evenly matched, and their fights increasingly violent.

The boiling point came when John searched his room and found two thousand dollars. He took the money and when confronted his only response was "anything in this house belongs to everyone in it!" His words set Robbie off. In a blind rage he swung and connected flush on John's chin with a right hook knocking him to the floor senseless. Without hesitation he was on top of him, smashing him repeatedly with driving right hands, before forcefully choking him. As he turned pale, blood mixed with saliva and ran from his mouth as his eyes began to roll. The commotion got the attention of everyone else in the house and they rushed to John's aid. The eldest dived on Robbie tackling him off of John, the other following up with a full stride kick to his ribs while Maria tended to John. Robbie managed to get back to his feet, grabbing the younger brother and slamming him through an end table and lamp. John had regained his senses and rejoined the skirmish, subduing Rob from behind with a choke hold while the rest began attacking him with a flurry of fists and kicks until he blacked out.

He woke some time later, bruised and swollen. The family had left. For the next few weeks the incident went unaddressed with everyone continuing with business as usual.

It was a Friday and John yelled to the boys that he and Maria were going out for a while and would be back later. They usually frequented bars in the area when they went out and on this night were at one off on W.72nd and Lorain that they had been talking about visiting. The bar was off a side street, a somewhat secluded residential area with low light so they parked on the side of the building as close as possible to the entrance. The warm summer night was vibrant and the bar was crawling with patrons, but by 2:30.m. a slight rain had set in and the night had lost its electricity. The street had gone dormant as most the people had cleared the bar at last call. John staggered out with Maria closely behind him, both talking loudly in their drunken states. As they approached their car a dark hood figured arose from behind the dumpster at the back of the building gun drawn and accosted them.

"Gimme your money!" he demanded one time.

As John reached for his wallet without argument the masked gunman fired into his face point blank, the bullet forcefully exiting his skull with a misty spray of blood and brain mixing with the falling rain. His body twisted awkwardly and the fell against the car as the dark figure fired twice more through his chest while Maria stood frozen in panic screaming. He then turned toward her and their eyes met. The familiar look in his eye broke her from her frenzied paralysis and she turned to run. Before she could get a full step multiple hollow tips entered her back, the momentum of the mushrooming bullet entering violently lifting her off of her feet before she hit the ground. The shooter ran over and grabbed John's wallet, then the purse as he headed over to her. He paused for a moment while aiming down at her with an uncanny look of hatred in his eyes, the gasping and gurgling of John's last reflex functions and the pouring rain being the ambient noise to the scene. Maria squeezed her eyes tightly bracing herself for the impending shot. Suddenly the back door of the bar busted open and security guard wielding a 9mm pistol came running out, catching the shooter off guard. He quickly turned back to his target firing two more shots, before turning to the security guard and unleashing a flurry of shots as he darted away. In his haste his shots were off, one bullet grazing Maria's head deeply and the other missing completely. The security guard managed to get hit in the leg below his knee.

It was about 4a.m. when the homicide detectives arrived. The couples son's were still awoke playing video games in their room when the police came to deliver the crushing news if the attack. Both began crying hysterically, causing Robbie to come up from his room in the basement. Upon explanation of what happened to Maria and John, Robbie appeared somewhat shocked though not distraught as the others. The boys just attributed his dull reaction to the issues of recent. The officers explained to them that John was pronounced dead at the scene and Maria had been taken to Metro Trauma Center from three wounds. Though she was touch and go and extremely critical she surely would have died from her injuries if the hospital hadn't been so close. The two boys ran around the house gathering the things they needed to head off to the hospital. Robbie was already partially dressed and offered to drive. The detective standing behind him placed his hand on Robbie's shoulder, expressing his condolences. Being observant questioned, "How'd your shirt get so damp?"

"I had to run out to my car in the rain earlier and got drenched." He calmly replied. "Just grabbed it and threw it on to come up when I heard the crying." The officer nodded at the answer and they soon were all off to the hospital.

Though Maria would survive the robbery her injuries were life changing. The bullets had ripped through her severing her spinal cord making her a paraplegic and permanently damaging vital organs. The bullet that grazed her skull also fractured it and gave her a concussion. Her memory of the ordeal was shaky at best so the officers quickly wrote off finding an assailant. She had constant nightmares of seeing the killer's eyes staring at her through his mask though.

After several weeks she was finally allowed to come home. Maria was having trouble speaking so her sons cared for her while they were home until a home healthcare provider would be established in the following days. Robbie had given up on school and was in and out of the house throughout the day. The day the nurse was slated to come her son's had to attend school so they left her in the care of Robbie. Once alone he entered her room and sat at the side of her bed awaking her. She hadn't seen him since the attack, and now he was at her side with a menacing stare. As he stood up from the bed looking down at her she broke out into a cold sweat, crying, trying to move as best she could. The nursing aid had arrived to an open door and let herself inside. Checking the house for its residents, she walked into the room and found Robbie restraining Maria by her arms. The aid quickly stepped in, asking what was going on. He explained her suspicion away by telling her that he simply heard her thrashing and rushed in to check on her, only to find her in a panicked state.

By the end of the month she had chose to take the boys and move back out of town, much to Rob's pleasure. He was finally alone again and plugged back into the streets.

When Robbie and Bird met it was actually off of a near incident between him and Tuffy. Parking lot pimping one Sunday night by the Mirage in the Flats the two got into an argument in the wall to wall traffic jam. Before it could escalate Bird and Lynx swooped in and smoothed things over. The two would see each other on a few occasions and exchange hand shakes out of mutual respect. He and Lynx would ultimately hook up and do business from time to time.

As Bird was leaving his desk for lunch, Dave walked up just as he had anticipated that he would.

"What's up Dave?" Bird greeted him. "You're just the man I was hoping to see."

"Hey Chris, what's happening?" he replied. "I'm hoping you've got something good to tell me then."

"I'm headed to the cafeteria. We can politic there if you have time? Bird asked.

Dave nodded and the two headed over to the café area ordered lunch and had a seat. Bird began discussing the issues that he had encountered the past weekend and listened to the feedback. As the two talked Bird noticed Double R moving about the room in his peripheral.

"Hold that thought Dave." Bird said excusing himself. He got up from the table and walked over to Double R, who was heading to a table with his meal. He was his trademark flashy self, with two long gold chains around his neck with diamond encrusted charms hanging from both and his Yankee fitted cap sitting lowly over his eyes.

"You blend in real good" Bird said as he approached.

"What's up yo!" he replied with a smile as two dapped each other up.

Bird took a seat with him at the table and explained to him that he was hot around the school from his dealings, and advised him to refrain from his activities for a while to let things die down. He listened and thanked Bird for letting him know what was going on.

"On another note nigga's talking wild shit on you money." Double R said. "Like you done got rich and disappeared since Tyco hit the dirt. Left ya crew and everything!?"

Bird laughed heartily. "Man, I could give a fuck about what a nigga think about me!" he said. "Muthafucka's stay talking. I ain't gotta answer to nobody. Real nigga's do real shit."

"Yeah I can dig it." Double R said. "You ain't strike me as the sucker type anyway. Appreciate the heads up on them people though. I'ma have to fall back from pumpin' that white shit out here. Nigga need to find a good hook on some Purp or something, they eat that shit up just the same. You ain't been doing nothing though?"

Bird paused at the information that had just been presented to him. "Nah, I ain't been doing shit. But if I find a link I got you." he said. The two exchanged numbers and he made his way back to Dave.

"My bad Dave had to holler at my people right quick." he said.

"It's cool young blood." Dave replied. "But I need to be getting up out of here. I'll give Mikey a call on that custody situation for you."

"Thanks O.G." he responded. "I appreciate it."

"Not a problem son." Dave said as he got up from the table. "Did you happen to give any thought to what we talked about the other night? The stores should be restocked in about 3 weeks."

"Haven't really had a chance to give it much thought." Bird said.

Dave nodded at his answer, "No problem. Just let me know." Bird nodded back as Dave turned and left. He glanced back over at Double R's table whose seats were now filled with three white girls, then down at his watch. His lunch break was almost over so he hurried back to be on time. Soon as he entered the employee entrance and reached his station a message was on the keyboard prompting him to come see his supervisor when he returned. Bird had no idea what the problem could be but and didn't want to wait to find out.

He knocked on the office door and was quickly asked to enter and to have a seat. His boss wasted no time and pulled no punches in his monologue explaining to Bird that do to the unforeseen expenditures the budget had become tight and cuts needed to be made and him being the lowest man on the totem pole made him the first candidate to have his hours cut dramatically. The remark of him being the low man prompted Bird to inquire further.

"How am I the low man in the department when Todd came in after me?" he asked.

"Well though that would seem to be the case Todd's role has changed dramatically placing him under the budget of another department, although he still helps out on our side a lot." his supervisor said with a ridiculous smirk.

Bird was furious inside at being subjected to such bullshit. "So when did this TRANSFER take place?" he asked smugly.

"I'm not really at liberty to speak on the affairs of other employees for legal reasons." he said. "These are just some tough times we're all going to have to work through."

Bird didn't bother to push the issue any further than he had. The proverbial writing was on the wall. His supervisor went on to explain that his hours were being cut in half, from roughly thirty-two per week down to fifteen. Even further insult was his incessant insinuation that the reduction in hours would give him more time for his studies. Bird hurried him through monologue by savoring any remarks he had.

"Thanks Chris." he said in closing. "I'm sure things will turn around soon. I appreciate you being a good sport with this."

"Well I'll start helping you today by leaving after this." Bird said getting up from his seat and walking out of the office. The department head sat there in shock as Bird casually strolled out. He wanted desperately to call him back to scold him for his nonchalant attitude and disregard of his title as his supervisor but opted not to push his luck.

The walk across the campus to his car gave Bird an opportunity to mull over what had just transpired. Once inside of his car he was still fuming, in disbelief that the discrimination that he faced could become so blatant. As he pulled from the lot on to the main street his phone rang from a number that he didn't recognize. Though he was reluctant to answer the unknown call he did anyway, hoping that it would be good news.

"Hello." He answered. It was Dave.

"What's up Chris?" He asked. "I just spoke to my guy about your situation. he said the approvals a lock but you're going to need an attorney to file the proper documents."

"Man . . . I thought it was a given as part of the deal we made!?" Bird responded.

"You know how it goes son." Dave replied calmly. "If you need a little help handling it just say the word. I'm here."

"I appreciate it but I'm gon' take care of it." Bird said. There was no doubt that he could use any help that he could get in the matter, but the last thing he need was to be indebted to anyone and Dave's motives were still unclear to him.

Once the two hung up Bird scrolled down his call log, thinking of who knew a custody attorney. Near the middle of the list he saw a familiar name, Langdon. The two hadn't talked since the day they had left the office of D.A. DeLuca several months earlier. Before he could think twice about their last encounter and how Langdon felt about him he had pressed send. In a split second he answered.

The two spoke for twenty minutes, most of which was a rehash of the last ten months of their respective lives, capped with a sincere thank you from the young litigator.

"Truly have to thank you Chris." Langdon said.

"Thank me for what?" Bird laughed. "All I did was fire you."

"True." He laughed along. "But it made me re-evaluate my skills and I'm where I need to be now."

He went on to explain that after finishing up with everything for Bird he realized that the criminal law, though lucrative as it may be for established lawyers, was a realm he wasn't suited for. He channeled his skills down the corporate lane, servicing companies in matters of formulation and structure down to counsel on acquisitions, and had garnered a fair amount of success in it. So much so that he was currently in the process of founding his own legal firm.

"So what can I do for you? Not another criminal case I hope." He asked with a chuckle.

"No!" Bird replied emphatically before detailing the situation to Langdon.

After hearing the matter out Langdon agreed to help Bird resolve his custody issue. The two set up a meeting the next day to discuss the intangibles and costs that would be associated with it.

CHAPTER 10

"It's just my flavor I guess . . .
like to spice shit up, ya know what I mean."

-Sauce

True to its rugged, hard-nosed ideology there was no middle ground in Cleveland, and the same held true for Mother Nature. Spring and fall merely maintained the elements of their predecessors. Two months had past and the summer was now fast upon them. With the sun came cabin fever and Bird wasn't immune to the bug. The city was alive again, emerging from the depths of winter hibernation. Young hustlers from every corner and hood of the city had stashed away prized autos in customizing shops over the winter awaiting the perfect day to introduce their candy painted toy to the sun. Others took the increased flow of traffic throughout the city as an opportunity to debut the fury of a myriad of intricately wired sub's, mid's and tweeter's to bopper's perusing the streets. Strips from 117th to Harvard vibrated at night, their curbs lined with chrome rims, their sidewalks crawling with onlookers. Indeed there was nothing like it.

This was the first summer in Bird's memory that he didn't have Tyco and Flex around. Tyco was known for his summer toys and Bird had full access to play with any of them at his bidding. Now he was simply riding a tinted black on black J30 that Tyco had gotten shortly before his disappearance and trying to stay low key. The months leading up to summer had proved to be taxing. Not only was he barely working but the custody filing for Jace turned into an all out battle and not solely because of Sheena. The parenting program was new and government funded, so prison officials wanted desperately to show the benefits of the system. The last thing that they wanted was to show their numbers receding in any way other than a mother being released, especially not in a custody showdown. With Langdon hard at work on the job he was out ten thousand already and that number was sure to go up, but Langdon assured, that by the end of summer the two would be reunited.

Bird had also begun kicking it with Dave more frequently. He had actually become a confidant of sorts, becoming privy to the inner most workings of Dave's life. It came to some surprise to find out that Jessica wasn't his biological daughter, but his wife's' from a previous relationship. Her father died before she was old enough to remember him and Dave stepped in not that long after and was the only dad she had known her whole life. In many ways she was Dave's ideal daughter, hence his overprotective nature with her—even still she had no idea of the family secret that she wasn't a product of her mother and Dave. The even bigger secret was his alternative business interests. Absolutely no one knew about them and that's the way he planned to keep it.

The revelations by Dave made it difficult for Bird to express that he and Jessica had been having light communication since he had seen her last but he did anyway. Maybe it was his honesty that gained Dave's blessing in the matter with only one stipulation. "Respect her. Never put her in harm's way by exposing her to the shit in the streets." Dave requested. Being that Bird wasn't in the streets anymore he quickly agreed without thinking twice. He actually had grown quite found of Jessica during their long distance conversations, accepting her invitation to spend the week before Independence Day with her in DC and driving back home with her and her friend Penelope.

Bird planned on leaving on Saturday in the middle of the night and as the day came he found himself cruising through the city, windows half down enjoying the evening breeze in the Denali that he had Dave rent for him. Glancing down at the gauge he realized he needed to fuel up. He pulled into a Sunoco on Lakeview and took his place in line behind the usual gas and Swisher purchasers when a 67' Cutlass screamed in to the station behind his car, a tall figure stepping from the door with music screaming from the cabin. By then Bird had paid for his gas and was walking back to his car as the young man was approaching, fitted cap sitting low and two chains swinging, the diamond charms refracting the light. Staring at each other, it wasn't until they were within a foot or two of each other that Bird could make out the face in the starkly lit lot. It was Double R.

The two greeted each other with a hand shake and laugh at the release of the tension that had mounted in passing.

"Yo!" Double R exclaimed. "So what you into tonight homie?"

"Shit I'm bout to ride a lil' bit and then hit the road up out this bitch." Bird replied.

"Oh yeah?! Where you going?" Double R asked.

"DC. Got this lil' chick out that way." Bird answered.

"Oh ok . . . shit I woulda made the trip wit you if you wasn't kicking wit ya lady." Double R said. "Been trying to get out that way anyway. I got people out there."

Bird considered the offer. "Shit, you can roll if you want. I don't give a fuck." Bird said. "It's her and her girl. They riding back too."

"I'm on it then!" Double R replied. He had Bird follow him to a twenty-four hour storage garage where he kept his car and he got in with him. In line with his extreme character Double R had ten stacks on him for no reason and was prepared to blow every dime of it. It was well approaching club time and after a stop at the weed man for Double R and a leisurely ride through the flats the two hit the I-76 headed southeast.

Eight hours in a vehicle was plenty of time to analyze anything and Bird learned a lot about Double R on the trip. The two shared stories of prior exploits, women and urban myths that both had been close enough to have witnessed themselves. They also gave their histories and plans for the future. Contrary to his outward extravagance Double R was a loner Bird learned. It was interesting how someone who knew everyone could be in a room full of familiar places and feel alone. It was a feeling that Bird thought only he had known.

Since she expected him to be alone Bird didn't know exactly how Jessica would react to him bringing someone along, Double R suggested they stop and reserve a room for the night somewhere before heading over. Bird agreed that it was probably best that they both did and after a quick check in the duo made their way to Jessica's. Bird knocked on the door a few times and got no answer so he stepped away to recheck the address. While he did Double R went to knock right behind him just as the door opened. There was brief moment of silence before either spoke.

"Hi, I'm Penelope." she said with an ear to ear smile, her attention aimed fully at Birds partner.

"What's up, I'm Roberto." He politely introduced himself. "Nice to meet you."

"Roberto?" she said confused.

Bird quickly jumped in. "Hey. I'm Chris." he said. "This is my friend that came with me."

"Oh ok!" she replied with a laugh, turning her attention back to Double R. "You guys can come in."

Penelope was a young statuesque Latin brunette with an infectious laugh, and fun-loving personality to match. Growing up as minorities in a predominantly Jewish school district, she and Jessica naturally gravitated to each other, becoming best friends and ultimately aligning their futures together by choosing the same college.

As he and Double R came in and took a seat, she still hadn't stopped grinning. Bird could tell the sentiment was mutual with him introducing himself with his birth name, in a studious tone. The two would continue to click over the course of the week, his over the top adventure-junkie nature complementing her inner thrill seeker perfectly, turning the trip into an unforgettable time for both.

Bird carefully analyzed his surroundings while the others talked. The apartment was simple and classy. A comfortable living room with the dining area combined with a couple bedrooms and bathrooms. The hardwood flooring a décor was reminiscent of the Greenfield's home. Once Jessica joined them the four talked for a while before deciding to hit the streets.

They were at dinner at Clyde's that evening when Double R's excessive nature made its first appearance of the week gaining him a new nickname.

None of them were over twenty-one still Double R signaled the waiter over, insisting they all have drinks. The ladies were nervous of the likelihood of rejection and subsequent embarrassment, pleading with him to not even attempt it. Bird stood by, quietly observing things play out even though he was also skeptical that Double R would be able to pull it off in such a swanky place.

Still he dismissed their concerns, pulling a large stash of bills from his pocket and cycling through it nonchalantly as the server reached the table.

"I'd like two pitchers of Sangria and a round two rounds of Cuervo." he said, staring into the waiter's eyes as he struggled to stuff the wad of cash back into his pocket. The waiter looked at the faces at the table then at the bills still spilling out of his bulging pocket.

"Ok I'll get that in for you right away." He replied with a nod, looking squarely into Double R's eyes.

"You couldn't just get one pitcher, huh?" Bird said with a laugh, enjoying the exhibition of paper muscle. "I see you do everything to the max!"

"Go all in or don't go at all, right?" He replied with a laugh. "It's just my flavor I guess . . . like to spice shit up, ya know what I mean."

"I feel you! You need a better handle than Double R . . . nigga's need to start calling you Sauce or some shit!" Bird joked, bringing the table to laughter.

A hustlers' moniker changed in the streets as they evolved in the game, making the acronym "a.k.a." a part of every police officers lingo. Neither knew at that moment just how much the name Sauce would stick.

After dinner the group visited a few nightclubs and soaked up the native atmosphere before calling it quits at about 2 a.m. It was clear that "Sauce" and Penelope hadn't gotten enough of each other and didn't want to part so the couples went their separate ways, Bird and Jessica ending up back at her apartment. The tension in the room materialized like a dense fog as the two realized it was the first time that they were alone together. It was a feeling like Bird had never experienced before, his nature rising with butterflies in his gut as thoughts of possibilities and desires danced in his mind. He hadn't taken his time to get to know Jessica on purpose, it just happened. Now the mental attraction had come to a head with the physical and his mind was conflicted with the question of how to appease both without derailing either. Under normal circumstances it would have been a no brainer but this situation was different. Not only was she Dave's daughter but a rapport had grown between them making her unlike his typical conquest.

As he tried to relax himself in the awkwardness of the moment, his only concern was not to move too fast—though the alcohol in his system was prevailing in slowly diluting what little inhibition remained. Bird flopped down on the couch as Jessica went to the bathroom to prepare for bed, all along making small talk. The humid night air jumbled with the drinks inside him had Bird's skin coated with a thin perspiration sitting in the living room. By the time Jessica had finished her shower Bird had taken off his shoes and shirt and was laying on the couch torrid, in every sense of the word. She walked out from the bathroom and stood in the hallway leading to the living area in view of Bird.

"You should take a shower to cool off." she said, standing with her towel wrapped around her, water still running down her legs.

"Yeah, I think your right." He replied calmly, gathering himself to his feet and following Jessica to the shower where she gave him towels before heading to her room.

Without further thought Bird hopped in the shower hopping that the refreshing rinse would give him a much needed moment of clarity. After fifteen minutes or so the sobering effects of the shower had set in and Bird got out and began to dry himself, becoming conscious of an overlooked fact in doing so. He had no change of clothes.

Bird knocked on Jessica's bedroom door to explain and she invited him in. The cool draft of the air conditioning in her room grazing his face as he stuck his head inside as it opened.

"I left all my clothes at the hotel." he said still half drunken. "And I can't just be on the couch dick swinging if Penelope comes back right?

Jessica laughed. "Whatever boy!" she said as she jumped up from the bed and attempted to find some old jogging pants that he could sleep in.

Bird watched her as she moved about the room, the shorts that she was sleeping in so short and tight that he could slightly see the cusp of her ass peeking for underneath them as if it was taunting him. Her tank-top hugged her closely as well her braless nipples pierced through. As she bent, squatted and knelt looking in drawers and storage bins Bird's eyes never left her body.

"I don't think I have anything for you." she said as she stood and turned to him.

"Ok." Bird said dryly. "So where you want me to sleep."

"How are you gonna sleep with that!?" Jessica said taking notice of his erection showing through the towel wrapped around his waist.

Feeling that the jig was up Bird shed the towel and his self restraint with it. "What you talking about? he said guilelessly.

Jessica showed her own unwillingness to back down, walking up to him and wrapping her hand around his swollen appendage. "I'm talking about this." she said with a sensuous stare.

Bird couldn't maintain his composure any longer, reaching around Jessica and sliding his hands down the back of her shorts and cupping her round smoothness in his hands. He could feel her body relinquish itself and flow deeper into his embrace. Jessica grabbed his face and brought her supple lips to his, sliding her tongue between as they met. It was amazing how a simple gesture of intimacy that he rarely partook in had him mesmerized. Bird was engulfed in the moment squeezing her tightly as she slowly backed up, guiding him to her bed before breaking their grasp.

Jessica sat down on the bed and reached into the nightstand, grabbing a trio of condoms from it and tossed them on the bed near where Bird was standing. She quickly slid out of her tank-top and stretched out in the bed flat on her back, legs half cocked, rocking back and forth as she waited for him. Bird climbed on top of her, bracing himself over her, working his way up her body with his tongue to the sound of her subtle moans. At her breast he slowed his northward progress, taking time to give each nipple its own attention. The more he gave the more her moans intensified, her body writhing in pleasure and anticipation of the moment he would enter her. Bird lifted up from his position to slide her shorts off, noticing the dense damp spot squarely in the center of the crotch. A fine string of her juices clung to the shorts as he slowly pulled them from her body. Once completely off, Jessica closed her eyes and spread her legs giving Bird an opportunity to fully admire her shaved beauty in entirety. Within a minute Bird had gotten the protection out of the wrapper and down the length of him and was poised to enter her.

The instant the head of him slowly began sliding into her she gasped deeply, grabbing Bird's forearm with one hand the other on his stomach bracing herself. He clenched the sheets on both sides of her, overwhelmed by the heat traveling from her body to his as he gradually penetrated deeper and deeper inside of her. Each time he withdrew wetter than the last. Once half of him was inside Jessica let out a long moan almost simultaneously her muscle relaxed plunging all of him in to the hilt.

They rolled around the bed for the better part of an hour, their sweats mingling, changing positions and taking turns following each other's leads in a passionate sexual tango. Without notice Jessica's body constricted, her legs and arms which were both wrapped around Bird, squeezed tightly as she climaxed. Struggling to maintain himself, he continued to drive deeper, increasing his pace, forcing her breathe from her in a loud sensuous moan. Her walls collapsed around him, bringing him closer to eruption each time he flowed and ebbed from her. Jessica buried her face in his chest—racing to catch her breath as what seemed like every muscle in her body pulsated, bringing Bird to his peak. He gasped himself as his essence raced from within with such exuberance that he saw stars once his eyes finally reopened.

As the two lay with each other talking, attempting to understand the magnitude of what had transpired a bond was formed between them. That night would repeat itself the duration of the stay. They had no clue that Double R and Penelope had done the same, making the couples ride home just as enjoyable as the trip. The expedition to the District would not only mark the first time he and Jessica made love but also the birth of the bond between he and his new comrade, "Sauce".

It was as if the stars were aligning and the streets were calling him back. His burgeoning relationship with Dave in conjunction with his newfound friendship served to create the perfect platform for his re-emergence into the game at a moderate level. The attraction proved to be too much and

Bird decided that he would put the play in motion with Dave once he got back home.

Bird pulled Dave to the side after he dropped Jessica off, telling him what he proposed to do. Needless to say Dave was ecstatic at the news in a strange way. Too excited to wait he went down to his office and came back with a duffle bag.

"There's five pounds of some good reg in here." Dave explained. "This'll be good for a trial run. Send me five hundred a piece back and we'll go from there." Although it wasn't the high grade that Dave had promised Bird accepted anyway. He left the rental with Dave to return and headed out to make things happen. Bird didn't want to waste any time on getting rid of the packages so he called Sauce and arranged a meet at a location half the distance between the two. After quickly giving him the instructions on the play Bird was on his way home. Judging by the quality of the buds Bird figured they could get upwards of a grand a piece. He tacked on a few hundred dollars on each parcel and left the rest of the room for Sauce to work his hand. As soon as he pulled into his apartments drive his phone buzzed with a text from Sauce that simply read, "Done." The message brought the infamous smile to Bird's face. Making fifteen hundred dollars in thirty minutes didn't hurt either. And with that he was again reeled in—the addiction to emerald paper resurfacing by one simple third person transaction. That one transaction would only serve to ignite the hunger for more. The same went for Dave the following afternoon when Bird handed him his portion. He didn't expect the young man to come off of his hiatus and move so expediently. Now he was more than willing to front him more.

Just as Langdon had told him the custody struggle was over by the end of summer and Bird was officially a single dad. Having the baby changed everything even mending Bird's relationship with his mother, her desire to be in her grandchild's life forcing her to overcome the disappointment in her son's past decisions. In the same sentiment Bird allowed her to be in his son's life, regardless of his feelings about her. Over the past year the practice handling a baby caring for Lil' Tyco from time to time proved invaluable and by all accounts, he was a great dad.

The whole experience of fatherhood brought a different level of maturity and awareness to Bird. He was focused like he had never been before trying to make as much money as possible while keeping everything in perspective with regards to his young offspring. Bird and Jace had become an extension of Dave's family with Mrs. Greenfield and the twins occasionally babysitting, down to Sunday meals. Bird and Jessica's relationship had also developed into a strong connection and she was great with Jace. Even Sauce had toned down his flashiness and handled business in a more discriminate manner. For six months everything had seemed to fall into its proper place, capped off with him and Jace spending Christmas and New Years with Jessica and her family. That was until Langdon contacted Bird.

Sheena was being allowed an early release in as little as six months, eight at the max. After losing custody officials at the prison deemed it was more beneficial to mask the custody issue with releasing Sheena before the yearly government audit of the program came around than returning her to general population and keeping her on the programs log as a failed attempt. At the point of her release custody would automatically shift back to her making it simple to boast a claim of success and there was no way around it. Bird hadn't even spoken to Sheena in months and knew that she held some contempt towards him for taking Jace from her. It was also safe to assume she knew he was with other women and wouldn't mind, but surely she had no inkling Bird had fallen for a girl like Jessica. The two were as different as night and day with absolutely no similarities other than a common interest in Bird.

He pushed his love life woes aside to focus on the bigger issue which was the change in parenting styles for Jace. As Bird lay in his bed next to the baby he watched him. He was a happy infant, his young eyes full of awe at the world around him, so full of potential. Every day was a new one, a new adventure. His young existence was unpolluted with the ills of life and the crimes that preceded his conception and birth. Now all of that was at risk not only because Sheena was coming home but because she was bringing a chip on her shoulder with her.

CHAPTER 11

"Anthony gon' be so happy when I talk to him!"

-Mz. Tami

The calendar rolled over in the blink of an eye and Jace's birthday was coming up. Bird relished the experience that being a single father had given him. The baby had begun walking late January and hadn't stopped moving since, mouthing everything that he could get his tiny hands on. Bird's welcome at the college had slowly worn out and was now highly volatile, dealing with questionable attitudes from coworkers and faculty on the regular made things extremely frustrating. Under the advice of Dave, Bird put a transfer in motion from the small junior college to Cleveland State University. Not only would it remove him from his situation it would also eliminate his long morning commute, as well as keep him closer to his son should he need to get to him. Jace was the main selling point in the decision.

He had been under the watch of Laura, his mom, Mrs. Greenfield and sometimes Sheena's family. It had become too difficult to manage and Bird didn't like the juggling around, so after a fair share of vetting he found a suitable daycare for his seed. The only catch was the substantial cost. Even if he went and got county assistance the toddler campus was still expensive and Bird didn't like the idea of having his name anywhere in any government system anyway. Leaving the college meant he'd leave the job as well, which, though not much still helped. Things with Dave and Sauce were constant but not as heavy as it could have been. Dave was under constant scrutiny from his partners for his closeness with Bird for fear it would jeopardize everything, causing a rift in their business.

Heading back into the city on a somewhat regular basis sorting out his college situation put Bird in view of a lot of familiar faces. Questions of "Where have you been?" and "What you been up to?" always came right behind "Hey". It never bothered him though, until a strange voice called to him by name as he was leaving his new counselors office. He turned quickly only to see a burly woman headed towards him. It was Mz. Tami.

"Bird?! Is that you?" she called out as she steadily approached. Reluctant to respond he slowly shook his head.

"I'm so glad to see you!" she said.

"How you doing Mz. Tami?" Bird asked.

"I'm doing okay, down here trying to get my shit right to go back to school. These people giving me the fuckin' runaround. It's a blessing I ran into you though. Ant and Brandon had asked me if I could reach you not too long ago but ain't nobody no where you was." she said referring to Lynx and Tuffy respectively.

"Oh yeah?" Bird feigned interest. Tuffy and is mother were crooks of the same cloth and closer than siblings. There was no doubt in Bird's mind that she already knew all the details of what happened as well as Tuffy's true feelings about him. "What's up?"

"The lawyer contacted Anthony and said that he think he can get him out or at least a reduced sentence with an appeal." she began. "Something about the police ain't have nothing but circumstantial evidence and the judge will probably throw it out when they got back . . . all type of stuff I can't remember. You know I don't know too much bout what's going on." she said with a steady eye and smirk both signs of a veteran conniver.

Bird listened to her tale and watched all of her mannerisms, selling the plan to Bird in a performance befitting of an Oscar. Outside of the fact that it was Tuffy's mother, she was also handling things for Lynx. The situation with the case had changed things so much yet so little. He never got the closure of knowing exactly what went down and who said what. Yet and still, the wound of being betrayed was raw and now faced with the opportunity to get the two released Bird felt torn. His mind shifted to the bigger issue, being the fact that a portion of the money was rightfully theirs and if the tables had turned he hoped that they would have done all they could for him regardless of personal stances.

"So how much they talkin'? Bird asked.

"Twenty-five thousand to do it for both of them." Mz. Tami shot back quickly. "Said it might take him a year to get it all done."

"Got damn!" Bird exclaimed. "I'll make sure you get it but that's high as fuck though! You might wanna find another lawyer."

"He good though Bird!" she said, now grinning like a Cheshire Cat. "You gon' see he gon' beat that shit Bird!"

"He better for twenty-five more stacks!" Bird replied. "I'll come through the hood to you by the end of the week."

"Ok Bird! You be safe baby!" she said giving him a tight hug before they parted. "Anthony gon' be so happy when I talk to him! Oh and I heard you and She-She got a lil" baby!?" she asked. "I know you got some pictures!"

"I'll bring some when I come by." he replied walking away, checking his pockets as he did to make sure Mz. Tami hadn't lifted anything off of him. She knew that he wouldn't say no to anything that could help Lynx out whether they were on the outs or not. She made sure to mention his name every chance that she got, even in front of her own son's.

The past few months' rocking with Dave and Sauce, Bird had managed to get the money back up to about seventy thousand. Even though the twenty-five thousand was a hefty portion of it Bird felt as if he was buying his soul freedom by giving it up—a buyout of sorts. It would give him the clear conscience to truly break ties and move forward.

The following weekend Bird kept his word, arriving at Mz. Tami's with the money as she had asked. Bird gave her a picture of him and Jace, and hurried on his way. It was actually his offspring's birthday and the Greenfield's had helped him organize a birthday party for Jace. Dave made sure that Bird invited some of Sheena's family along with his mother, Laura and Lil' Tyco. Even Jessica was flying home for the weekend just to be there for the babies first birthday.

Bird didn't know exactly what the outcome would be like of all the different family's interacting with each other and expressed his concerns to Dave. But Dave held fast explaining to Bird that the party wasn't about him but Jace and everyone who cared for him had a right to attend.

Contrary to his feelings the party went well and ended without incident. But Bird couldn't help but notice Sheena's family's eyeballing of Jessica and her relationship with Jace and he. Surely they would run back to Sheena with all types of far reaching stories, stoking the fiery explosion that was already smoldering. With Jace sound asleep in Jessica's arms Bird loaded his car with the mountain of gifts his son had gotten. Watching Jess with Jace he accepted the situation as Dave had told him, happy that his heir was content and poised to handle the Sheena issue when it arose. At that moment he had no clue if that moment would be sooner or later.

It was only a few months later in May the question of when would be answered. Bird had dropped Jace with Laura for the weekend, and was waiting on Sauce to swing by on him to plan out the moves for the weekend. He had gotten undressed and ready to get in the shower when the doorbell rang. Assuming it was Sauce heading up Bird haphazardly hit the switch unlocking the security door. Within a few moments there were three soft raps on his door. Towel wrapped around him, Bird began talking as he made his way to the door.

"Nigga don't be knocking on my door all soft like a bitch!" he goaded as he walked to the door to open it. As he grabbed the handle and pulled it open the smirk on his face subsided as his eyes met with those of a completely unexpected visitor.

"So you gon' invite a bitch in or what?" she said with a smile.

"She-She?!" he said in a confused tone. "What you doing here? How you find out where I live?"

"Damn! No "Hello." or "Glad you home."? She replied stepping past Bird and through the threshold.

"You know it ain't like that." Bird said closing the door behind her. "You still ain't answering my question though."

"Nigga, it wasn't hard finding you!" she laughed as she turned to face him. "I know you think you Batman all ducked off and shit."

Bird looked her over. It had been months since he saw her last, right after she had given birth to be exact. Her body had snapped back like it was made of elastic with a few major improvements, her small waistline remaining while her ass and thighs had maintained some of the thickness child-bearing brought. Bird also wasn't accustomed to seeing her dolled up in a form fitting spring dress with heeled sandals exposing her French-manicured toes.

"Don't be looking at me like that!" she smilingly flirted as she switched around eying Bird's living space. "I heard you got a little girlfriend since I've been gone."

Bird laughed to himself as he watched her strut around like a peacock with fresh feathers. "It's been a long time right? That was to be expected." He answered. "And I'm just looking."

"You looking cus' you know you miss this shit." she said leaning back against the table in his dining area, bracing herself with her hands. "It's reeaaall tight too!"

Bird pretended that he didn't see or hear Sheena's advances as best that he could and continued on with preparing for his shower. "Jace with my sister right now." he said walking the narrow passage past the dining area. "But I've got a couple of dollars I've been holding for you."

He quickly headed to the back bedroom and re-emerged with a bag in hand and placed it on the table next to Sheena. "This should help."

Sheena reached past the bag and between the towel Bird had wrapped around him and grabbed his dick. "I appreciate all that but I need this right now more than you know." she said as she began to slowly stroke him.

"Come on Sheena . . ." Bird said, trying to convince them both that he didn't want her but the stiffness in Sheena's hand alluded to otherwise. As much as he hated it he could hardly fight off the desire to see what she could do with her new curves. Whether he wanted to or not she wasn't one to take no for an answer and knew just how to persuade him.

"Come on what?" she asked playfully as she spit into the palm of her off hand and glid it across the head of his now fully erect member. It wasn't like Bird at all to back away and Sheena was clearly enjoying every minute of it, like a cat playing with a mouse before it devours it. As the moments progressed his resistance only fueled her, turning her on even more.

Bird was speechless finding himself physically defenseless against her advances as his body gave in, his only hope was that playing possum would make Sheena call off the hunt. But that strategy faded quickly.

"Oh so you gon' get quiet? My dick must want me to put him in my mouth huh?" she asked rhetorically as she bent over and took him down her throat, stripping away the towel and any remaining apprehension he had.

Bird was just as angry with himself as he was turned on. Mad at the fact that this was the same She-She that had decided had no place in his new life but still was incapable from breaking away, Sheena again knowing exactly which buttons would trigger her desired reaction out him. The mixture of the two contrasting emotions made the energy so intense that it was like splitting an atom. Unable to analyze the situation with his mind clouded by his feelings while Sheena simultaneously was trying to choke herself on his manhood, he let go and allowed himself to be consumed in the event. Sheena must have felt him relax because she refrained from sucking him momentarily to taunt some more.

"You missed that shit huh?" she said as she looked up, now squatting in front of him. "Tell me you missed it nigga!"

Without answering, Bird grabbed a hand full of Sheena's hair and guided himself back down her throat until she gagged, giving rise to an amorous moan from her. She went faster, twisting her head left to right as she went up and down his shaft, the excess saliva dripping from his sack. Bird looked down, watching as she went through every technique in her oral repertoire, moaning loudly as she did. She raised her dress waist high, pulled her thong to the side and began rubbing her lips and clit with both hands while balancing perfectly. As Sheena changed position to her knees she braced herself by putting her hands on Bird's abdomen he could feel that her hands were drenched with her juices, sending a jolt of adrenaline through him.

Bird pulled away from her and on clue Sheena stood, shedding her dress. As she backed up to the table the two shared a lustful gaze before looking each other over, their eyes speaking what words dare not say. Bird throbbed as he looked at Sheena in her nakedness, her body amazingly preserved after having Jace. Watching him eye her, she parted her legs as his eyes made their way south of her navel exposing the glistening wetness that had begun to run down her thighs. With that vision Bird had surpassed the limits of his wherewithal to act in his higher self.

He took her boldly to him, his grasp met with a gasp as he turned her around and bent her over the table. "I need you to fuck me right!" she exclaimed looking back over her shoulder.

He agreed with an almost caveman grunt as he glide his head back and forth between her lips, coating it with abundance of natural lubricant that ran from her. It had been so long since she had sex that rushing inside was nearly impossible. Instead he gripped himself tightly, slowly pushing in, opening Sheena back up.

"Oooh . . . get in it that shit!" she urged.

Eyes closed she dropped her head, resting it on her crossed arms, back arched awaiting his complete penetration. Bird pulled out and stroked himself, manually spreading her thickening fluid down his shaft before reinserting. Sheena spread wide and accepted all of him in one motion, pushing her ass higher in unison with his thrust.

Bird's knees weakened for a split second at the rush of pleasure when his head touched the bottom of her, the heat and snug fit inside of her being almost too much for him to bear. After getting acclimated to the feeling, he instinctively began stroking her with longer, more forceful jabs. Holding her waist, he pushed inside her at a furious pace, the collision of their bodies shaking the table violently. Bird looked down, watching his dick slide in and out of her, the thin stream that had been running down her leg now thickening into a creamy mixture.

Sheena was completely uninhibited, thrashing about the table knocking its contents to the floor. Not being one to be dominated she began to throw her ass back, their combined energies making a thunderous clap. Bird now leaned back against the wall adjacent to the table bracing him as he watched her work. Feeling the reduction of effort a panting Sheena pulled away and turned to Bird, seductively leaning back on the table.

"Uh un nigga . . ." she said panting. "I told you, you gotta fuck this pussy right!"

Bird couldn't help but smile at Sheena's challenge and the notion he would do anything other than just that. Bird stepped up to her, wrapped an arm around her waist and hoisted her unto the table. He lifted her left leg with his other arm, aligning himself for re-entry. Just seconds after climbing back inside of Sheena she was flowing like a river. Bird quickly regained his brisk pace, pounding away to her command of "Harder!" in between screams. With one arm wrapped around Bird's shoulder holding herself closely to him and the other hand trying desperately to steady herself on the violently shaking table. She attempted to muster the composure to speak but her racing pulse held the words captive. Only a long bellow escaped her lips as her body shuddered as she came.

Bird never missed a beat, continuing to stroke her writhing body relentlessly. The sensation from climaxing after her judge imposed hiatus had every inch of her erogenous zones hypersensitive making each thrust torturous pleasure. Legs shaking she tried feebly to push him out but Bird wouldn't allow it, grabbing her outstretched arms by the wrists. Seeing her typically abrasive demeanor compromised gave him a surge of excitement that rushed him to his own peak suddenly. Bird hastily withdrew from her just as he began to erupt, cumming all over Sheena's sweat covered breast and stomach.

The sexual release brought a mental clarity that came rushing back as if a flood wall had been breached by cascading waters. An air of disgust permeated the room, he with himself for indulging Sheena and her for enjoying it so much. He scooped the towel from the floor and handed it to her to wipe off.

"Its towels in the cabinet in the bathroom if you wanna take a shower." he said. "I'ma use the other one."

"Hmpf . . ." She exclaimed staring at him. "Ok."

Sensing an implosion Bird grabbed him another towel and headed to the bathroom off of the master bedroom. He waited a moment before getting in, waiting to hear the main bathrooms door close and after it did he hopped in.

The hot water raining down on him was sobering, giving him even more lucidity. The question of how she found out where he lived plagued him and had him going through different scenarios in his mind. Then without warning Sheena called out to him, "When are you bringing me my son?"

"Let me get outta here and we'll talk about that." Bird replied.

There was no answer in return. When he came out of the shower he found that she had left already, taking the bag of cash with her. Bird had no number or address on her but was sure she would make her whereabouts known to him. They had unfinished business in the matter of Jace and there was no way that she would let it go. Bird's deeper concern was her living arrangements and what she planned to do with herself now that she was free. He wasn't even sure that she knew herself. With Sheena there were no indicators of intentions or motives. She was a wildcard. And one that Bird would be forced to deal with for the rest of his life.

True to form he blocked his thoughts on the situation out and continued with his regular order of business which was meeting with Sauce, who was uncharacteristically late. Two hours went by and Bird's calls to him were going straight to voicemail. Feeling that something wasn't right he hit the streets in search of his crony only to find that common acquaintances were already in search of him to deliver bad news. Sauce had been shot.

Bird rushed to the Westside trauma center where Sauce had been taken. Details were limited but Sauce had survived his wounds. For the next few hours Bird lingered around the waiting room hoping that he would be allowed to see him before the night was out. The feeling he was experiencing was somewhat new to him. With the exception of Tyco, Bird's close friends didn't come up on the tail end of felonious assaults and the fact that it happened didn't sit well with him. His mind was set to make things right the moment he had a direction to go in and for that he needed Sauce.

It was well after visiting hours when the doctors finished plugging and patching Sauce up, but being as that no one else was there to see about him they allowed Bird in the room. As soon as the nurse left the room Bird quietly began his interrogation.

"How you feeling my nigga?!" he asked.

Doped up on anesthesia Sauce responded slowly, "I'ma be aight."

"What the fuck happened?" Bird whispered.

Sauce began to give Bird the play by play. He still had been maintaining his cocaine business as well as his operation with Bird but recently things had gone dry. In search of a new connect he contacted some young hustlers from the far south side of town off Miles who linked him with an old head named Lefty. After politicking the past few weeks when they saw each other in clubs and in passing Sauce finally decided to give it a shot, taking twenty five thousand dollars to buy a kilo from him before his scheduled meet with Bird. But the reality was that everyone who had work was riding out the drought capitalizing on the inflation and the transaction was purely a setup. Once in the house where the deal was to be made two masked men stormed in weapons drawn. Sauce reacted straightaway pushing the setup man into the gunmen before making a daring escape crashing through the sliding glass door off of the kitchen, tumbling down the short group of stairs.

Cut and scraped he hopped to his feet and darted towards the garage as a barrage of bullets gave chase, one striking him through his back near his left shoulder. Once under the cover of the car stall he got his gun from his holster and fired back several shots before taking off to climb the fence behind the garage. With one arm and gun in pocket it took what seemed like an eternity to scale the railing, giving his attackers enough time to creep from behind and blast another shot, this time through his lower right side. The shot carried him over the fence, landing in excruciating pain from the burning sensation he pulled the Glock from his pocket and fired what remained in the magazine before using every ounce of strength left to take off running, making it a few blocks to the main street before collapsing in traffic. Last thing he remembered was digging in his pocket and giving a samaritan that stopped, everything he had in his pocket to take him to the hospital without calling the law.

Bird looked at him, choosing the wording for his next question carefully. But Sauce had learned him well enough to already know what he was thinking.

"I gotta do my thing B." he said. "That lil' weed shits ain't doing enough for me. This how I survive."

Bird could only empathize. "Well why didn't you call me on it?" he asked. "I woulda rode with you."

Sauce's drooping glazed eyes looked squarely into Bird's. "My nigga I fuck with you tough, but this ain't yo game no more. You got ya lil' man to think about and I respect it." he said slowly. "Look how many people came to check on me. You see what it is with me."

Bird left it at that and shifted the conversation to the identities of the setup man—which Sauce gave him along with the exact address of the house. Shortly after that the sedatives took a hold and Sauce drifted into a deep sleep and Bird was off into the night.

He made one stop at his place before he went back out to hunt. Dressed in black from head to toe he grabbed a Magnum snub-nose revolver and speed loader from his old bag of toys and headed out. He hadn't used any of the relics from his past in a while but Flex had long taught him the handiness of the six shot. They never jammed in tight situations and never left shells for evidence as automatics did. No witness, no motive and little evidence equaled a cold case.

In the car his phone rang incessantly with calls from Dave. It was no doubt that word had hit the proper channels and gotten back to him about Sauce. Bird didn't want any words of deterrence so he powered his phone down to focus on his mission. Under different circumstances he would let the heat die down before going on the offensive, but no one knew of the closeness of their relationship—so it was highly unlikely he'd make a suspect list. Added to that fact, Sauce had the presence of mind to get to the hospital without rescue assistance so no report was ever made. The only thing keeping his target's heart beating was that the opportunity to stop it hadn't presented itself, but he was hell bent on changing that.

Sauce had done quite a bit of homework on the bait man that lured him into the ambush, giving Bird his general whereabouts and his baby's mother's house. For most unschooled thugs calling themselves lying low after dirt, it was the first stop. It was the wee hours of the morning and Bird was in route when a text came through. Without giving it a second thought Bird opened the message, it was from Dave and simply read, "Think chess not checkers." The simple sentiment almost immediately diffused Bird's rage and caused him to question his mode of operation in the matter. With the streets being so tight everyone was hurting. Times like this brought the savages to the surface and the price of a body down dramatically. For that he would need a heartless goon with a passion for his craft. As his train of thought changed tracks to murder-for-hire only one individual came to mind, Sleepy. "Having a reliable mercenary would always prove handy." He thought to himself. Not to mention Sleepy was borderline psycho with murderous tendencies, masking them as a pathological robber with a deep disdain for the law. The odds he would ever cooperate with them if things went wrong were nil. An offer of five thousand dollars and the assurance that added spoils of the hit were his for the taking would insure the blood contract was taken.

Since he was already out Bird decided to do some recon himself to make sure the info Sauce had given him was valid before passing it over to Sleepy, along with five thousand of his dwindling stash. Bird arrived in the early hours of the morning, positioned his car several houses down the street from the marks hang out. Bird didn't know anything about Lefty other than the name and description of him that Sauce had given him. It was a mild weekend night so Bird staked the location out in hopes that his quarry was foolish enough to come in after bar hours.

Judging from the look of the neighborhood he sought refuge in, he was definitely no Jeopardy contestant. The house sat on a sullen street, lined with multiple abandons on both sides of the street. Shots could be reported and police would care less about response times. After only a couple of hours Bird's hunch paid dividends as a late model Cadillac STS pulled on to the street only a few cars ahead of him and a large bald figure stumbled out of it matching the description with a young woman closely behind him. "I hate to even have to be on this shit!" Bird thought to himself as he watched. In a perfect world nigga's would play the game straight up or at least save the bullshit for the truly meek and timid. Some will never learn dogs that don't bark bites can be more vicious than those that chase cars.

Watching closely, he saw another figure open the door of the apartment to let the two inside. Bird stayed posted until sunrise, waiting to see if there was any more movement in or out then left, confident that he knew exactly where Lefty would be when he became a memory.

Bird didn't sleep. First going to get the money, and then to look for his ghetto assassin—locating him in a trap house with his small clique of bandits. Wasting no time Bird pulled him to the side and got straight to the point, extending his proposition. It wasn't often Sleepy got commissioned for a move upfront and got to keep the complete haul so he readily accepted—assuring Bird that it would be handled with uncanny speed, efficiency and most importantly discretion. The two exchanged contacts, and with his play in motion Bird headed home to catch up on some much needed rest.

By the time he walked through the door and settled on his couch his phone rang again, this time it was Jessica. Bird answered and exchanged their usual pleasantries before she began to ask him what was going.

"What do you mean Jess? He asked.

"Well my Dad told me to give you a call to check on you because he had been trying to reach you." She explained. "And Pennie told me she's been trying to reach Robbie the past couple days and hasn't been able to get a hold of him either."

Bird didn't know that Sauce and Penelope had kept such close contact since meeting, each of them visiting the other periodically. After learning it he considered telling Jessica everything that happened but Dave's request of him to never expose her to the life echoed on his head.

"Well . . ." he began reluctantly. "Robbie got robbed last night and got hurt pretty bad."

"What?!" she exclaimed.

"Don't overreact." he said quickly. "He's going to be okay. Tell Pennie he'll call her later."

"Okay. Okay." she said, obviously distraught from news of the events.

He hung up with Jessica with a feeling of distress himself. Bird had seen so much drama in the streets over the years that dealing with the lifestyle had become second nature. Just in Jessica's reaction he knew that he could never disclose certain things from his past to her, let alone the present. How could he tell her he had paid for the life of Sauce's assailant? Or that he'd done the same things before himself? Dave had managed to raise a beautiful soul, unperverted by the chaotic world of the underhanded. Now he found himself withholding his thoughts, trying to keep her that way.

Finding himself now unable to sleep, he laid there with his thoughts rambling. It was times like this when just verbalizing the situation to an understanding ear helped. If Sheena was good for anything, that would be it. It was nothing to tell her the most dastardly of deeds from shootouts to slip-ups with other females she was there, a true rider. But with that unconditional acceptance came the deeper underlying issue. There was no accountability or expectation of better living, which only brought the worst out of him. Sheena had lived hard so long she didn't desire or even want to exist differently. Embracing it as she was who she was destined to be—a G, and subscribed to the ideology wholeheartedly.

Bird slowly began to drift when the phone rang again, this time from a number he didn't recognize. He usually didn't answer such calls but under the circumstances he did, figuring it may have been Sauce. The instant he answered and Sheena's loud voice came blaring through the speaker.

"When the FUCK are you bringing me my son nigga!" She screamed. "Don't fuckin' play with me!"

Her timing for calling couldn't have been any worst. The combination of frustration and fatigue made his blood come to an immediate boil at her comments.

"Bitch don't call me yelling on some bullshit!" He hollered. "Recognize who the fuck you talking to. I told you we'd handle that shit right?"

Sheena was frozen for a moment stunned by Bird's immediate reaction. Before she could offer a rebuttal Bird was back at her.

"How the fuck did you get my number anyway?!" He asked. "I'm tellin' you now don't fuck with me!"

As the last word left his lips he pressed end on the call and powered his phone down. Still fuming from the call, he turned on the TV while he sulked for a bit. In the midst of the issues with Sauce the issue of Jace's custody had fell from thought. Thinking about his son soothed his rage and relaxed him. It was dealings like these that he wanted to spare his seed from—the hassle of bearing unfathomable burdens all in the name of survival. The emotional release depleted what energy remained and before long Bird drifted into a sleepy coma.

His sleep was deep with no dreams or thoughts just blankness. Over the next day he drifted in and out of his slumber in a drunken daze, finally awaking 6 a.m. Sunday to the local early morning newscast. The breaking news shook the cobwebs from Birds mind as they detailed a late Saturday homicide.

"Details are sketchy, but officers have confirmed that 3 bodies were found in the home behind me, murdered in a bloody scene." The Reporter said as he stood with the house Bird had staked out as his backdrop.

"Have any of the victims been identified?" The Anchor question. "Do they have any leads?" Bird watched attentively with his stomach in his throat, waiting for the response.

"The authorities have positively identified the trio but are only releasing the names of two as the one was a juvenile whose family has yet to be notified." *He answered. Raymond "Lefty" Carlyle 38, and Latasha Williams 23, both of Cleveland were found along with the minor whom police are withholding releasing. Investigators are scouring the crime scene but say they have very little evidence and no motive in these gruesome slayings. In a sad twist though, there was one survivor, Latasha Williams's 5yr old son who was asleep in his room*

when the attack began. The toddler survived by hiding in his closet until being found by one of the victim's brother who came and discovered the massacre."

Bird breathed a bittersweet sigh of relief. Things got done though not without collateral damage. His change in parental status over the past year brought a disheartening feeling over him like he'd never endured before with the news of the teenager and child. In that moment he found making the call to take a life was no easier than doing it himself. Yet after powering his phone back on and checking his messages and hearing Sauces labored breathing as he told him to call him brought the contrasting view back to light.

The next few days Bird spent his time with Jace, stopping in on Sauce from time to time as he recovered discreetly at his Aunt's old home. Bird taking care of his enemy served to cement their relationship as well as make the streets rumor mill chatter. It was an expected reaction so Bird remained unconcerned until a few containing his name hit the streets. Even though they contained nothing more than the fact he and Sauce had close ties he felt compelled to get back with Sleepy to make sure the leaks weren't coming from him in away.

They setup a meet in the open air of the high schools nearby football ball field. With the team practicing and runners walking the track it was safe to congregate there without drawing suspicion. Sitting in the aluminum bleachers, Sleepy came up and sat next to him.

After exchanging "What's ups?" the two got down to business.

"So how you like my work?" Sleepy said with a tone of pride.

Bird just looked at him for a moment, wondering just how demented he was. "Was cool . . . you got it done." Bird replied. "I'm hearing shit swirling though . . . just want to make sure we don't have any problems."

"Ain't shit bout me. But I've been hearing nigga's talkin' how you and dude cool and shit." Sleepy replied. "Don't know who put it out here though. Was gon' ask you bout it. That talkin' shit ain't my thing."

Bird could see that he was telling the truth. He was a man of little conversation.

"Fuck them. As long as we're good I could give a fuck what the gossip is." Bird said staring Sleepy in his eyes, extending his hand to shake. "But what was the deal with the kid?"

Sleep reciprocated, shaking Bird's hand and going into a detailed account of the lethal undertaking.

He stalked the house just as Bird had the night before. For some reason Lefty came in near the same time Bird had told him. He sprung from the car, walking from up the street, timing it perfectly with Lefty getting out of the Cadillac. "He was slipping . . . drunk and shit." Sleepy described.

As soon as Lefty reached the sidewalk Sleepy was in passing, or so it seemed, quickly pulling the Glock from his waistband and aiming it to his head. He quickly escorted Lefty to the door, mindful that someone would come to open it he stayed low, directly behind Lefty of the peepholes line of vision. Once the door began to open he kicked it hard as he could, knocking the woman opening it to the floor and then threw Lefty inside landing on top of her. The young boy there, seventeen years old or so, rushed to the door with a pistol at the commotion. Sleepy spotted him as he got within sight and with no choice fired, hitting him in the throat caused a huge spray of blood. Fear and disbelief crippled the two as they watched frozen still. From there Sleepy went on with his business demanding the money and drugs.

"So what was there?" Bird questioned.

"Man!" Sleepy began. "Shit was like the lottery. This dumb ass nigga kept all type of shit there, guns, dope . . . . shit was all out in plain sight. I was amazed. I hit for like seventy-five if I cash everything out."

"Shit. I might need my lil' paper back!" Bird joked.

The two laughed and soon wrapped up their talk. Once in the car Bird sat for a moment, soaking up the whole scenario. Oddly he was comforted knowing the youngster, as the news described it, was a young adult capable of understanding the risks of the wrong affiliation. With closure he could put the event behind him and allow all the talking to fizzle out. Or so he thought.

Three days had passed and the weather was continuously warming up. So had the rumors which now had somehow segwayed from the killings to Sauce and Bird. It was a ghetto version of "Where Are They Now", with Bird being at the height of inquiry. He hadn't talked to Dave since dodging his calls nearly a week earlier but received another text from him out of the blue reading, "I told you chess . . . get it together son."

Bird dismissed it all, simply attributing the prolonged chatter to his absence from the streets. That was until he ran into a familiar face as he exited the elevator one morning while taking Jace to daycare. Snags, a young goon that was a close associate of Sleepy, was getting on as he exited. Although they never had any problems between them and were cordial that day, Snags had a penchant for aggressive and obnoxious behavior. Bird didn't like the idea of anyone knowing where he was, let alone a newly christened jacker, especially with his name swirling around. Realizing his cherished sanctity had been compromised by the retaliation, he wrestled with the idea of giving up his custody sooner than he would have liked. The fact was, now was as good a time as any to let Jace go be with Sheena. Weighing his options he finally gave in and decided it would be the safest thing for his son.

With a hesitant heart, Bird called the number that she had called him from during their last conversation and arranged the drop-off. Sheena gloated inside during the proceedings as Bird unloaded bag after bag from his car into her Aunt's house. He could feel the jubilance radiating from her as he painstakingly made sure his son was situated as best as possible. Still he manned up and handled it, knowing that he couldn't allow his own ego risk the most important thing in his life. On June 10th he would be glad that he had.

Bird was in and out of the house running now. With Jace gone he had a lot more time which he tried desperately to occupy with something worthwhile like studying. It was a balmy night and rather than head in from school Bird decided to stop by and see how Sauce was doing since he was still nursing his wounds. He got in around 10:30p.m to what seemed like a normal parking lot. It wasn't until he reached his apartment door and found it opened as he went to push his key into the lock that his senses began to tingle. Bird could see that the door trim had been kicked through with splintered remains on the floor outside his doorway. He looked down both ends of the eerily quiet hallway cautiously before making his mind up to enter. Luckily he had been keeping his revolver with him since he had seen Snags in the vicinity. With gun in hand Bird burst into the dark apartment, checking every room in the small living space as if he was a member of a SWAT team.

No one was there.

The apartment had been ransacked from top to bottom. Every item in every room was displaced. First he checked the coat closet where he kept a black duffle bag with a few pistols and ammo. Everything was gone. Bird rushed back to the bedroom to see if the safe he had hidden was intact only to find it gone too. Instantly his knees got weak and his stomach turned. Everything was in it. In one fell swoop Bird was flat broke.

He sat on the bed before calling the apartment management and the police. His mind racing through possibilities. Along with the money he had lost irreplaceable items like his picture of he, Jace and Jessica from Christmas. Thinking on it infuriated him even more that the cash. He thought to himself long and hard but every effort to calculate who did it was overtaken by thoughts of what he would do now. There was no job to lean on. Sauce was still down, relying on his own reserves to survive. Dave had slowed with the weed and would only slow even more now with Bird's spike in popularity. Even in hindsight, trapped in his own memories Bird couldn't foresee any other alternative in the situation. With any trace of apprehension about returning the streets full throttle being swallowed by his will to survive, he succumb to the pull of the game. But this time he would play on his terms.

CHAPTER 12

"Y'all betta let my lil' nigga through!"

-Brennan

With no money and no connections jumpstarting things would be difficult but there was one favor Bird knew that he could call on. Brennan aka Boss B.

An old head that Big Tyco often dealt with, Brennan had flourished after Tyco's death. Bird had picked up large amounts of dope that he had battered into nothingness a half a dozen times for Tyco. Each time Tyco would use the cake mix as cut for his own, paying Brennan healthily. Without Tyco Brennan would have easily been dead or dead broke from his mishandlings. A forty year old with the mind of an eighteen year old, he stayed into something reckless, demanding his underlings called him Boss B. But word on the streets was that his new woman held things together and was responsible for his continuous success, yet no one really knew who she was or much about her. Even still, he managed to draw the attention of law enforcement landing him into hot water.

Bird went to Brennan's bar in University Heights where he could often be found. It was a nice place, one he likely had no say in and let his mystery woman pull together. As Bird entered he could hear him talking loudly in the back. He attempted to approach but was stopped and patted down by two men who awaited Boss B's blessing to allow him through.

Brennan looked up and saw it was Bird and laughed loudly. "Y'all betta let my lil' nigga through!" He yelled.

Burly and dark, Brennan was unmistakable. At first sight he looked like a figure that should have been some franchises offensive lineman, standing 6' 6" and over 300lbs. Never one to be conspicuous, everything about Brennan was obnoxious, from his speech and size down to his dress. With Mr. Albert's latest linens, gator sandal's on his hooves and a large faced watch on his wrist, ornate with jewels around the bezel and bracelet he sat and stuffed his face. Bird walked over and greeted him with a handshake as he stood and towered over him.

"Where you been nigga!?" He asked in a low bass heavy tone.

"Been trying to stay out the way." Bird replied.

"Must not be too much money out the way or why would you be here to see me?" Brennan jeered.

Bird bothered not to reply, giving a hard look into Brennan's eyes. He too knew the role that Bird and his crew played for Tyco. Rushing into danger with what seemed to be insane bravado, yet with schemes crafted with a razors edge—all to maintain the balance of power. Now he was alone like a young hungry prince with no country seeking asylum.

"So what can I do for you lil' nigga?" Brennan said strongly.

"Front me a track." Bird replied plainly. "I'll be back to you in 24 hours with your money plus a lil' interest.

Brenna wiped his hands and sat back in his seat. "A track of?" He replied as if he was confused.

"I'm not gender biased. Girl or boy it doesn't really matter to me." Bird said.

For a long moment there was silence, each of them staunchly maintaining their poker faces until Brennan broke the silence with a thunderous laugh.

"I don't know who you remind me of more Tyco or Flex." he said.

"Whichever one you would front some work to." Bird replied still focused on his goal.

"Here's the situation." Brennan began, lowered his tone as he spoke. His talk shifted from boisterous to methodical detailing out his current legal issues to Bird. The extravagance of his nature had rubbed quite a few important people the wrong way yet he had managed to avoid the snares that were set for him. A chance police stop and gun charge later and he was going to have his probation violated. His lawyers had an inside track and knew that a warrant was imminent—notifying him in enough time that he could get his affairs in order. With jail time awaiting Brennan had fell back, allowing his mystery woman to handle both sides of the business at her own discretion.

"So where do that leave me?" Bird asked. "I ain't tryin' to be jumpin' through hoola hoops for a lil' track."

"You and I both know it's fucked up out here." Brennan said. "If my girl is cool wit' doing business with you we can make it happen. If not . . . it is what it is."

"So when can we link?!" Bird asked emphatically.

In turn he was invited to a private party that weekend that Brennan was having, a farewell celebration of sorts. There his lady would be able to watch Bird's movements anonymously and see if she felt he was worth extending a hand to without endangering herself. Without another hook on the line Bird accepted, with the pretense that even if she declined he would still be able to sift through the crowd and capture her identity.

The night of the event came and Bird was prepared. He had talked to Sauce about the move and he was all in, guaranteeing Bird that the money was secure for whatever he bought as a failsafe for his self imposed 24hr deadline. With that information Bird was supremely confident that he'd make good on the connect.

The party was invite only and due to the circumstances the location wasn't disclosed until that evening to throw off any agents that might have been have wanted to partake in the festivities. At around 7pm the call came through, The Touch of Elegance was his destination.

Bird arrived to the location shortly after 11:30pm, driving past first to peep the scene. The venue was a hall, located in a decent neighborhood yet not too far from the hood. Its facade was unassuming, absent of any glitzy signs or awnings. Inside it was another story. Brennan had the party going full throttle with an open bar pouring nothing but top shelf. Bird was amazed at how many people were in the building since no one knew where it would be at five hours earlier. But nevertheless the place was slowly getting packed. Once inside Bird could understand why Brennan took such precautions. The attendees were made up of a virtual who's who on the urban scene in the city. From hired guns and drug mules to career crooks and the lawyers that protected them. Panning over the crowd it was evident Brennan had his thumb on the pulse of the city. Bird even saw he and Sleepy exchange daps as he faded to a location near the back wall where he could observe the whole room.

Giving the room a second glance over Bird saw a familiar shape that caught his eye but in the low light the face was hard to make out. Making his way through the crowd the woman turned, allowing him a slight glimpse of her profile, still he wasn't certain of her identity. Determined to satisfy his curiosity he hurried through the crowd and directly behind the woman.

"Ummm. Excuse me?" he said gently tapping her shoulder. "You're not supposed to be on this tier C.O. Williams."

The woman swung around with a puzzled look that quickly turned into a beautiful surprised smile. "Heeeyy!" she said cheerfully. "Don't play like that in here."

"What else can I call you?" He asked. "You know you still owe me your name right?"

Bird's recollection of her words brought a blush to her caramel face.

"Natalie." She replied. "And I'll have you know I'm not a corrections officer anymore.

Bird walked over and sat on the side of the bed, picking up a tightly rolled cigarillo from the nightstand and sparking it. He inhaled the thick vapor as the thoughts of his encounter with the vixen swirled through his mind like the smoke in the air.

"So what do you do now?" Bird inquired.

"Well . . ." she began, but then got distracted by something behind Bird in the distance. "Excuse me, I'll be right back."

Bird turned just in time to see her be swallowed into the crowd. After 15 minutes she hadn't returned and Bird dismissed it, attributing her disappearance to the probability of a male friend at the bash. Wading through the crowd he found his way back to his original position and stayed there for the rest of the night, surveying the atmosphere while watching Brennan's self-aggrandizing antics. Not once did he or his people address Bird in the matter of business so he left, still in the dark on whether he would be one of the chosen few his madam would consider doing business with in his absence. Certain that he would get word of the decision either way he discarded it from thought and left. Yet the chance encounter with Natalie remained. She was even sexier than he remembered from his short stint of lockup. She plagued his mind until his eyes closed for rest.

The next morning Bird awoke, still thinking about the night before. He wasn't used to wanting something and having a clue where to find it. Shuffling to the bathroom to piss and brush his teeth, he made a promise to the man in the mirror that when the next opportunity with the coquette presented itself she wouldn't steal away so easily.

Moments later he received a call. It was a request for his presence at Brennan's bar for lunch which he readily confirmed. Bird fell asleep as he casually awaited the meeting, ending up slightly oversleeping by a half hour. He quickly got himself up and soon enough was pulling up to the bar only to find it flooded with police and federal agents. Bird drove up another block and pulled over, studying the scene in his rear view mirror as officers escorted Brennan into the back of one of the cars. "Thank God I fell asleep." He murmured to himself, knowing that if not for divine intervention he'd have been sitting there next to him when the FED's stormed in. As he watched a young kid knocked on his passenger window startling him. He powered the window down to see what the boy wanted, but he didn't say anything; instead he dropped a piece of paper on the seat and walked off. Bird picked it up and saw it was a receipt from the restaurant he was parked in front of with an address and time scribbled on the back. *2720 Hampshire Rd. Apt C., 8p.* A wave of anticipation overtook him. His first inclination was to disregard the note and head home but curiosity had gotten the best of him, urging him to turn around and at least see what was at the address. Before he knew it he had rode down the street twice, checking out the layout of the building the apartment resided in from different angles. He drove home thinking about who had sent the little boy up to his window to deliver the message.

"It couldn't have been the police." he thought to himself. They could have grabbed him right then and there. Went he got home the question of who and why remained. Maybe it was one of the people that were privy to his meeting with Brennan, but if so who could that be? He pulled the receipt from his pocket and analyzed it closely, finally he noticed something. The time stamped on the receipt was only minutes before he received it which meant the individual that composed it was right there, watching him the whole time. Bird came to grips with the fact that the only way he would know the answer to his question was to go find out. So 2720 Hampshire Road Apt C, 8p.m. it was.

7p.m. came and Bird was already there, scoping the scene. There was absolutely no activity in the quiet neighbor let alone the building he was going to head into. The hour had pasted by and Bird still sat. Patiently waiting to see what would happen if the appointment was disregarded. He waited until the digital clock in his car read 8:50p.m. before heading up to the door to enter. As he walked up a group of young white kids were walking out the building and let him inside past the security door. By not having to ring the bell and be buzzed in gave him the slight advantage of surprise. After walking up three flights of staring he was at apartment C. He took a deep breath and tightly gripped the handle of the pistol tucked in his waistband before his knuckles reached the wood. Knock! Knock! Knock! A minute went by and there was no answer. He tried again, this time harder. KNOCK! KNOCK! KNOCK! Another minute went by and still there was no response. Bird knew that no one had come or left in the last two hours except the skateboarders that he passed on his way in. Whoever wanted him was still on the opposite side of the door in front of him.

His hustler's instinct told him to try the door. The knob turned and the old wooden door slowly creaked open. He pulled the compact .45 he had his hand on from his waist and slowly entered the dimly lit entrance. As Bird got inside he saw that he was in a short hallway. Back against the wall he slowly crept through, keeping his eyes peeled for any sudden movement or shadows. He checked room after room finding no one in them. He couldn't help but notice that the apartment was an immaculate dwelling and expensively furnished. It was obvious that whoever stayed there had money. And was also a woman. Bird made his way to the master bedroom to get a better idea of who lived there. His transitioning thoughts caused a momentary slip in the cautiousness of his movements as he entered into the bedroom too quickly, neglecting to turn the light on. As he got past the bedroom door he felt cold steal touch the base of his skull. He froze in his tracks as his heart dropped beneath the sole of his shoes.

"Who the fuck did you come with!?" A woman said in a hushed tone from behind the gun.

"Don't shoot." Bird said calmly. "I'm by myself."

"So what you plan to do with that gun muthafucka!" she said tensely, nudging the barrel into the back of his head forcefully as she spoke.

"Never go anywhere without it." Bird replied. "Looks like I'm bout to die wit it in my hand though."

In the midst of the moment Bird couldn't recognize the voice for the life of him, literally. A million outcomes flashed through his third eye in the span of 10 seconds. His first inclination was to pivot and squeeze rapidly, letting the outcome be what it may. Yet his conscience mind got a hold of him, inciting him to go along and see how things would play out. Then just as suddenly as it was applied, the pressure of the barrel against his head subsided and the voice ordered him to drop his gun then walk over to the bed. Bird complied, slowly taking a seat on side of the bed, sitting in almost the same exact position in reality as he was in his memory.

Still in the darkness he couldn't see the shadowy figure. At that moment the light came on. Bird was stunned.

"Natalie?!" he said confused. In front of him she stood with tear stained cheeks, nervously fidgeting with her guns sights trained on him.

"Did you set him up!?" she asked.

"What the fuck are you on?! I ain't set anybody up! I don't fuck with the law like that!" he said as he rose to his feet.

Natalie paced back and forth distraught but when Bird went to stand she instantly focused back on him. "Sit back down!" she yelled.

"You gon' have to kill me standin' baby!" Bird said staring in her eyes.

She stared back, unmoved by his display of heart. "Nigga I will blow your head off!"

Bird could see the strength in her eyes. She meant every word she had just spoken. He chose his next reply carefully, attempting bring the tension in the room down from its fevered temperature.

"So you invited me here to kill me Natalie?" he asked calmly.

"I don't know." she answered. "Brennan had asked if I'd take on your business. he said you could be trusted with the front. But I don't know if I can trust anybody right now."

Even in the midst of the drama Natalie was sexy beyond comparison. Beyond her tear soaked eyelashes her beautiful brown eyes welled up from fear and uncertainty. Bird slowly walked towards her until the gun in her hand was flush against his chest. "You can trust me." he said sincerely. "I'll help you through it."

The words that he spoke couldn't have been more welcomed. Natalie dropped the gun to her side as the reservoir of tears her eyes held began to pour freely. Bird took another step forward and wrapped his arms around her as she buried her face in his chest and relinquished her pain. He walked her over to the bed and the two sat down. Holding the loveliness of her face in his palm he turned it to him and implored her to talk. "Tell me what's wrong."

"It's a long story." Natalie said regaining composure.

"Well I guess I should get comfortable then." Bird replied wittingly. "Take it from the top."

With a soaked face she flashed her perfect teeth as she laughed and began into the story. Natalie grew up in the hood and like a lot of other pretty young girls got wrapped up with a hustler. She had been dealing with Brennan since she was twenty-one and he was thirty-five, but due to his off and on prison stints no one ever knew. She got pregnant during a stretch of probation when she was twenty-five—their daughter had actually just turned eight years old two days earlier. Brennan married her right after the baby in an attempt to keep her to himself. By all accounts they were total opposites in every category imaginable. Her, a young working single mother going to nursing school, him a much older career criminal with other kids, his oldest child just twelve years younger than her. Over the years they separated too many times to count. Still she loved him and because of it she began smuggling drugs in for him while he was in the county his last go around.

"I was good at it." she said. The money became the glue that slowly mended their relationship, transforming it into more of a business partnership. Brennan was smart enough to respect that Natalie was better at managing the money than he was. And Natalie was loyal enough to not exploit him because of it.

"Then I met Carlos." she said. "And everything went crazy from there."

"Carlos?" Bird questioned, the name sounding familiar. "The Mexican dude I was locked up with?!"

"Yeah!" she exclaimed. "Los."

She had explained that he had hollered at her before she brought him into the cell that day, giving her a number and telling her, "Call whenever you need a vacation." She looked at the number in her locker at work for six months before finally calling it and leaving a message for him, curious if she would get a call back. A week later she did and after talking periodically for a couple of months she was flying first-class to meet up with him in Puerto Vallarta. The two partied hard night after night for four days with Natalie holding off his sexual advances before getting drunk and giving in. Before leaving she expressed her regret, explained her situation with Brennan and that she wouldn't be in communication with him anymore. After a little opposition to her stance he respectfully accepted bidding her safe trip back and happiness in her future. Thinking that was it she got back home and to her life until a month later there was a knock on her door. When she opened it no one was there just a small package addressed to her from the resort she stayed while in Mexico. Figuring it was some item she had left in her room she opened it without thinking. Once she pulled the box open the contents threw her for a loop. Inside was a Louis Vuitton box containing a brown damier toiletry bag, obviously a gift from Carlos.

"I was thinking to myself why the hell he didn't just send a purse?!" she said with a smirk. Then she took the bag from the box and noticed it felt weighted which made her open it to expose its contents, a half a kilo of cocaine and a cell phone. Immediately she deciphered the message that the package was intended to convey. Natalie didn't pick up the phone and call right away instead she left the package sitting on her dresser for several hours as she thought out her options. What would happen if she didn't call, would someone come to reclaim it? Or did Carlos take her explanation in Mexico as a confirmation that she was down to play? Then her thoughts spun rapidly on to other things. How good was the cocaine that he'd sent? Was it possible that it was more pure than everything else that was out here? These were all questions that she didn't know the answer to but wanted to know before she made up her mind.

In the coming day she was supposed to bring in two ounces that had been dropped to her the day before. Natalie decided that she would split the package swapping half of it with what Carlos had sent. If it was better surely the feedback would tell her. And it did. Brennan was so impressed with it he instructed her to get as much as she could and cut it down so they could make even more profit. "I didn't know what I was doing so he had his cousin come show me."

After getting her cut game down, Natalie repeated the procedure and had even begun selling to select individuals on the outside through his cousin, on Brennan's orders. It took about two weeks for her to knock the half kilo out, but it had gone addictively well to say the least. With the drugs gone and the supply chain calling for more of the same Natalie was compelled to get the phone from the bag.

After powering it on she saw that there was only one number in the call log so she intuitively pressed send. Upon answering the voice on the other end never said hello or goodbye it only gave a time and place—a tactic that she would later incorporate into her own operation. Facing the decision of backing out or going back in for more she chose the latter, arriving at the Westside meeting place 15 minutes early. The place was low-key without many patrons at the time, nestled deep in the Ohio City neighborhood. Natalie sat and ordered a coffee and by the time it came a female customer in the establishment had already walked over and took a seat next to her. Again not wasting time she quietly began detailing out prices and the rules that which she must adhere to. Natalie never responded but only nodded in agreement.

The number she was given was twenty thousand per ki and assured the quality would always be impeccable. She could take the front or outright purchase, but either the money or merchandise had to come back as it was given. No exceptions. And she would never use the same phone twice, one would be given to her with each order, and would only be used to confirm the time and place nothing more. Natalie's heart pounded as she committed every word to memory, skipping a beat when the woman began detailing information on her daughter, brother and niece. Their safety would act as the insurance policy in the venture.

"I just felt like I couldn't say no." she said, the tears streaming down her pretty face replaying vividly in Bird's mind. Natalie accepted figuring a short run would limit their risk and the quality was sure to sell itself. She was told where to pick up the next bag and where to leave the money for what had been fronted already, also that she would never talk to or meet the same person twice as not to cause any alarm when she met an unfamiliar face. With that information disclosed the conversation was over almost as fast as it began and the two went their separate ways.

Things went smooth for six months and then Brennan came home. "The problem was he lacked the focus and attention to detail." Natalie explained. Brennan flashed and flaunted, forcing her to fall as far off the radar as possible. Natalie ran things like a business, investing the profits in the several businesses that they had. She quit her job to stay as far out sight of the law as possible, using her going back to college as an excuse for her exit. But Brennan had drawn not only the attention of the police who had been watching him since leaving jail but also the supplier.

"This dumb ass nigga, running around acting all dumb and shit!" she panted as her tears subsided. "And my ass is dumb for steady fuckin' with him!"

Brennan must have sensed that Natalie was about to give the game up after all the talk that was swirling as he began urging her to go all in on the next trip. After constant lobbying she finally conceded, viewing it as her way of ending things with him on amicable terms. She took the two hundred twenty thousand dollars that they had stashed and made the deal, which also came with the usual front. There was no way around taking it, it was all or nothing. Carlos and his crew used it as a sense of control, keeping their buyers indebted to them making it almost impossible to ever stop. But Natalie's plan was to simply drop them what was owed at the location given to her and fade from contact with them, completely even.

But events wouldn't allow for such a simple retreat. Things went haywire after the last packages came through. First Brennan caught the gun charge leaving the bar one night. "The gun wasn't even on him, it was on the passenger." she explained. "They just wanted him so bad they made it his."

Once they saw how determined the law was to get him they switched things up, Brennan falling back completely and moving the drugs storage to an apartment his best friend had. At the same time the "hook" called to meet, which she found was in relation to the heat Brennan was bringing while still in possession of a quarter million of unpurchased product.

Natalie assured them everything would be fine, though she wasn't sure that it would be herself.

The operation slowed to a crawl with Brennan and Natalie taking their time and every possible precaution. The streets weren't happy with it, Brennan's best friend in particular. "I guess Ray was still out in the streets doing his thing." she said as her eyes again began to well. "All I know is somebody came in and killed him . . . . and my niece!" Natalie broke down, sobbing uncontrollably on Bird's shoulder. "I didn't even know they were messing around! I wouldn't have let her. I wouldn't have let her." She repeated over and over.

Bird listened quietly to Natalie as she vented, absorbing every detail of the story that sounded eerily similar to one he'd heard before. He comforted her in his arms waiting for her to go on.

"She let that muthafucka bag up in her place . . . even hide it there . . . in her baby's room of all places!" she said angrily. "Thank God they didn't go in there or they would've found him and it in the closet."

Bird swallowed hard at her string of statements which were falling in line with what he was already thinking. Seeking confirmation he gently probed further. "So what did they take anything?" he asked.

"They had two ki's out. And some money Ray had left there." Natalie told him. "Her brother came over that morning and found them all. He got my nephew and the drugs out before he called the police."

Natalie's answer fortified Bird's feared conclusion. The news broadcasters voice resonated in his mind, "Raymond "Lefty" Carlyle", followed by Natalie's, "I guess Ray was still out in the streets doing his thing."

She then explained to Bird that Brennan had told her how loyal he was in making his bid for her to take his business on, but had a jealous fit the night of his party when he saw her talking to Bird inadvertently. "I didn't even realize you were who he wanted me to consider." she said. "Then the very next day all hell broke loose!"

Before the FED's had even put Brennan in the car the special phone began ringing incessantly from Carlos's people. Out of fear she didn't answer the call. Since the slayings she often wondered if the whole thing may have been a message from them to get things together. As she watched the events at the bar develop from the coffee shop she saw Bird pull directly in front. Having no one to trust and recollecting Brennan's account of Bird, she sent a lil' boy that was passing by to hand off the receipt.

Natalie waited, not knowing whether Bird would come or if she would meet her maker first. But now she was curled up in Bird's arms being coddled yet still fearful for her life. She had sent her daughter to stay with her parents and sought refuge in the apartment that they leased after the murders to be a safe house for the drugs. No one could possibly know of her whereabouts and still she was a nervous wreck. But with a heavy debt looming over her head and every tangible outlet for moving the product to cover it gone she had good reason to be.

Bird lay down on the bed and Natalie crawled up alongside him, resting her weary head on his shoulder. There was no way he could leave her in the condition she was in. Soon she closed her puffy eyes and dozed off to sleep. Bird stayed awake watching her vigilantly, his mind moving at the speed of light. He felt no remorse for the lives that were taken—it had to be done. But he did feel conflicted inside knowing his decision was part of what was causing the woman he was staring at so much pain. Or maybe it was the fact that he knew their futures were intertwined from that moment forward and he would have to take his transgression to his grave.

The footsteps he had heard in the house had closed in, slowly creeping into the room behind him as he daydreamed of a time long gone. Bird's mental flight was finally broken with the clicking of a hammer coming from directly behind his head as he sat on the edge. Bird took one last sip of his drink and slowly placed it on the nightstand.

"Don't shoot." Bird said calmly, closing his eyes tightly. "I'm by myself."

The gunman giggled while coming around the bed to face Bird.

"You think that's going to work this time?" he was questioned as a soft hand rubbed across his freshly lined cesar. "You know what I came for. And I came prepared to get it by any means necessary!"

"Well do what you gotta do." Bird replied.

"Open your eyes and take it like a man then!" the voice challenged.

Bird opened his eyes and slowly began panning up seeing first perfectly manicured toes, tracing their arch up into 5 inch heels and then the toned thickness of sculpted calves that disappeared underneath a three-quarter length maxi coat. It was tied snuggly around the woman's waist and accentuated her frame perfectly. His eyes sailed up her body, finally setting anchor in hers.

"I have to admit I didn't expect this Officer." Bird said.

"I thought we established long ago that's not how you greet me?" she quipped as she untied her coat exposing her matching lace top and bottom. "I bet my name will roll off of your tongue now." she said seductively as she posed in front of him with her .380 still in hand.

"You sure about that?! It is Natalie right?" Bird jokingly quizzed as he grabbed her by the waist and pulled her to him. Without hesitation he ripped the frilly panties off of her, spread her thighs and licked between her lips. Natalie dropped the pistol and grabbed his head, grinding on his outstretched tongue. Her legs began to shake as the coat soon dropped to the floor and placed her foot on the bed for better positioning. The tongue lashing had her passion running down her thigh as she thrashed around moaning erratically. Bird devoured her tenaciously, yet cautious not to drown in her climactic ocean—a lesson he'd unintentionally learned the hard way during one of their initial sexual trysts.

That was one of many things he'd grown to love about her over the years. Natalie was completely in tune with her sexuality, going into a zone so deep that at times it was like seeing another person emerge from within. Her usual unassuming quiet demeanor gave way to a loud rambunctious nympho that knew just what she wanted and how to get it.

The sensation from the oral massage Bird was giving her became overwhelming. Natalie wrestled to pry his herself away but he held her firmly by the ass and continued unimpeded. Finally she broke free, feeling some type of way about Bird pleasuring her as he did. Her competitive streak ran deep.

Forcing him to his back Natalie quickly removed his garments and returned the favor. She ran her hands across his lower torso as she voraciously went up and down him from the tip of the head almost to the hilt. She had mastered her gag flex and had the uncanny ability to take him well beyond her throat for extended periods while flicking the tip of her tongue on his balls. The feeling was almost too much to bear for Bird as he watched her in utter amazement. Soon he found the roles reversed as he fought to extract himself from her mouth before he came.

"One-one." He joked as he stood, picked her up and playfully threw her on the bed. Natalie smiled and rolled over on her stomach, raising her ass high while resting her face on her folded arms. Bird quickly mounted her and went back to work.

Natalie's body was a thing of beauty, the byproduct of consuming the best delicacies and five day a week workout regiment, both luxuries that the game had afforded her. She had only gotten better with age, more polished in every imaginable way.

Bird held her by her waist and pushed deep inside her as the beads of sweat began to form on her silky caramel skin, slowly pooling in the deep curve in the small of her back. As her moans got louder so did the force in which she threw herself onto him, spreading her ass with both hands begging him to go deeper. Admiring her Brazilian wax he slowly slid his thumb into her ass as he satiated her, grabbing a handful of her flailing hair in his other hand as she bucked wildly. Sensing that she would soon be reaching her peak Bird thrust harder and faster, each thunderous clap of their bodies colliding beckoning her river to flow. Within a few minutes of rapid strokes she neared her summit and began to quiver uncontrollably as she screamed his government name between breathless heaves. Bird pulled out of her as she fell to the bed gasping, the remnants of her eruption still dripping from him.

Natalie's flawless skin glistened in the pale light motivated Bird to not leave well enough alone. He grabbed her still trembling legs, turned her onto her back and pulled her to him. Holding them wide apart he sucked her swollen clit as she cursed him in agonizing pleasure while trying frantically to push his head away. When he finally came up, he grabbed her hands and pinned them over her head as he aligned their bodies and re-entered her. The two shared moans as Bird grinded the length of him deep inside of her with each stroke. With her meticulously maintained hair now frizzied all over her head and her legs wrapped securely around his waist, her French manicured toes were now curling as her second serving began to brew.

Wanting to turn the tables before the feeling overtook her, Natalie clenched Bird with her thighs and quickly flipped him onto his back.

Now she was fucking him.

With her hands planted firmly on his abdomen she rode him aggressively, sliding herself down his dick and rolling her hips all in one smooth motion. She clenched him inside her as she rose up and dropped down as hard as she could literally trying to extract his nectar from him with her muscle. Bird's expletives of passion only fueled her fire, driving her to her own brink once again. In typical fashion their encounter turned into a race to finish last, each grimacing and gasping down the stretch. It would be Natalie who couldn't hold out, succumbing to a second orgasm that was even more powerful than the first.

She lift herself from him, hands still planted, just in time for him to see her love rain all over him as if the levy holding them back had finally been breached. The sight of Natalie unleashing her tsunami on his throbbing manhood brought Bird to the brink of eruption and with no hesitation she took him beyond it. Her love was still dripping as she again took him down her throat repeatedly. This time she didn't stop until well after he exploded in her mouth and she had swallowed it all, savoring every drop. The two both collapsed in the bed. Drained from their releases, the duo passed out before waking an hour later and picking up where they left off.

CHAPTER 13

"Fuck that!"

-Natalie

Bird was up at the crack of dawn the next morning admiring the early rays of the sun as it entered into sight. His mind was restless with what lay ahead. Glancing over to the bed he took note of how the sheet hugged Natalie's luscious curves. Even after knowing her for a decade it still amazed him that she could be beautiful even in the depth of sleep. Moving through his condo to the bathroom he was even more amazed how far he had come since their first encounter long ago.

That very next day after consoling her he got in motion, formulating a run that would make him a hustler of lore. He linked with Sauce and collectively conceived a plan to move the seventeen units in a matter of days. To pull off the feat without causing too much attention to themselves they procured a rental and took their show on the road. Sauce knew hustlers all over so the two hit every major city in the state and surrounding locales, choosing each destination on a whim so that they couldn't be tracked. By the following Monday they had gotten everything off. Natalie was in disbelief when the two reappeared at the apartment with two duffle bags stuffed with cash. Relieved beyond words she swore to one day repay Bird. Carlos's people were also thrilled, gaining a newfound respect for her coming through in the face of adversity. From that point forward Natalie would be Bird's plug to the connect, doing whatever he requested without question. And Bird reciprocated by vowing to never put her at risk.

The streets were wide open with the absence of Brennan and Bird and his Capo took advantage by filling it ever so discreetly. The past twelve years had blown by and though many things changed just as many stayed the same. Though Bird and Nat, as he liked to call her, had an undying bound it was mutually understood that they could have no future together. The fact was he and Jessica were finally ready to take the next step in their relationship with her leaving the medical post where she had begun her residency in D.C. and moving back to take a position Dave had secured for her at Cleveland Clinic. Although Bird went back to his hustling roots he still dealt with Dave and the two were as close as ever. Penelope opted to come back home to do her post graduate work at Case after Sauce got shot and in an odd twist were now married with two kids. She worked in the county coroner's office as a medical examiner and in irony had unknowingly inspected more than a few cases of her husband's handiwork over the years.

With the duo being major movers in the city Robbie's name "Double R" had completely evolved into Sauce even though he had long deviated from his excessive ways. Having a family gave him something to live for, something worth coveting. Taking a cue from Bird he relinquished the big rims and loud music for a subtle silver and black late model Range Rover.

The restaurant his mom had went under financially. She now ran a modest catering service out of her home. Though Bird and his mother had mended their relationship through Jace, things were never quite stable and after his return to the streets their ties severed again. Although he had never gotten over the hurt of her turning her back on him when he needed her most his heart wasn't cold enough to do the same, making sure she stayed afloat via Laura.

Laura had managed to fair pretty well finding a career in accounting. The trials and tribulations of being a single mother and widow had made her an amazingly strong woman, though her son was the source of constant worry. Lil Tyco was going on 16 and without doubt his father's son.

It was if the hustling was a virus that lay dormant in his veins periodically flashing signals of its existence, to which there was no cure. Yet to his benefit he inherited Laura's brain and was always on his toes. Still the fear of his transformation was visible in her eyes at the slightest mention of Tyco and his namesake in the same sentence. It didn't help that her beloved little brother essentially had become nothing more than a refined version of her former spouse either. For L's sake Bird applied his influence on his nephew as positively as he could without being hypocritical, in an attempt to deter him from the game. He made sure he had everything he wanted in hopes it would offset the allure of the life, while downplaying his own exploits. He schooled his kin with knowledge few would ever be privy to. Explaining that the money, cars and attention were all coping mechanisms to numb hustlers to the underlying reality in the back of their mind—the game almost always ended badly and in a way that couldn't be anticipated, with either bullets or bars somewhere in the equation. Despite it all Lil Tyco's disposition alluded to him that he was only prolonging the inevitable.

Jace was a young teenager now as well and the split image of Bird at that age. He took after him from his smile down to his very mannerisms, yet Sheena's influence couldn't be avoided. With a mother that condoned nonsense he stayed in trouble much to Bird's dismay. Jace was incredibly intelligent but the trait was often nullified by his ill tempered behavior that he'd absorbed from Sheena. The past five years Bird had begun to spend more time with Jace again with Sheena going up and down I-71 to Cincinnati. It was Bird's understanding her new boyfriend lived there, a robber masquerading as a hustler from what he gathered. He had never seen him or had any details on him and truthfully didn't care. Whoever the character was he seemed to keep Sheena occupied with something other than him or his son which was a much welcomed turn of events. Alone with him Jace was a different person. Free to be himself the cloud of dark idiosyncrasies fogging his mind dissipated, allowing his finer points to shine through. Realizing his son's future was in jeopardy with Sheena, Bird knew something would have to give. Sooner or later the final turn in the game would come, either in the form of an opportunity to exit or a judicially imposed retirement. He had no idea two months ago that "sooner" would become "now".

Brennan's violation had turned into a fifteen year stretch after the FED's indicted him on conspiracy from wire conversation obtained from his going away party. Up until then Natalie hadn't had any run-ins with the law. She caught their undivided attention the day he was due to be released though. As she and their daughter sat patiently outside the gates for Brennan in a pearl white BMW 745 she had gotten him as a gift, so were the FED's, waiting outside the prison the day of his release from the eighteen month stint for the violation to take him directly into Federal custody. The reunion was ruined the moment he walked outside with them swooping in quickly. With their daughter balling as they cuffed Brennan again Natalie lost her cool, exchanging a barrage of words with the agents. Even after nearly ten years since the incident the news she received within the past month came as no surprise. The FED's had been investigating her for the past year already, under the assumption that she had continued his criminal enterprise.

Brennan's legal woes with the FED's created massive bills from litigation that would have been insurmountable for an average citizen, which they knew. A similar case could easily be eaten at state level with budget concerns and cost over runs. But the Federal agents had the bottomless pocket of Uncle Sam backing them. Anyone with ability to enter into a prolonged legal battle in drug cases signaled a red flag and Natalie certainly met that prerequisite. That in conjunction with the disdain created by the release fiasco made the situation especially combustible.

With Bird and Sauce's hustle combined and her business acumen she had amassed a small fortune, with her worth being nearly a million on the books and likely double off of them. In the first few years of Brennan's absence Natalie struggled to manage them alone prompting Bird to turn her on to Langdon for help. Overseeing her business matters for the last five years, Langdon was crucial in taking them to new heights, cleaning up the paper trail as he went. Still, the idea of her business being swept with a fine toothed comb by a suspecting eye wasn't the least bit appealing to her. If her experience with Brennan taught her anything it was that when they wanted you they never adhered to the rules. Rather than chance getting caught red-handed she decided it was best to quit while she was ahead.

The news of her exodus didn't shock Bird much. He often toyed with the question of why she still underwent the risks involved but never asked, fearing that he and the answer were one and the same. Bird greeted the decision with encouragement, happy that Natalie would likely make a peaceful exit. The only hindrance was the matter of the connect and the chain that fed from it. How could she introduce someone she cared for to the lethal dangers that she'd unwittingly accepted and lived with? And if not someone she knew, then who? Could a stranger even be trusted? The questions piled on top of each other to no end like a losing game of Tetris.

Bird could see the distraught look in Natalie's face as the two talked things over. By no means was he financially set, yet he would survive should the well run dry. The cost of being on the front line didn't afford him the luxury of stacking as heavily as Natalie. Maintaining his fronts, while dodging the pitfalls of streets didn't allow room for it. The real estate and carwash businesses that Langdon set up for him didn't generate much revenue with him not actively giving either much effort. They only functioned as shells to launder enough money to justify his lifestyle. Yet the notion of walking away had been prevalent in his mind, and Natalie's situation only stoked the desire.

He sat and listened to the dilemma and her hinting to the fact that she didn't want to put him in harm's way. But he felt the same way in regards to her, and there was no way he'd stand-by and watch her self destruct. What could be worse than to feel trapped in a situation that will be your undoing if not abandoned?

"There's only one solution Nat." Bird said.

"And what's that?!" she said curiously.

"I'll take over." Bird replied.

"Fuck that!" she exclaimed vehemently. "You're too visible. Too much could go wrong!"

After an hour of negotiating Bird finally managed to dispel Natalie's fears but she still wasn't sold on the idea.

"Just one move." Bird proposed. "One shipment and we both can be done."

From the look in his eyes she was certain that he wasn't going to give in. Reluctantly she agreed, but only under the pretense that he'd keep his word and only make one move and walk away. Bird found himself heavy in retrospect ever since her compliance. Thinking over the life he had lived and the things he'd done. Many had come and gone in a game marred with ups and downs—yet Bird was still standing, and finally poised to take the final turn in his race to the finish line, and exit from the fast life.

His mind churned, formulating an ingenious plan to score a major shipment and fade into obscurity. Natalie had met with one of Carlos's handlers weeks ago and gave them the rundown of her quitting and naming a successor. She had just gotten the feedback the previous night, prompting her surprise visit to deliver the news before getting sidetracked.

Bird was up long enough to have breakfast ready by the time Natalie got herself together to join him.

"Long night, huh?" he asked.

"Something like that." she replied coyly. "Must have been for you too. Gotcha up early making breakfast."

The two shared in a laugh and threw a few more witty puns at each as she made her plate and took a seat adjacent to him. Before Natalie could settle into the chair Bird enquired into the business that was handled the night before.

"So what happened with your people? Bird asked.

"It's a go." she replied slowly.

Bird could tell the apprehension had crawled back into Nat's forethought by the brief response but decided not to waste time to reign in her emotions. Instead his mind shifted into hustle mode. All he wanted to know was who, what, when and where.

"So?" he said looking squarely in Natalie's face.

She placed another fork full off eggs into her mouth in an attempt to buy as much time as she could before ushering Bird towards the point of no return. What she had failed to realize in her concern was that in his mind there was already no turning back.

"He wants you to meet with him." she said after swallowing the last food in her mouth.

"Ok. Where?!" Bird asked becoming visibly aggravated by the constant short responses. "You realize this is gon' be hard enough without you makin' it harder right?

"I'm sorry . . . it's just . . ." she said trying to gather her thoughts.

Bird cut her off before she could finish her statement. "Don't be sorry. Just cooperate."

Natalie put her personal opinion to the side and gave him the information just as it was given to her.

"Mexico." she said blankly. "He wants you to come down to discuss it."

"MEXICO?!" Bird replied in shock. "What's that shit about?"

"That's what I said when I heard it." Nat remarked, the angst visible in her wrinkled forehead.

His mind began to reel as he tried to understand the reason for such an encounter when Carlos had outlets much closer. Bird thought back to their encounter in the cell before he was taken into federal custody. He went over every detail in his mind repeatedly. The light bulb finally went off when he recalled him mouthing "Find Las Cruces" as he was escorted out. But a lot had changed in Mexico since then. The region was now embroiled in heavy drug warfare, that Carlos no doubt was a part of to some degree. A trip there presented a different element of danger. But his mind had envisioned what his life would be like if things went through seamlessly, so bowing out wasn't an option. If making it happen meant going into the dragons lair then that's where he was headed. But before he did, everything would have to be in place.

After breakfast Bird spoke very little. He went straight to the shower to begin his day. Natalie had seen him in this state before and knew the best thing was to give him time alone with his thoughts. As he emerged from the shower she stood by the sink preparing to get in with the infamous cell phone in hand. In the quiet of the steamy bathroom their eyes met and communicated what words wouldn't. Bird hugged her tightly and after he let go she handed it to him, all without uttering a word. Before she finished her shower Bird was fully dressed and sliding into his Bally sneakers preparing to hit the door. Before leaving he slipped his head in the bathroom door for the two to exchange good-byes and then he was off.

As he walked down the lush brick hallway he greeted his neighbor who was heading in from his morning jog and then random yuppies that were waiting on the elevator to take their dog for a walk. His life always amazed him in contrast to those around him. Many of the people that were living in the high priced Pinnacle were executives and athletes. Their beginnings and daily lives were worlds away from his. They stressed over problems with bosses at work, their credit scores and portfolios. While Bird's stresses were that his life didn't end abruptly. "But soon that would all be a thing of the past," he thought to himself as he stepped from the elevator into the parking structure. He climbed into the all black CLS parked near the entry to the elevator and took his phone from his pocket to text Sauce. It was a bright sunny day and Bird felt good about where things were about to go in his life. He pulled from the structure and emerged onto the downtown Cleveland streets with the carwash set as his first destination. After checking things out and getting a wash he would get with Sauce and give him the scoop, then from there see if Dave could pull together a meeting with The Partners' that evening. Planning a move of this magnitude would take all of his resources. There was no point in not calling in all favors seeing as this was his finally hurrah.

Bird reached the carwash and found it having a good day with the line of cars extending from the bay onto the street. He parked and entered figuring he'd wait a little while for the crew to handle the paying customers before having them get to his car, greeting all of the workers with daps and pounds as he made his way into the office and flopped into the seat. He was cycling through the mail when a tall lanky figure strolled inside.

"What's up Uncle Bird?" Lil Tyco said.

Bird glanced up with smile. "What's up boy? What you doing around here?" he asked.

"I'm chillin'. Just was ridin' by and saw your car out front." Lil Tyco replied. "You seen Jace?"

"Not today. I spoke with him a couple days ago though." he answered. "Why what's up?"

Lil Tyco paused as if he only wanted to disclose information if Bird already knew.

"Talk." Bird said strongly.

"He out here wildin'." Lil' Tyco began. "Him and another lil' dude jumped on some cat real bad and put him in the I.C.U. Nigga's know we fam so they put me up on it. They say the police looking for him. I just was askin' you to see if he was cool."

Bird sat back in the chair with a blank look of disgust on his face. His rage wasn't shown in the ways most people exhibited theirs in loud cursing. Instead he got totally quiet, almost emotionless, yet his blood was boiling over. How could something like this happen and Sheena not even call him? He sprung up from the chair and made his way from the office to his car quickly.

"I'll take care of it." he said as he hopped in the driver's seat. "You need anything?"

"Nah I'm good." Lil Tyco responded.

Bird's tires screeched as he pulled from the drive and sped up the street in route to Sheena's. The whole way he tried to understand the thought process behind her not telling him what was going on. It was things like this that he had always dreaded with Jace and Sheena's parental approach. But every time he questioned the way she did things he was met with the argument that his feet were still planted in the life and the reason his son was only following in the footsteps. He knew her whole take was nothing more than a ploy to get under his skin but it was effective. Maybe it was his conscience that made her words burn with such intensity. Regardless of what he did, the fact that was Jace had begun doing things that could ruin his life and needed to be corralled. Being a positive influence to a teenage son with the stigma of his reputation was difficult enough, but with a mother like Sheena it was almost impossible.

Pulling into the Euclid home where they lived Bird could see there was a new Audi A8 in the yard with thirty-day tags in the window. As Bird walked to the door and rang the doorbell he promised himself that he wouldn't fly off the handle during his conversation with Sheena. After only a moment Sheena came to the door and let him inside.

"Where's Jace? he asked.

"Damn, no hello?!" Sheena replied with her usual zeal. "He ain't here right now."

Bird swallowed the hard as the tension mounted in his throat. "So what's been going on She-She?

"Same shit." she answered as she sparked a cigarillo. "How you like the whip my dude got me?"

"It's nice." Bird replied smugly. "He must really love you."

Sheena laughed. "He's been wanting to meet you. Y'all might be able to make something happen."

Her words drew Bird's ire. Knowing her it was something shady in the mix. Bird wouldn't ever consider doing business with anyone remotely related to her. "I got a few houses he can buy."

"Nigga don't play with me." Sheena said in an elevated tone.

"Who are you that I have to play with?" Bird said with a smirk. "You know I don't fuck around like that."

Sheena jumped from the couch enraged by his smirk, feeling like he was laughing at her. "Cut the bullshit nigga! You still on the same shit . . . you ain't no different muthafucka! You ain't better than nobody!"

Bird couldn't help but laugh again. It was clear that there was something much deeper bothering Sheena about him and not just his words. "Really? I'm sorry you feel that way."

"You got yo lil' doctor bitch and think you something!" she screamed. "I ain't gon' never let my son turn into no pussy ass nigga like you!"

The very mention of Jessica and Jace re-ignited Bird's frustration. "Speaking of my son, why the fuck you ain't tell me what the fuck happened?"

Sheena simply rolled her eyes with a look of disgust.

"Yeah. I thought so." He continued. "You know you ain't shit compared to Jessica. Don't be a punk bitch about it. And you know I ain't gon' let you fuck my son up!"

The comparison of her and Jessica pushed Sheena over the edge. She jumped up, ran to the kitchen and grabbed the longest knife she saw. Bird could see the hatred in her face as she walked back with it at her side. Still he didn't move, opting to slide his hand into the rear waist of his jeans to get a firm grip on the .45 he had on him.

"I got yo punk bitch muthafucka!" she said as she closed in on him.

Still Bird stood fast with his grip on the handle tightening. Sheena got within a few feet of Bird and was timing her strike when he pulled out the pistol and positioned it at his side.

"Oh you gon' shoot me now?!" Sheena screamed as her eyes welled.

"I ain't got shit to prove . . . you know what I'm about." Bird said calmly. "But if you think I'ma let you poke me you got life fucked up baby." For a split second his mind flashed glimpses of him shooting Sheena point blank as she charged him with the knife. The aftermath of him calling the police to report it and then explaining it to Jace.

As she clenched and drew the knife up, Bird raised the pistol and positioned himself for the moment to fire. Suddenly the door flew open and Jace ran in. They stood, frozen in embarrassment with their son looking on. Bird quickly slipped the gun back into his waist band, grabbed Jace and headed out of the door.

"You were gon' shoot my mama?!" Jace yelled as he struggled to pull away from Bird.

Bird pinned him against the car. "What?! Now you wanna go and get ya' lil' nigga and put me in ICU too?! What the fuck is your problem?"

Jace stopped struggling and gave Bird a defiant look. "Who told you that!? Lil Tyco?"

"Don't matter who told me and don't look at me like that!" Bird said angrily. Jace complied and relaxed himself. "You know better than to be doing that type of shit!"

"It ain't even that serious." he pleaded. "It just happened like that. Ma ain't trippin'."

Seeing that his son was already defensive about his mother he opted not to share the reasons why she wasn't tripping. He told him to get inside the car so he could speak to him candidly out of earshot of Sheena's open door. The two sat in the driveway and talked until he had gotten his son to understand the error in his ways, or at least appear to. He could tell Jace's feelings were still raw about what he witnessed. Bird understood that it was only natural for him to draw to his mother and want to be her protector, despite the fact she was the instigator in most matters. He hated to have to leave him there for another night. It was getting more and more difficult to deprogram him from his mother's teachings. The only way to truly help him was to get him away from her completely, a fact that only refocused him to what was at stake with his plan. He exchanged hugs with his son and pulled off, headed straight to Sauce. He didn't have a minute to waste in aligning the elements of his scheme.

He and his partner met at a discreet parking lot and got out to talk in the open air. With all the technological advances the law had at its disposal Bird left little to chance. He never spoke in vehicles for fear that the Onstar or onboard phones could be monitoring his conversations without his knowing.

Bird got straight to it, detailing out his whole plan to Sauce. More importantly, the intricate role that he would need him to play to pull it off as he listened quietly.

The plan was to secure as much cash as they could from every ally they had. Being that the drugs were coming further up the supply chain meant the quality would significantly better than anything most of them had ever had before and at a better price than the going rate. Street prices fluctuated like the Dow Industrial. A bust here or lost shipment there could drive prices through the roof instantly. Currently a whole unit was going for twenty-four to twenty-seven thousand, depending on the quality. With the type of number Bird was trying to spend coupled with the fact he would take care of the transport he was certain he could negotiate a price of seventeen thousand a piece for product better than anything that was currently in the streets. That alone would net them ten thousand per unit, with them barely handling them. With the slightest cut on them they would make a killing. Just one hundred grams of cut on every kilo would bring them a free unit and on top of that they would purchase some to move themselves and make even more.

Sauce stopped him there. "If we flood the streets with raw like that to everybody we deal with how are we going to sell what we pay for?!" he asked. "Doesn't make much sense to me."

"That's the beauty of it!" Bird laughed. "We make the switch and walk that Dog . . . make that heavy flip!"

Sauce thought over what his friend was proposing. He was no stranger to heroin by any means. Running back and forth from city to city and state to state, he had become familiar with the opiate trade to some extent. The cost and jail time involved with it deterred him from dealing with it extensively, though he knew that the money it could generate was astounding.

"So how much we talkin' about spendin' yo? Sauce asked.

"$Two million or better." Bird said plainly.

"Two mil?!" Sauce scoffed. "You talkin' bout takin' on bread from every cat we know! You know shit go wrong all the time B, and this the first move with these dudes!"

He knew that everything Sauce was speaking was the truth and under normal conditions the advice would have been well received. But with time being of the essence he was going in all or nothing. Bird leaned his back against the truck and explained his reasoning to his partner.

"This is it bruh." he said.

"What's it?" Sauce replied.

"I'm done out here." Bird answered. "It's a good a time as any. Nat quitting. FED's everywhere. Nigga's snitching. It's time to get ahead and fade to black."

Sauce stood there watching Bird after he finished as if he was waiting for more. "FED's ain't just get around and nigga's been snitching. And I know it ain't just Nat that brought this shit on B! So what's really good my nigga?"

If in an eight hour car trip you could get to know a lot about someone, then in twelve years you knew everything. Sauce had pulled his card. He went on to explain what had just happened with Sheena and Jace. There was no way he could get legal custody of him while he was in the streets and as long as he stayed in them his words of reprimand held little weight. Added to the fact that Jessica was finally moving back to the city, it all put his mind in the realm of quitting. Throughout the years he and Jessica had broken up and made up several times, yet because of the distance he was able to keep his business discreetly away from her as he promised Dave. But now they had decided to give it another go when she was last home to interview for the position and soon she'd be back.

"It's like all the signs sayin' quit." Bird said.

He gave Sauce his detailed vision for the plan from top to bottom. Needless to say he was impressed with the brilliant scheme Bird had devised but still was reluctant to buy in. He looked away out into the distance then back at his friend. "It's a risky move B . . . but I feel you. Maybe it's that time."

Bird hadn't expected Sauce to cave so suddenly. "So what's on your mind?" He asked. "Keep it one hundred."

"Penny's pregnant." he said. "A lot of shit on my mind too."

Bird congratulated him profusely, but something was different in Sauces strained smile. He quickly dismissed it and suggested they go have a drink in celebration of the conception. Sauce's first inclination was to decline but he knew Bird wouldn't cease until he agreed so he accepted.

Since it was a personal celebration the two went to a bar in the warehouse district where they knew they wouldn't see anyone in their industry. An hour and six shots of Patron later and Sauce was off edge and back to his lively self. The two laughed heartily as they reminisced on past exploits and conquests when Natalie called to check on Bird.

"So how Nat feel about you and Jess? Sauce asked as he hung up. "Did you tell her?

"Yeah, she knows what's up." Bird answered as he took another sip from his bottle of water. "She know's what it is."

"What is it?" Sauce said with a laugh. "All these years I always wondered why y'all been sneakin' around and shit. Y'all might have well been a couple."

"We're at two different places in life bruh. I mean . . . we got the best chemistry but just in different places." Bird explained. "Hell, and even though Brennan ass been down forever, you and I know that bitch would go crazy if he knew I was fuckin' his wife."

Sauce responded in agreement with a wrinkled brow and nod. It was obvious the night of his party when he pulled Natalie to the side that he was highly possessive. Surely he knew that she would be seeing someone but certainly not a peer. There was no gauging what he'd do if he knew that Bird, of all people, was the culprit.

Happy hour had long since ended and both were intoxicated. Bird excused himself for the night to prepare for his meeting with Dave. Sauce decided to call it a night as well to go home and relax with Penelope. Bird congratulated him again and sent Penny his regards while exchanging handshakes as the valet pulled to the curb in the Range. As Sauce got inside Bird called out to him.

"Everything's gon' go as planned!" he said.

The window on the passenger side rolled down as the valet pulled behind in Bird's Mercedes. "I wouldn't let you go in the lions pit alone bruh, so you know I'm in." He screamed out before peeling off.

Bird got into the CLS, still halfway inebriated and touched by his friend's belief in him. The short ride home gave him just enough time to make the call to Dave to coordinate their meeting. He answered on almost the first ring.

"What's going on Chris?" he answered.

"Hey Dave. Just seeing if all were still on for tomorrow." Bird asked.

"We're doing lunch tomorrow anyway but haven't chosen where, so that'll be fine." Dave replied. "Any suggestions?"

Bird paused for a moment. "Zanzibar. Shaker Square."

Dave wasn't familiar with the location but agreed. Bird chose it for several reasons. It was an upscale eatery with a hood twist and typically African-American patrons. The only place in the city where wine or mason jar of kool-aid. The environment would be safe yet unsettling for Mikey and Josh and serve as a great stage for negotiating.

As Bird and Dave's conversation segwayed into another topic his call waiting interrupted. It was Jessica. He stopped Dave short just as he began to complain about the service at the last restaurant he and his wife dined at and let him know he had to take the call from his daughter on the other end.

"Ok . . . ok . . . Tell her to give me a call when she gets a chance." Dave said quickly. "Oh yeah, I forgot to tell you Mikey's finally getting into politics! Remind me to tell you about it tomorrow."

Bird okayed him on the request and swapped calls.

"Hey baby?" he answered. "How was your day?"

"Hey!" she said happily. "My days been crazy! Didn't think you'd answer, I was just going to leave you a message."

"Was talking to your Dad, he wants you to call him when you can." Bird explained. "So what's up?"

"Um . . . . well they moved my start date up so I'll be back for good next week!" she said excitedly. "And the other news I'll wait to tell you when I see you!"

Bird was stunned for a moment at the news. He expected it to be at least a month or two before she returned, but was still ecstatic that she'd be closer after all the years of back and forth traveling.

"That's great! I can't wait." he said with a smile. "But what's the other news?"

"I can't tell you over the phone." she said. "I need to see your face when I tell you."

Her words only made him more curious. "Come on Jess!" he pleaded. "How are you going to say all that and not spill the beans?"

Still she declined. Jessica knew he wouldn't give up until he found out, and after several minutes of back and forth banter on her leaking her secret she bid him farewell. In his semi-drunken state he couldn't deduce what Jessica's secret was. He had reached his place and walked in to the unlit living room. The row of long windows lining the outer side of the condo gave the illusion of a glass wall and allowed the glow of the city lights shine through, drawing him to the balcony. The view sobered his mind and brought his thoughts back to his upcoming day of business.

Everything hedged on having The Partners onboard with his plan. To make a move as big as he was planning required an unfathomable level of risk, whereas allies like Mike and Josh could make it a cake walk. The last decade had been a period of exceptional growth for them both.

The Goldman family's shipping company had garnered a lucrative contract with Home Depot to handle their excess shipping and warehousing needs in the region 3 years ago and slowly transitioned into transporting goods from the north coast port throughout the Midwest and southwestern. Moving everything from loads of shovels to tons of manure, Josh was at the heart of his plan. Bird's goal was to get his load picked up at the southern most regions of a shipping run and back to the Goldman's storage in the city. Being that it was a commercial trucking company meant that it would likely go unabated by law enforcement, not to mention give him unbelievable leverage with Carlos to get the numbers where he wanted them.

Mikey would only serve as insurance that there would be no interference once the truck got to the state with his deep political ties. That would give them the freedom to take their time to take inventory while unloading their parcels. But he also was the more out spoken and outwardly aggressive of the two, and Josh typically sided with him. Still news of his recent political aspirations couldn't have come at a better time.

For the past eight years Mikey had enjoyed a seat on the bench as a circuit court Judge. Bird had played a key role in his bid for the seat by generating enough money from business with Dave to push his campaign over the top. Now he was seeking to further his career in public service which meant money could definitely sway his opinion. In a sluggish economy campaign donations would be tremendously hard to come by and he'd likely have to use a significant amount of his own money. What better way to subsidize his endeavor than with a hefty donation from Clark's Realty?

Bird turned to his laptop to see what he could turn up on Josh's shipping company. He needed all the information that he could get to force his hand and make his deal happen. Thirty minutes of research and he had read enough to feel comfortable in his knowledge of the Goldman's and their business. Now it was time to sleep the rest of his drunkenness off and awake fresh for his meeting.

CHAPTER 14

"Well I'm not so sure about it."

-Mike

That day Bird was up bright and early. He couldn't go back to sleep but didn't want to get off into anything that would distract him, so he took his extra time and tension to the gym in the basement of his condo. He hit the treadmill like a boxer training for a prize fight, running mile after mile. After a few hours of working out and shower he was ready to get to the business of the day.

He rarely had any personal interaction with Josh and Mike over the years so there was no doubt in his mind that they assumed he was purely some gun toting thug with a penchant for Timberland's and t-shirt's. Opening his closet to select his garments for the day, he decided to dress for the meeting as he would any legitimate business deal. He pieced his outfit together from various items in his wardrobe, teaming a white Purple Label polo with grey Zegna slacks and Farragamo loafers. He studied himself in the mirror. With his cesar and face still freshly lined from his last cut he could fit the bill for a millionaire already. After few soft mists of Creed he was off to his scheduled appointment.

He arrived at the site before the others and quickly made his way inside and secured their seating. As he sat sipping his drink Dave was the first to stroll in, checking out the atmosphere as he walked over to Bird. The two exchanged greetings as Dave sat down and ordered an orange juice. In his haste Bird had yet to disclose the purpose of the meeting to him either.

"So what's the word young man?" Dave asked. "What are we here for.?"

"Long story short I'm quitting Dave. For good this time." Bird replied.

"Glad to hear that." Dave said, unaffected by the news. "But what's that have to do with Josh and Mikey?" he questioned.

"I'm putting together one last move." he explained. "And it's a BIG one. I need their assistance on this one."

Dave had a skeptical look on his face as Bird went into some of the details of his proposal. Before he had a chance to offer a rebuttal Mike and Josh walked in. As the gentlemen acknowledged each other Bird could see that his choice of venue would pay off. Josh's eyes scampered about, bouncing off of the myriad of faces in the mahogany room. Mike was a little more focused on the cause for such a meeting and wanted to get right to it.

"So Chris, you've been staying out of trouble?" he jabbed at Bird. "The arrest rate is up ya know?"

"I've been good Mike. And you?" he said with a widening smile. "I hear the arrest rate is up for politicians in the county too!"

The others at the table shared in the laugh at Mike's expense, much to his resentment.

"So what are we here for kid?" Mike questioned. "What's the big news?"

Bird slowed him down. "What's the rush? We're eating right?" Bird said as he summoned the waitress.

Mike nodded as he and Josh shuffled through the menu lined with soulful delicacies with posh twists, confused on what to order. To not appear uncultured they ordered meals similar to Dave's. With their attention bombarded by their surroundings Bird felt it was the right time to begin his pitch.

"So gentleman I won't beat around the bush any further. I asked you both here to propose a bit of business." Bird began. "I'd appreciate if everybody pulled the batteries out of their phones before I go any further."

After everyone complied with his request Bird went into a detailed synopsis of what he needed from them and their roles in the scheme of things. All three men actively listened what he was saying to them without question. He had gone over in his mind just how much he would disclose to them and how more times than he could remember. There was no doubt in his mind that he had addressed every angle that pertained to them. He finished his explanation as the food arrived to the table. Josh and Mike found themselves struggling to formulate an adequate response to his offer as they sampled their meals. Being removed from their typical white collar steak and salad environment of Morton's, into a lavish hideaway with a rich afro-centric theme had their senses on overload. Dave couldn't help but smile to himself at the strategic foresight of Bird's meeting, but sensing his friends discomfort in the moment he moved to break the ice.

"So what do you guys think?" he asked Josh and Mike.

"Sounds interesting to me." Josh answered.

Then Mike spoke. "Well I'm not so sure about it. How much stuff are you moving? Who are you getting it from?" he questioned. "There are a lot of questions here."

Bird anticipated friction from Mike. As much as he would have liked to circumvent him totally there was no way to do it without ruffling his feathers and causing him to poison Josh with his negativity.

"None of that's any your concern." Bird said matter-of-factly. "Ignorance is bliss in situations like this."

Mike sat up from his plate ready to fire back but Bird quickly guided the conversation to the ultimate motivation. Money.

"What's the most you have made on moves in the past?" Bird questioned Josh rhetorically. "Fifteen . . . Twenty grand at the most? I'm prepared to give each of you twenty-five grand. Upfront."

"Twenty-five grand upfront for a so-called simple transport!? What's the catch?" Josh said warily. "This must be ridiculously risky."

"The risk is in not taking advantage of the opportunity here." Bird said back. "So I'm willing to do what it takes to make it happen."

"I don't know about this." Mike said still apprehensive. "This is an election year and I'm trying to make a major run. I can't risk being tied up in this."

Dave jumped in, "It's a little too late to NOT be implicated in anything, don't you think?!" Drawing a cold glare from Mike.

"What seat are you gunning for this time?" Bird asked.

"A seat in the state House of Reps." Mike said proudly. "Finally going to follow in the family footsteps."

"So you're going to take on an incumbent huh? That's going to take a nice piece of change." Bird said with his trademark smile. "How's financing that campaign coming along?"

Mike almost choked on his wild rice at Bird's knowledge of the political landscape, swallowing hard before replying. "It's coming along. It's a process."

Bird had him right where he wanted, pausing for a moment like a lion eying his weakened prey before going in for the kill as Josh and Dave looked on. "How about this . . ." he began. "Thirty thousand from Clark Realty to your campaign. In exchange you get with some of your friends in high places and get the Goldman's safe passage through the trucking route."

Mike sat quietly thinking while Bird turned to Josh. "And I'll make it thirty thousand to you too." he said. "All you have to do is give me when and where your next large load will be furthest south and allow my load to hitch ride back."

"Well that load will be on the road within the next two days." Josh replied. "It won't reach south Texas for three days after that. It's due back next Friday. The next is six weeks from then."

The time constraints put Bird in a precarious situation but he couldn't turn it down. If he gave Josh and Mike the option of waiting it would give them time to back out. But there was no way that he could guarantee Carlos would be able to produce such a large amount of narcotics so quickly. With no time to waste he'd have to leap that hurdle when he came to it.

"Let's do it." he said confidently. "I'll have the money for you tomorrow."

With the ball in their court Mike and Josh froze, wishing that they had time to confer. Before they could say a word he backed them further into the corner.

"What's there to think about?" Bird questioned. "We don't have to over think this. It's actually really simple."

Mike's pride wouldn't allow him to back away from the money, especially with the majority of the risk being placed squarely on Josh. But he wouldn't allow Bird to take complete control of their dealings either.

"If Josh is willing I'm with it." Mike said.

"I'm with it." Josh echoed.

Bird was elated but dared not to show. As soon as he heard them agree he wanted nothing more than to leave, but had to do it tactfully. There wasn't a moment to waste in making sure he could make good on the promises that he had just made.

"Well we're on then." Bird nodded as he gathered his belongings.

"Leaving so soon?" Mike said. "I thought we were eating?"

Bird extracted a wad of cash from his pocket, pulled one hundred fifty from it and dropped it to the table. "Who has time to eat when there's money to be made?" he said with a chuckle as he turned toward the exit. "I'll be in touch with each of you gentlemen tomorrow. Dave, we'll talk."

Just as quickly as the meeting had started it was over, with Bird handing his ticket to the valet. Once in the car he breathed a sigh of relief and grabbed the cell phone from his armrest to dial the number that he had been longing to call. After three long rings a woman answered and immediately began giving instructions when Bird cut her off, "I need to talk to him". The voice on the other end went silent, followed by the dial tone. He had anticipated a reaction somewhat to that degree but grew more concerned by the minute. As he neared home he checked the phone periodically, debating on whether he should call back. He walked into his place and flopped down on the couch. It was becoming difficult to stay positive in the matter. Things rarely went according to schedule in the game so he was used to it, but the stakes had never been so high. To keep himself ready he continued to prepare, going to the various stashes of cash he had in the condo and consolidated them on his bed. The total was just shy of three hundred fifty thousand stacks, more than enough to take care of Josh and Mike but not enough to force the hand of his would-be supplier. He planned to call Sauce and have him go half with him on making the initial down payment one that Carlos couldn't turn away, but couldn't until he knew it was going to happen for sure.

It was the early evening and Bird had gotten everything packed up and still the he hadn't heard anything. With the time constraints looming over his head he began to feel the pressure. There was no way that he was going to give Mike and Josh sixty thousand without knowing that Carlos was at least on board. He grabbed his phone and began to dial Natalie to vent when the other phone began to ring from the bedroom. Bird nearly killed himself racing to the handset, flipping it open on the fifth ring.

"Yeah." Bird answered.

"Parajos!" A man said with a thick Spanish accent.

"Long time, amigo!" he replied. "I need to see you ASAP."

"A lot's changed. My passport is not too favorable with your country anymore." Carlos replied. "How soon can you get across the border?

Bird looked at the date marker on his wristwatch before answering. "Hell, I'll fly down tomorrow if I have to." He shot back.

"Fly into El Paso International and I'll have my people there to pick you up." Carlos said plainly. "Call the number you have back and simply give the arrival time and we'll go from there."

Bird agreed and immediately began looking up flights flying into the airport that Carlos had suggested but had no luck. He also wanted to take a large amount of cash as a down payment on the shipment to seal the deal which was a huge gamble and also presented its own array of problems. How could he take that much money on a commercial flight? What if the truck got intercepted after he paid? Even worst, what if he got robbed and murdered for the money? Bird shook the notions of failure loose from his mind and opted to continue his urban high wire act.

He called Sauce, who just happened to be at home and told him that he was on his way. In less than a half hour he was walking through Sauces front door to the cries of "Uncle Bird" from his kid's. Sauce heard the hoopla and came up from the basement, summoning Bird back down with him. As he approached the kitchen to head down the stairs he was greeted with a smile from Penelope who was at the sink preparing to cook.

"Hey Penny!" Bird said with a smile back as he ran down the stairs behind Sauce.

Sauce had gotten so accustomed to being in the basement at his Aunt's house that it became the area he was most drawn to in his own home. He had turned it into his own private lounge area reminiscent of Dave's, with a few theatre seats and huge flat screen on the wall.

"So what's the word B?" Sauce said as he poured himself a Patron and sweet lime at his bar.

"I got everything going my nigga!" Bird said in an excited tone. "But I'm gonna need that bread to make shit go for sure."

Sauce was amazed that Bird had managed to get The Partners to comply with the move. "What kinda bread we talkin' yo?" Sauce asked.

"Two hundred and fifty stacks." Bird said.

"Gotdamn B!" Sauce exclaimed. "That ain't a small piece of change! How you gonna get it to him?!"

"I feel you nigga but it is what it is." Bird replied. "I'm taking it down to him . . . I'm trying to figure out how to fly with the paper though."

"So you goin' solo, with half a mil in cash on you?!" Sauce said in amazement at his bravado.

"I don't give a fuck nigga!" Bird said aggressively. "Chances make champions right? Hit or miss I gotta shoot my shot."

Sauce looked Bird squarely in the eyes. Then he rose from the chair, slid it over and stomped on the parkay paneling causing it to spring up. Under the flooring was a hollowed out space containing vacuum sealed bundles of cash that Sauce began pulling out one after the other. Bird was impressed by the stash spot. He thought his spot inside of the exhaust vent in his bathroom was ingenious, but this was a new level of craftsmanship. After tossing several of the bags on to the floor he closed the floor and slid the chair back over it. The whole time he never spoke a word, not breaking his silence until he got everything back in place.

"We can just charter a flight to fly with the money." Sauce said. "Have Natalie schedule it so we won't draw any attention."

Although he hadn't invited Sauce along he knew he wouldn't let him assume the risk of getting killed in the desert alone so he just agreed with a nod. The idea was perfect. They would charter through Flight Options and fly out of the small private air strip in the Richmond Height's suburb. That would give them the ability to simply walk on with their money.

"I'll hit UPS tomorrow and send couple of straps next day so we won't be down there naked." Sauce explained. His mind was like a war chest of knowledge when it came to efficient violence.

"Ok. I'm about to call Nat when I leave here and have her do that." Bird said as he and Sauces palms met in a handshake. "We bout to pull this shit off my nigga!"

"Shit. Failing ain't an option yo!" Sauce replied.

Bird ran up the stairs to leave, shouting goodbye to Penelope and the kids as he headed for the door.

"Hey Chris!" she shouted pleasantly. "You're not sticking around for dinner?"

"Wish I could Penny!" he shouted back. "Got a business trip that popped up out of the blue and I have to get ready."

He backed out of the driveway and had Natalie on the other end before reaching the stop sign at the corner of Sauce's street. She was at her shop collecting rent on the eastside not far from where he was heading, so he told her to wait there until he came. It was getting late so he mashed the pedal half-way to the floor to make sure he got to her as soon as possible, turning a twenty-five minute trip into just under fifteen. As he pulled into the rear parking of her salon he spotted her, already there waiting in her Cayenne when he backed in. Natalie got out and walked to the rear of her SUV and perched on the bumper until Bird got out and met her. Under the shadows of the overhanging tree and out of the sight of the possible onlooker's from the shop she gave Bird a tight hug and kiss. He explained to her just where the plan was at and what he needed her to do, which she agreed without question.

The look in her eyes was unexplainable. Observing Bird on his million dollar power move, maneuvering through the traps and alluding pitfalls was a turn-on for her. Bird however, was experiencing tunnel vision, feeling like he was three moves away from doing the impossible. He kissed her face softly and told her goodbye. She stood there as he got back into his car and disappeared in the black tint.

Bird sped off back to his house awaiting Natalie's message, which came by 11p.m. that night. The flight was scheduled for 3p.m. the next afternoon. Just setting the whole play in motion was becoming costly. Between Mike, Josh and the flight Bird was out almost seventy. A large portion of the rest of his money was going to Carlos to lock him into the transaction, a move even his conscience mind questioned. But his gut feeling was opposite, and he had learned long ago to trust his instincts in tight situations so he allowed it to lead him.

He made the call to the mystery number to give them the arrival time, then to Sauce as well. Lastly, he contacted Dave to coordinate a drop off time for Mike and Josh's payments. With everything intact he got into the shower and let the water rain over his head in hopes that it would ease the pressure. "One week Chris." he said to himself. In seven days his life would change, hopefully for the better but potentially for the worst. His gauntlet had him going at a break-neck pace trying to pull it together, while balancing all of his responsibilities. As he got out of the shower he wrapped himself in a towel and fell back onto his bed into the moonlight that shined in. Thinking over the next two steps of his plan, he knew things would only get more perilous. His thoughts held his sleep hostage as he tried to take into account every plausible outcome. Bird closed his eyes for what seemed like seemed like five minutes only to open them to the morning sun blazing through at him.

It was almost 12:30 p.m. and he was due to meet Dave at noon. Bird jumped up and was brushing his teeth when his door buzzed. He ran to the monitor to see who it was. "Dave.", said the voice coming through monitor. He quickly buzzed him up and waited for him to get to the door. Dave walked through the door, took one glimpse at Bird and laughed.

"Long night?" he asked.

"My bad Dave." Bird apologized. "Been going nonstop trying to tie up loose ends."

"I figured that much." Dave replied. "You sure you're up for this?"

"I guess I'll find out if I'm not." Bird said as he headed to his bedroom and returned with the bags of money that he had for Dave.

Dave looked down at the bags, then up at Bird. "You know . . . on the highway of life it's sometimes best to take your time." he said allegorically.

"Ain't no speed limit on the road to riches either!" Bird replied.

"True. But it's always wise to pick your points." Dave said with a shy grin and wrinkled brow. "Dead man's curve done claimed many a soul who thought they could take it with their foot to the floor."

Bird tried to come with a witty comeback but Dave turned to leave after offering that food for thought. As he followed him to the door Dave gave him a strong handshake and hug.

"I know your minds made up on whatever your plan is." Dave said. "Just be careful. You've got a lot at stake."

His words slammed against the back of Bird's mind like the door as he left, then reverberated in it the rest of the afternoon and even through the flight south. On the plane he looked out of the window as it raced the sun west. He had a certain fondness for riding metal birds, amazed how beautiful the world was in the purity of the unmolested sky—unlike the murkiness that was found on the ground.

During the flight he found a brief moment of solace from the chaos that his life had become in the past week. He dozed off for the remainder of it and got the best rest he could remember in recent memory, only to be awakened by the thunderous sound of the small planes airbrakes as its wheels came in contact with the pavement. The pilot announced their arrival along with the weather and local time, which were 87 degrees and just past 6p.m.

The sweltering heat assaulted the two as they exited on to the tarmac causing them both to break into sweats within seconds of their exit. He had no clue what the next step was to get to Carlos but knew that they'd be in touch with him somehow. The two stuck out like sore thumbs, dressed like city slickers in a city only a few hundred miles from the Mexican border. Normally the attention wouldn't have bothered them, but with half million dollars on them it was the last thing that they wanted. Bird decided it was best they got out of sight as fast as possible, so they hustled to the car rental shuttle with a hotel as their final destination.

As they walked through the terminal a young Spanish woman manning the register at a small store selling beverages and magazines caught Bird's eye. There was something about the look on her face that invited him over.

"I'll catch you outside." he said to Sauce as he detoured over to the counter. He gave Bird a nod as he headed off to find the courier service that he'd shipped the package to.

"Can I help you?" she said slyly as Bird approached.

"Let me get two bottled waters." he said looking her in the eyes.

"Ok." she obliged, reaching into the cooler behind her. "May, I suggest a map as well to help you travel while in the area?"

"I'd appreciate that." he replied back. The young woman reached under the counter and produced a rather bulky map. "How much do I owe you?"

"It's on the house." she answered with a smile after bagging his goods. "Enjoy your stay."

Bird thanked her as he grabbed the bag and raced to catch up with Sauce at the shuttle pick-up. Once outside the building the blazing heat again engulfed him. He reached inside the bag and pulled out the bottles, handing one to Sauce as they boarded the bus. Even after removing both of the drinks the bag felt weighted, causing him to take the map out and inspect it. When he unfolded the first fold a small bar shaped phone fell into his lap.

"The chick at the lil' store!" he said as he showed Sauce the phone.

"You gon' call it or what??" Sauce asked.

"I'll wait until we get settled into a spot first he replied as he powered it on."

Bird took in the landscape of the area on the short bus ride. The sky was beautifully clear with tall palm tree's reaching high into it, reminiscent of somewhere tropical, yet with an unabated view of the mountain ranges on the far off horizon. After picking up the rental they stopped in the postal courier near the airport for Sauce to pick up his parcel before checking into the Radisson on the main boulevard. Expecting a brief stay they only bothered to bring one change of clothes in each other their bags. If he had it his way they wouldn't have brought any and flown back out in what they wore in—like true hustlers heavy on the grind, but chose otherwise under Bird's suggestion that they needed luggage to avoid suspicion. Sauce kept complaining that he was starving from the trip so they ordered room service and sparked a burner to take the edge off. While they waited Bird double checked his bag to make sure everything was in place before making the call. Simultaneously, Sauce loaded up his weapons, patiently awaiting the knock on the door. Before long the knock came and Bird answered, receiving two trays before tipping the kitchen servant and sending him on his way. As he sat on the bed to eat an unfamiliar ringtone began sounding incessantly. He and Sauce looked at each other dumbfounded until Bird realized it was coming from the phone he'd gotten to contact Carlos's people. He sprung from his seat and rushed to answer it like an Olympic sprinter, answering the unknown caller on what was likely the last ring.

"Leave your room and be in your car alone in ten minutes." the voice said.

Bird was speechless as the voice hung up after giving the directions. The notion that his potential suppliers knew his every move made him more than uneasy. Now he could empathize with Natalie for being constantly paranoid, thrown off by the idea that they were always close enough to touch her yet invisible. But the constant fear for one's safety was simply the cost of moving up the supply chain. And at the moment they were closer to the apex than most would ever be.

"They want me to come alone." Bird said.

"Fuck that!" Sauce said with a mouthful of food. "I'll follow you."

"That shit ain't gon' work!" Bird exclaimed. "These muthafucka's already know our every move."

Sauce was quietly considering the options to himself when Bird walked over to the bed and grabbed the duffle bag full of money off it. "Hold up!" Sauce yelled. "What's to stop these nigga's' from robbin' you B?!"

"The way I see it is if they wanted us dead by now we would be. Besides, this money ain't shit to them." he said as he placed the strap over his shoulder. "He had lost six times this when I first met him."

"Ok, but take this." Sauce said handing him a Glock. "And if I don't hear from you before long I'm going on the hunt."

"Don't worry. It's going to be cool." Bird reassured as he hurried out the door.

The truth of the matter was that he was even more wary than Sauce. He looked at his reflection in the mirror of the elevator—gun in waist, a half million dollars hanging from his shoulder and butterflies in his stomach the size of a newborn. The only calming idea in the moment was that he'd have an unbelievable story to tell after it was all said and done, which he reminded himself of constantly in an attempt to overshadow the more morbid scenarios fighting for his thoughts. As he walked through the lobby and to the valet, he made a mental note of all the faces around him, wondering if any of them were working for Carlos.

Bird tipped the valet and climbed into the car. Before the door closed the phone was again ringing.

"Drive to the rear lot and park." The voice again instructed.

Bird did as asked and pulled into a parking space in the temporary parking in the rear of the hotel. Just as he put the car in park a tinted SUV pulled on side of him and the window slowly rolled down. With his head motion the driver signaled for him to get into the rear. Bird swallowed hard and got out of the car with his bag secure around his neck and gun on his hip. The back door opened and a man stepped from it. With the door open he could see inside were three more men—one in both the driver and passenger seats, and an older one in the rear waiting for him to get inside. When Bird's foot touched the rail too climb inside he knew that he was beyond the point of no return. He exhaled all of his worry and put his game face on.

As the truck pulled from the lot it on to the main road Bird sat back and observed. Other than periodic comments between the men in their native tongues the ride was in quiet. He spied them closely, as well as the route he was being taken, but the sun had made its pass through the sky so his ability to commit landmarks to memory was hampered. What he did notice was the small machine guns the men on each side of him toted. He wondered how they would get through the checkpoint with such an arsenal but after only a quick glimpse inside of the vehicle at the border and a nod at the patrolman they were allowed in. Bird had never considered that the border was only minutes away from a large American city, yet within moments he was not just in another country but one of the most violent cities in it.

He'd heard the tales of Juarez and the battle for the valuable real estate in the narcotic trade, but now had a chance to see it firsthand. Only minutes away from the largest drug consuming nation in the world, its dangers were evident in the brigade that Carlos had sent to escort him. There was a certain sense of ever present menace that sent a continuous dose of adrenaline coursing through his veins as the truck sped through the dark side streets.

After several left and right turns the truck pulled onto a lively strip and parked in front of a lowly bar with a flashing neon sign. Bird found that the day's air had cooled into a comfortably warm night as he emerged from the truck and was ushered inside. With everything in Spanish he hadn't noticed that the bar was actually a strip club until inside the double doors. He was guided past the stage though a shallow sea of locals getting lap dances and through a doorway behind the bar, leading to a short dusty hallway with a storage room on his left and doorway at the end.

Once at the end of it his lead rapped on the door and announced himself. The door was opened by an older Mexican man covered in tats with a large prison build. Bird stared into his lifeless eyes as he was allowed inside the room. As the door slammed behind him Bird accessed his surroundings.

The room was clouded with a thick mixture of weed and cigarette smokes being blended by the ceiling fan. To the naked eye it would have appeared to be a simple private party, with several half naked women indulging men around the room and, if not for the random arsenal of weapons peppered throughout it.

As his panning eye recognized Carlos he was halted by the Mexican doorman.

"The bag?" He questioned to the driver as he stood almost chest to chest with Bird. The men froze, realizing that they had neglected to check him let alone the duffle bag. Sensing that they men hadn't followed protocol he began to pat Bird down. His aggressive nature was beginning to raise Bird's own as he reached in his waist band and felt the Glock he had tucked inside of it. He removed the gun with a grunt of disbelief, giving Bird an intense stare as if he wanted to use it on him. Bird stared back into the man's eyes with a taunting look, almost daring him to do something. The tension had built precipitously when Carlos diffused it.

"Puch!" he called out. "Relax." His henchman backed down and allowed Bird over to him. "I apologize for Ah Puch's behavior. It's a trying time so my Uncle keeps him with me."

"I see." Bird said as he walked over to the table where he was sitting. After the two exchanged handshakes they got right to the business.

"So I understand you're taking over for Natalie. How's she doing anyway?" he asked in a rivaling tone. "You've been taking care of her, no?"

Bird laughed off the jab—not interested in having a pissing contest with a Mexican gangster in his backyard. "She's good. She's really good."

"So what brings you here Parajos?" he asked sternly. "This isn't typically how business works but since you came this far I'll entertain you."

As Carlos took a long draw from his cigarette Bird unzipped the bag and allowed him a small glimpse inside at the contents. His jaw loosened after seeing that the guts were full of rubber banded bills. He called out to Ah Puch again, "Clear the room!" His muscle did as ordered, clearing everyone out before coming over to Carlos's side. "It's not my birthday. So what is this about?" he asked Bird.

"It's about price and the next order." Bird said calmly.

"The prices are the prices." Carlos replied. "Not much that can be done about that."

Bird scoffed at his comment. He stood from the table and poured contents of the bag on the glass table. "I've got 3x's this that says otherwise." he said. Street money never came in crisp bank notes like the movies suggested but in stacks of tattered bills of various denominations. The five hundred thousand that he emptied on to the table looked like a million, spilling from the edges onto the floor.

Carlos took a gulp of his drink, seemingly unimpressed by Bird's display. "What's the number like out that way Ah Puch?" He asked his henchman.

"Twenty-four . . . twenty-five thousand per kilo usually." He replied.

"See there." Carlos said with a smirk. "Twenty-four or twenty-five and Natalie's only at twenty-one. And it still has to get to your city which gets more and more difficult and costly."

"This is what I need." Bird said as he began giving Carlos the order and numbers that he needed to reach.

"Aye!" Carlos exclaimed. "I would love to help you but those numbers aren't possible. You're asking for too much."

Bird had savored his very best bargaining chip for last, hoping to get Carlos wrapped up in the dollar signs before forcing his hand. "How about if I pick it up just inside the border?" He asked.

Carlos laughed heartily and even his muscle cracked a hardened smile at his remark. "So you're going to come pick up over a hundred kilo's?!" He asked. "I thought you were loco when you brought this fucking money in here, but that takes the cake gringo!"

Bird sat back smiling like a poker player with five aces that had lured his challenger all in. He went on to explain to Carlos that he had a full proof plan to get the drugs from the region without interference and purchased political insurance to guarantee its arrival. He purposely embellished the timeframe that they could take advantage of the opportunity with the Goldman's to plant seeds of continuous transactions in Carlos's mind. Judging from the attentive look on his face the auspicious explanation had achieved just that.

"So can we make it happen?" Bird asked. "And I need the quality to be top grade shit. Anything less and you can have your people haul that shit back."

Carlos paused. There was no way that he wanted to cut his prices so steeply but was in a corner. It had gotten so hard to move massive quantities that far north undetected that he couldn't chance letting such a beneficial alliance pass him up. Bird's scheme had his mind roaming through the angles and potential profits a secure shipping route would bring him.

"What do you think Puch" Carlos asked.

"No se que . . ."[1] Ah Puch said in Spanish as he looked at Bird. "El me recuerda de los dos que Diego me envio a la manija en esa ciudad."[2]

"Hmpf." Carlos exclaimed. "Your memories too good Puch. You need to let it go bro."

"Es como el que dejé en el lado de la carretera!"[3] he sneered.

Bird grew agitated that they were speaking of him in his presence in words he couldn't decipher. Before another word between the two was spoken he quickly interjected. "No habla espanol muthafucka."

Carlos again laughed at his gall but his gunman didn't find it funny in the slightest. Before tension could re-escalate he sent his help to get samples of the product. He returned with two wrapped cubes and threw them on the table in front of Bird. Each was distinctive to him from just a glance. Carlos produced a razor for him to open them with and eyed him closely. Bird chose the pale white block to check first. Upon the plastic parting the distinctive odor of cocaine polluted his airspace. He took the tip of his finger and spread a small amount of the powder across the tip of his tongue. Instantly it went to work, numbing the tip then his whole tongue. The package was so potent that within a few seconds his mouth felt like he'd rinsed it with novocaine. Carlos smiled at Bird's reaction. Satisfied, he proceeded to open the other square. Outside of his casing the square was dense and hard as cement with a smooth tan gradient reminiscent of sandstone. The stench was so strong that Bird couldn't hold it close to his nose. Remnants of its original stamp were visible but Bird still wanted to check its insides to verify its grade. The brick of heroin

---

1   "I don't know?

2   "He reminds me of the two that Diego sent me to handle in that city."

3   "He's like the one I left on the side of the road!"

was so solid he had to use the corner of the table and his body leverage to break it in half. Once split in half, its color and texture was the same throughout, validating his opinion of it.

"What can it stand?" He asked Carlos.

"A four easily." He replied. "Maybe a five."

Bird kept his excitement concealed at the information but inside he was thrilled. In essence Carlos had just told him he could turn each unit into four and maintain its potency. That meant he could easily turn one into three without losing its strength and guarantee a return of well over a million dollars.

"So are we on?" Bird asked extending his hand to shake. "If so the truck will be through El Paso in a few days."

Carlos reached over and reluctantly shook his hand, unsure if he had just gotten hustled. After two came to the final numbers they drank a shot of tequila to celebrate the deal. He sent Puch to recall the others and resume the party, urging Bird to stay partake in the fun. Bird declined as he waited for the members of Carlos's crew to take him back to his hotel.

Suddenly Carlos asked, "How's that son of yours Parajos?"

"What?!" Bird responded it a stupor.

"I'm just saying, it's hard to keep kids safe when their into shit." Carlos said, lighting another cigarette. "You can kill a guy jumping on him like that."

Before Bird could muster a reply his men funneled back into the room.

"Make sure my friend here gets back to his hotel safely." Carlos said to the driver. "As always Parajos, it's been a pleasure."

Bird didn't bid him farewell, but only nodded as he followed the men back through the club and to the truck. Carlos's last remarks resonated in his head the whole ride back. He knew in mentioning his son that Bird would read between the lines and find the implied threat. His words were meant to let Bird know that their eyes would be on him and those closest to him at all times. As he climbed from the SUV back into his rental and drove back to the valet safely, he couldn't shake the feeling that had gotten a hold of him. What was a major coup had become bittersweet with knowledge of the underlying danger of the one person that mattered to him the most.

Bird didn't want to alarm Sauce in anyway, so he forced a smile to his face when he re-entered the hotel room. It was nearly 3a.m. when he walked into the cloudy dwelling and found Sauce on edge. The ashtray was full of cigar wrappings and fillings from his binge smoking. He hit him with a barrage of profanity laced as soon as he laid eyes on him. Bird calmed him, staying up the rest of the night giving him a detailed account of the meeting and its outcome.

The next morning they checked out of the hotel early in hopes of avoiding losing too much time moving forward through the time zones. They managed to secure a noon flight, giving them time to pawn the guns and get them back to Cleveland by the early evening. Sauce's level of excitement had grown tremendously since Bird's return. They spent the flight home laughing it up as they discussed their adventure, feeling the most precarious part of their mission had been surpassed. As Sauce fell asleep reality settled back in on Bird. Although they had gotten the deal situated they still had roughly a week to corral nearly two million dollars. Bird rested his eyes to sleep, knowing that once they reached their area code the real work would begin.

CHAPTER 15

"That would be me."

-Lynx

Fresh off of the plane Sauce jumped in his truck and headed home. The next few days for him would be endless as he burned a rental out racing up and down the interstate pooling funds. Bird chose to stay in the city and pull together all the contacts that he had. Off of three hours of sleep and a Red Bull he decided to get a jump on his responsibilities by hitting The Cocktail to see if any people that he had in mind to do business with were there so he could get the ball rolling.

Each side of town had a night spot legendary for being a safe haven for hustlers to congregate and unwind and The Cocktail was just that. Nestled deep inside the upper eastside of the city surrounded by trap house's and abandoned dwellings, it's following was unparalleled. A parking lot full of patrons was typical for the bar on any given day of the week.

Bird went home first to quickly wash the Mexican dust from his skin and get dressed for the night. By midnight he pulled off of the avenue into the parking lot. The bar was an urban version of Cheers, the place where everyone knew everyone. If there was anything happening in the streets it traveled through there, whether through conversation or ghetto gossip. Bird walked inside, gripping hands and greeting nearly every person he passed. A casual smile to the thick bar maid and a Ciroc and lime was quickly sliding across the bar to him.

As he moved through the crowded bar stopping from time to time to speak with individuals who he had hoped would be there, the staring eyes of what seemed to be familiar faces caught his eye. He made his way closer for a clearer view finally doing a double take as if he'd seen a ghost when his eyes focused.

"Lynx?!" he asked.

"That would be me." He replied with steely eyes. "Been a long time Bird."

Bird could sense the tension in his old friend immediately as their hands met in a weak handshake. Lynx had gotten rock solid from his long stint. He was a walking mural with jail ink covering his arms, hands and neck with various images. It was obvious he felt some type of way about how things had gone—maybe rightfully so. Regardless, Bird wasn't up for wasting precious time playing makeup or willing to entertain his attitude. Lynx's eyes looked past Bird, causing him to turn to see what was approaching. The large figure in sunglasses moved past him quickly and perched on the stool on Lynx's other side. Bird didn't initially recognize the dark skinned man with a large beard and tatted tear drops streaming down his jaw line. It wasn't until he heard Lynx greet the man that he knew who it was. Tuffy.

Some things never change and the same held true for him and Tuffy. Neither he nor Bird spoke as much as a simple hello to each other, though Bird bought them both a round of drinks. Lynx angled his body toward Tuffy and began talking energetically as if they were the ones that had catching up to do. Bird laughed at the message his body language sent.

"Lil' mama!" he called out to the bar maid once again. "Take care of their drinks for the rest of the night for me baby and keep the rest." Bird pulled two hundred dollar bills from his knot and tossed it on the bar. "Y'all nigga's enjoy yourselves and stay out of trouble, aight?" he said as he got up and left.

Bird had enough after seeing the ghosts from his past again and decided to call it a night. It was obvious that the feelings were still raw by everyone involved. Bird saw the whole situation as a non factor though. His mind was on things bigger than each of them could even fathom at the moment and it deserved his full attention.

The next day Bird's ghost phone almost exploded with phone calls. The city was so small that mover's and shaker's were amongst a small crowd that swam in shallow waters. From just his walk through the bar and choice interactions news of the pending move had gotten around to everyone he wanted to reach. The absolute beauty of the plan was that all Bird had to get with were the major players—those whose identities never reached street level hoods. They were peppered throughout the city under different guises, yet controlling the game anonymously. Realistically they may have all indirectly had the same suppliers the whole time while being oblivious to each other. Now Bird was funneling all of that same money down one channel, in essence leapfrogging to the head of the regional drug trade in one fell swoop. But he'd only hold the seat for a few months at most, vacating it well before any opposition could be mounted.

The next three days he compiled more than a million himself with Sauce bringing in nearly the same as the big day approached. He had gotten the call that the truck had reached El Paso and was headed back home right on schedule with no hiccups in the plan thus far. The streets low hum on the matter had turned into an official buzz. With everyone's resources put into Bird's major play nothing was moving anywhere in the city. The result was a city on pins and needles, as everyone anxiously awaited the drop day. Bird secured the money outside the city limits in a hotel room under him and Sauce's watchful eyes, taking turns spending the night with the ante to avoid any mishaps. Bird knew that everyone in the streets would simply assume that Sauce would be point man on the money drop, being his most trusted friend. But instead he enlisted the most unlikely of those closest to him. Lil Tyco.

The only person who knew the drill was Sauce. Bird couldn't afford the possibility of a double cross by having the money and drugs in the same place at one time. Lil' Tyco would drive a car loaded with the cash for the transaction into a long term parking lot of his discretion at the airport, and then send the information to Sauce. He would give it to one of Carlos's men at the warehouse to pick up as they unloaded the shipment. After parking the car Lil' Tyco would take the shuttle to the rental station, get the car Bird would have waiting for him and pick up Jessica, whose flight would be landing around the same time. He had everything strategized down to a science like clockwork.

With everything in place Bird decided to celebrate the final stretch of his plan and clear his mind. With just eight hours until the trucks arrival time, he was in his car heading to the MGM Grand Casino in Detroit to try his luck at the craps table to relax one more time before the feeding frenzy began when he got back to town. As the hours past he made his rounds from game to game, winning a little and losing more back while trying not to check his watch.

Bird had managed to strike up a hot hand at the craps table when his phone began going off. He looked down at the phone sitting on the railing and saw that it was Dave. Figuring he'd be off the table shortly he ignored the call. But as soon the call went to voicemail it began to ring again, this time it was Natalie. Bird stepped away from the table to take the call.

"Hello?" he answered.

"Bird!!!" she screamed frantically. "Where are you??!!"

Bird's stomach instantly sank at the sound of her voice. "What's wrong?!"

"Oh my God . . . . Oh my God . . ." Natalie repeated over and over. "Shits fucked up! It's all over the news!"

Bird's first thoughts were that the truck got intercepted by the police but he needed Natalie to calm down and give him the details. "Tell me exactly what their saying happened." he said.

"Their saying it was a shootout or hijacking or something . . ." she said in a panicked tone. "It happened in the warehouse. They're saying it's a bunch of bodies . . ."

All the air left the room. Instinctively he ran from the casino to the valet, with his mind still stuck where it was when he heard the news. The first thing that crossed it was Sauce. Bird almost jumped into the car before the valet had a chance to get out of the seat. Natalie was on the other end of the phone still, but now she was sobbing loudly making her communication incoherent.

"I'll be there!" Bird said as he hung up and raced onto the freeway.

As he pushed his cars governor to the limit on the freeway he toyed with the idea of calling Sauce. Something had to be wrong because he hadn't heard from him, but he also knew Sauce wouldn't call if it would bring heat to him, he'd get under the radar first. Before he could gather his thoughts his phone rang again. Without looking at the caller I.D he answered.

"Yeah Nat?!" He answered.

"Why Chris?!" The voice cried from the other end.

"L?" He hesitated. "What you talkin' about??"

"Why the fuck you get my baby wrapped up in your shit!" Laura sobbed. "I can't believe they shot my baby!"

Bird was confused by what he was hearing, Lil' Tyco wasn't at the drop. "What!?" he exclaimed. "Who shot him?! What happened?"

"The police said he got car-jacked in a car you rented!" She explained. "And they kidnapped your girlfriend . . . I'm at Metro with him now!"

Few in life have ever been unfortunate enough to know the despair that overwhelmed Bird after listening to Laura. His own thoughts were so intertwined that he couldn't think at all. "I've gotta be dreamin'." he thought to himself. But the hellish nightmare was all too real. Nothing but the sound Laura's tears being painfully shed came through his phone. Bird couldn't think straight with the sound of her soul aching in his ear. "I'm on my way." he said gently as he hung up.

The uneasiness of not knowing what was truly happening was unbearable. In the midst of the chaos the realization that Jessica had been taken set in Bird's but still he didn't shed a tear. Instead he shifted his thoughts to sift through the bits and pieces of information to figure out what was happening.

After making it through the toll road he punched the pedal to the floor, turning two hour drive into a little over an hour. Just as he was entering the city limits his phone rang with another call from Dave. Reluctantly he answered.

"Dave . . . I . . ." he began but was stopped short.

"I told you to take your time, didn't I?" Dave asked calmly. "Now you see what's happened? First the warehouse shit happens—got Josh all fucked up calling me trippin'! Mike's ass hoping the shit doesn't blow his way." tMrs. Greenfield's cries filled the background. "And then the police just left saying my daughters been kidnapped!" he explained as he fought back his own tears. "Now I don't know what the fuck is going on, but you better get my daughter back, you understand me?!" he scowled.

Bird didn't speak a word for the duration of the call. There was no adequate response to Dave's words. No reply could justify what was going on, or ease the torment that he and his family felt. He couldn't image how frightened Jessica was that very moment or what was happening to her now as a hostage. Bird prayed to God that she was ok and tried his best to not let his thoughts paralyze him. His heart wasn't willing or prepared to let his imaginings go as far as to consider the worst. He again attempted to refocus and the offensive, cycling through a mental rolodex of suspects. But that strategy only led his mind on a wild goose chase without any facts to sustain his theories. Maybe it was someone he'd done business with? Maybe Carlos's people nabbed Jessica after the drop went bad? With so many things happening at once the questions and possibilities were endless.

As he got inside the city limits he called Sheena to forewarn her of the potential threat that loomed.

"She-She!" he said as she answered.

"Bird! Where are you?!" she said concerned. "Everybody's talkin' bout what happened. Are you ok?!"

"I'm ok. I'm headed into the city now." Bird replied. "I need you and Jace to be careful. I don't know what the fuck is going on!"

"Ok." She peaceably complied. "Hook with me when you get back! You know I still got your back baby . . ."

"Ok . . . I'll get with you." He responded. "Please keep an eye on the boy until' I figure shit out!"

She again agreed as Bird hung up and pulled into the visitor parking at Metro Health Center where Laura was. Sheena's reaction was actually a welcomed one, offering to be there for him if he needed her meant more than she knew. It also allowed his nerves to calm some, knowing he could rest assured that under the circumstances Jace was in the safest of care with her.

Bird raced into the hospital to the intensive care unit where Lil Tyco was being treated. Laura wasn't in sight but a nurse just happened to be exiting his room. He ran up to her and introduced himself as an immediate relative then inquired into his nephew's condition.

"He's alive. But barely." she said. "Three gunshot wounds at point-blank range with a 9mm. luckily for him the shooter used a high velocity round and bad aim. We're purposely keeping him unconscious."

"Where exactly was he hit?" Bird questioned.

The nurse described the extent of Lil' Tyco's injuries. "The first round went through his face, entering through his left side and exiting the middle of the right." she began. "The second grazed his neck deeply but wasn't life threatening. The last shot was the one that landed him on the operating table. It entered his lower back and exited the front of him just under his collar bone. From the police accounts of the shooting, he was in the driver's seat when the shots began. That's how the third and final bullet entered his back and seemingly to exited upward through his lung."

Bird could only listen as he looked through the window into the room. With his plan being as solid as it was he had overlooked the fact that sending Lil' Tyco to pick up a rental car in his name and his future bride could possibly make him a target. Now he was in the hospital bed unconscious with a machine assisting his every breath. The nurse vowed that they would do everything within their power to aid in his recovery before she walked to her station. His eyes trailed her as she walked away, hoping she meant the words she spoke and wasn't just giving a conciliatory speech. As he was turning to the room he could see Laura walking slowing up the hallway. Her head hung so low that it looked like she was watching herself walk, so she hadn't seen him yet. Her hair was everywhere and her lips were slowly mouthing something. Laura was a few feet away when she finally looked up and saw Bird standing outside of Lil' Tyco's room. With outstretched arms he went to hug her but she stopped him, her puffy swollen eyes staring into his.

"Why are you here?" she asked softly. "Please just leave."

"Listen L . . ." Bird tried to explain.

"Just go!" she screamed.

Again Bird attempted to hug and console her.

"Get the fuck off me!" Laura spewed angrily. "You did this to him! And got that girl caught up in your shit! Just leave us alone . . . go fuck up your own life!"

Seeing Laura hurting like she was devastated him but the words aimed at him cut deeper than a surgeon's blade could. Bird had never imagined that he would hear words like that from Laura. She was his constant, his everlasting connecting to his life before innocence was lost. Now he had effectively destroyed that relationship as well.

By the time she got fully enraged the nurse had come over and politely asked him to leave, which he gladly obliged. The walk down through the quiet corridor was a solemn and sobering one. Bird's perennial, even-keeled temperance was shaken. "Maybe she's right." he thought to himself. As he got in his car to leave. He'd left his phone in the center console while in the hospital and came back to over a dozen missed calls and twice that in text messages. The majorities of them were from Natalie and Dave, with a couple from unknown callers and blocked numbers. The last call he missed radiated from the screen and sent his stomach wrong side up. It was Sauce's home number. Bird stared at it long enough to burn his retina before giving in and calling it. The phone rang for several minutes before the voicemail picked up. He left a message, exhaled and then powered his phone down. He couldn't handle another call of misfortune while he was still struggling to get a clearer understanding of what already had transpired.

Bird sped home to gather himself and recollect his thoughts. He turned on the evening news just to add soothing ambient sound to his domicile as he sat at the foot of the bed, his head in his palms. Suddenly there was a breaking news flash that caught his attention.

This just in. One of the victims of the deadly warehouse shootout that left seven dead has been positively identified as thirty-two year old, Roberto Roy of Cleveland.

Bird's heart almost stopped as he watched in shock.

"Have any of the others been positively identified?" the on-air anchor questioned.

"No other victims have been identified. I was told by investigators that the shooting was an especially brutal slaughter, leaving the work up to the medical examiners to sort out. Yet, in a horrible twist of fate a relative of Roberto Roy's actually was at work in the examiner's office when his body arrived and I.D.'d

him immediately. There are reports though that three of the men were Mexican illegals and that Federal authorities would be contacted for assistance. Again we will keep you posted as details emerge."

Bird's mind was so heavy it toppled him to the bed. His emotions were overwhelming him, experiencing more pain and anguish than he could contain as his thoughts transitioned to Penelope. He couldn't begin to imagine what she felt as she peeled the sheet back only to see her husband and father of her children lifeless on the gurney.

Maybe it was the bevy of things going wrong and the fact that his mind hadn't had time to register them all completely that made him unable to mourn and shed a tear like a normal person would have in his shoes. But he never cried, even though he wished that he could. He found himself thinking everything over once more, coming to the conclusion that things were inevitably going to get worst as the story unraveled.

Mike and Josh wouldn't allow themselves to be scapegoats by any measure of the term. He owed almost every major hustler within the state either product or a monetary refund and there was no clue to the exact location of either. With Lil' Tyco in a medically induced coma the location of the money that he dropped in the car was lost with him. On top of it all the fact that Carlos's men were murdered in the fiasco and two and a half million in drugs were gone was the most lethal of his issues, with Ah Puch undoubtedly in route to the city as he laid there.

And that was just scraping the surface. Sauce was dead. He had no inkling if Jessica was the same. His nephew was at death's door and his beloved sister was done with him. Surely Dave was awaiting the outcome of his daughter's situation before doing the same. Bird glanced at the Glock laying next to him with the thought of self murder dancing around the borders of his troubled mind posing as a panacea to his woes. Then he thought of the people that still needed him most. Jessica, Jace and Natalie. If she was alive she needed him to pull through and if he didn't Jace would soon join him at the hands of Carlos's henchmen. Natalie would likely meet the same fate too.

"Besides, the way things were looking, someone would likely do him in anyway." he thought to himself. "Why not die on my feet?"

His thoughts became increasing morbid as he came to grips with the possibility that his end was all but guaranteed if he didn't get a hold of the situation and fast. But with embracing death came an odd sense of freedom and peace of mind that was unexplainable. For the first time in what seemed like forever his mind was completely clear and everything simplified. His mind finally allowed itself a moment to rest giving his body an opportunity to do the same.

Bird awoke ready to get down to the business that awaited him. Moving around his house, he treated his day as if it was like any other. He stepped from the shower in the master bedroom only to hear a familiar voice come from his television. Bird hustled into the room, only to catch the tail end of Dave and his wife on the news. As he continued watching they went on to explain the new developments.

"Mrs. Greenfield's daughter was forcefully taken at gunpoint last night in a violent abduction. In the early hours the kidnapper's allowed her to call from her cell. Reading a written message verbatim, she voiced their demands that her fiancé produce a half million dollar ransom within 48 hours. In her panic Mrs. Greenfield tried to contact the fiancé who was unreachable before contacting the authorities who turned it over to the F.B.I."

Bird couldn't believe his eyes or ears. He immediately grabbed his phone and powered it back on to check his voicemail's and texts. Just as the reporter had stated he had a flurry of both from the Greenfield's. Bird turned his head back to the television after they went live to the Fed's press conference on the matter—his jaw dropping at what he saw on the screen.

There standing at the podium was Detective Blake, who had become Agent Blake and now was the lead in the F.B.I.'s Greenfield case. As he began to speak, Bird turned up the volume and listened close.

"We have received some leads in this matter and are currently pursuing them. Being a detective in the region for many years before becoming a federal agent, I'm familiar with certain individuals close this investigation and am looking forward to bringing Jessica home safely. We also have reason to believe that another incident that took place that night is directly related to this abduction."

As the camera angle went wide he could see everyone on stage which not only consisted of the Greenfield's but also Mike DeLuca conveniently holding a picture of his missing God-daughter. It was painfully obvious he was doing preemptive damage control, placing himself outside of the fallout zone as the investigation unfurled.

"Fuck!" Bird yelled as he grabbed his duffle bag from the closet and threw some clothes inside of it. He grabbed his work phone and called Natalie.

"Bird!" she exclaimed. "I've been so worried about you!"

"Listen to me carefully . . ." he said as he detailed the plan like a quarterback during two-minute drill. "I need you to go buy me a low-key whip, like right now . . . nothing more than five or six grand. Nothing hot."

Natalie agreed and Bird quickly got off the phone. He was moving at the speed of light around the apartment gathering everything he needed. The press conference was only four blocks from his condo, and judging from Blake's comments it wasn't hard to decipher their first person of interest. Bird ripped the exhaust enclosure from his bathroom ceiling to reveal his emergency stash of seventy-five thousand and tossed the bundles into the bag. He then tucked his Glock in his waistband a hurried out of the door.

Bird made it away from his downtown nest safely, but still had his cell phone which was a problem he couldn't avoid at the moment. He knew the FED's could triangulate his whereabouts with it, but he also knew there was no way that he could be contacted by the kidnappers without it being on. Until a call came through he would have to play cat and mouse by keeping on the move. For several hours he stayed on the go, only stopping for brief moments near highways so his movements wouldn't appear purposely erratic, but still giving him a chance to get away if cornered.

He was walking through Saks Fifth when Jessica's name flashed across his screen. Bird promptly answered.

"Jessica, baby?!" he said as his heart pounded in his chest.

Tearfully she replied. "Chris! Please help me!"

There was rustling on her end of the phone and Bird could hear her screaming. When it ceased she began to read a statement to him as she fought to speak the words through her cries. The instructions were for Bird to come alone to an abandoned building located right inside the East Cleveland border with half a million cash at 4a.m. that morning. Any deviations from the plan and they would kill her. No extensions.

"I'll be there baby! Don't worry . . ." he said.

The phone went dead.

Bird rushed out of the mall to his car. He had to keep the law off of his tail for at least the next eight hours until he could get Jessica back. The black CLS darted down the back streets from Beachwood until it reached St. Clair. "What better way to keep the police away than giving them something to chase?" he thought. Bird called the Greenfield's home phone knowing full well that it was being monitored, hanging up just as they answered. If he knew Blake they'd be tracking his whereabouts immediately. Bird rode through the streets where he'd grown up, bending corner after corner as he cleared out his phone, before coming to a stop in the back parking lot of The Open Pitt restaurant. He walked inside to the shocked expression on many of the faces of the patrons that knew him. Undaunted, he walked up to the window and nonchalantly placed an order like he usually would, then took a brief seat before rushing back outside. With everyone's attention on him they hadn't noticed that he had purposely left his phone wedged between the cushions of the bench seat. Hopefully that would be enough to make Blake mobilize and act, buying him time to handle what was in store that morning.

As he walked from the restaurant back to his car he called Natalie to see if she had him situated and also for help making the ransom happen. She again conceded and they were coordinating the drop when an SUV screeched to a halt. For a split second Bird thought that it was part of Blake's team until the passenger closest to him sprung from the rear driver's side and opened fire. The first shot was wide and high, giving Bird a chance to react and return fire, striking the first gunman three times with precision marksmanship before the passenger perched himself in the window and began to fire from the opposite side of the truck. Bird didn't have a clear shot at the passenger so he emptied his magazine at the driver, causing him to mash the gas to escape. The SUV plowed into a parked car, the impact ejecting the shooter from the window onto the curb. There was no movement out of the driver but the other man who had landed on the curb got to his feet and took flight. Bird jumped into his car and sped off headed straight to the freeway. With adrenaline flooding his blood stream he struggled to catch his breath. He didn't care about what happened as much as he did about who the gunmen were. "Could they have been some of Carlo's men? Already?" he wondered. Whatever the case, the police definitely had grounds for an arrest warrant now with the shooting likely being captured by the security cameras surrounding the business.

Bird called Natalie back after the fire-fight and finished their discussion on the switch. At the rate he was going, to see each other in person could be hazardous. He didn't want to expose her to any danger so he gave her a parking garage where she could park the car and leave the key inside of it under the floor mat.

He got off the freeway and made his way to the parking structure, slowly cruising through on the prowl for the grey Nissan that Natalie described to him. As he cleared the second level he spotted it backed in just as she said. Conscience of the cameras, he continued to the next level up before parking and took the stairs back down to the car. As he pulled from the garage he decided to head to a safe house where no one would be able to find him. Sauce's aunts.

Sauce had kept the property even after he and Pennie got married and started a family. She didn't even know that it still belonged to him. It was his safe haven away from the world, he used to tell Bird. Now it would serve as his, at least until it was time to head to the swap. Bird parked on the street and went to the back door and the hidden spot for the key. Inside everything was just as Sauce had left it the last he was there. He walked through the house looking at the pictures and knickknacks reminiscing on his friend. He couldn't believe that he was gone, leaving behind a wife and three children or not feel responsible for that matter. He never intended for it to end like this—on the run broke with attempts being made on his life. His world had been turned upside down in pursuit of the pot of gold at the end of the rainbow. The only saving grace would to get Jess back safely.

Sauce had a small arsenal of weapons and ammo at the safe house, along with several bullet proof vests. Bird took full advantage of it, stocking up and reloading his gun back to the brim as he sat on the couch in the basement. He turned the flat screen on and tuned in to the news to see what was going on. Reporters always had a way of releasing more than they should, making news broadcasts the perfect barometer to see how and what was transpiring after major happenings. A shooting outside of the legendary Cleveland restaurant was unquestionably major.

Just as he thought the cameramen and reporters were live on the scene with the top story.

"In the second night of extreme violence a gunman opened fire on a man as he exited this popular Cleveland restaurant behind me. Though details are still coming in, reports are the man then returned fire, killing both the gunman and driver. Witnesses at the scene indentified the man as Corey Milner also known around the neighborhood as Snags. Oddly, Federal authorities were already in route following a lead in the Jessica Greenfield kidnapping when the shooting took place and believe the incidents are again related."

"*The streets are becoming a battlefield.*" *the in-studio anchor said. "Do the police have anyone in custody?*"

"*The police do not have anyone in custody at this time. The shooter as well as a third passenger in the vehicle fled the scene but they have reviewed the security footage and feel that they have a suspect in mind.*"

"Snags?" Bird questioned aloud.

He was certain that it would turn out to be Carlos's local sector coming for him. Now he was dumbfounded as to how it came to be Snags and even more curious as to who the second gunman was who escaped. Snags had been part of Sleepy's team of bandits for the better part of ten years, robbing and murdering. But they only played for the money, either in taking it or by commission. The shootout was unmistakably a hit. The burning question in Bird's mind was who could have ordered it? He laid his head back on the couch to rest his eyes and to ponder what he was potentially walking into in just six hours. A few blinks later he was in another world.

It was an island setting and Bird was there with Sauce and his family. He looked at his side and Jessica was there with Jace. But there was no sound, not even when they laughed, but their elation was evident. Then he found himself suddenly following Sauce from the beach toward a jungle. But he stopped just short of entering, faced Bird and shook his head side to side. Bird couldn't understand what was happening and just stood there in the sand. Sauce's face contorted into an enraged snarl. "You gotta GO!!!" he screamed.

Bird sat up on the couch suddenly, covered in sweat. He used his t-shirt to wipe his face as he came to his senses and glanced at his wristwatch. It read 2:39 a.m. He took a deep breath to let his nerves settle. As his rubbed his forehead with his hand several slow creeks of the wooden floor above caught his attention. Seconds later he heard more creeks, some in unison. He had visitors upstairs.

Bird hurried to his feet and grabbed his gun. He first tried to escape through a basement window but it was stuck. As the steps got closer to the basement door he took cover behind the furnace and water tank, watching as two men dressed in black slowly came down the stairs and began sweeping through the room. A third stood at the top of the stairs waiting. Bird could only see him from the knees down but judging from his attire he was overseeing the job. He wasn't in murder gear like the others but blue jeans and Durango boots.

The men slowly closed in on Bird's hiding spot, assault rifles poised to fire. There was no way that he could take them out without taking on heavy fire. He took aim at the figure at the top of the stairwell, opting to at least take the head man with him. In a moment the men would invade the shadows and he'd be exposed. Without thinking further Bird fired, the bullet ripping through the man's knee, bringing him tumbling down the stairs. The fall startled the gunmen giving him the split second he needed to split twelve rounds between the two of them, rapid fire.

When he emerged from the shadows he could see that the man who he hit on the stairs had dropped a sawed shotgun during the fall and was now trying desperately to crawl to it. But the hollow-point .45 slug had blown a massive hole where his knee once was, leaving him in excruciating pain. Bird fired another shot through his shoulder as he reached for it. He crept slowly, cautious that he may have had another weapon. As he got within a few feet, the pale glow of the television shed enough light for him to see that it was indeed Ah Puch. Bird commanded him to roll over and face him. He did as he began to laugh between pants.

"You'll never get away." he said slowly. "Carlos is weak! But Diego is merciless!"

Bird trained the gun on his face as he stood over him, reveling in Puch's defiance even in the face of his fate. Growing weary of Bird casting his smile down on him, he became belligerent.

"Do it putah!" he screamed. "Diego's still going to kill you and your family. You all going to die!"

His last words sounded eerily familiar to Bird, though he couldn't put his finger on it. There was no more time to waist. Bird slowly squeezed the trigger sending a shell casing flying and a bullet through his face. The shot entered just below his nose and out his neck. The wound didn't immediately kill him, but left him gasping for air with his eyes bulging as he drowned in the blood pouring from him.

Bird grabbed his things and made a quick exit. With all the commotion it was safe to assume that the police were on their way. Once they put two and two together they'd connect it to every other crime and be on his trail. With nowhere else to go there was only one thing to do.

"Couldn't hurt to get there early." he thought to himself as he headed to the swap location. It was after 3a.m. when he got to the desolate area. The building the kidnappers had chosen was on a short street surrounded by vacant dwellings and tall grass. With only one entrance, there was no way anyone could scope the scene or enter unnoticed. Bird circumvented their strategy by driving by the building then parking one street over. He came through the yard of an abandoned house adjacent to the building and watched closely for any movement. The building was a shell with no doors or windows and caving ceilings.

After thirty minutes he finally saw movement inside. There were three of them in the apartment on the second story of the building. From what he could see they were scrambling to prepare for him. Bird hastily dashed back to the car and pulled around onto the street, effectively announcing his arrival. He climbed through the mountain of trash and debris that filled the entrance and headed up the stairwell, careful not to spark a shootout by surprising Jessica's captors inadvertently. The scene was surreal as he cleared the final stair and entered the doorway. In front of him stood three masked figures dressed in all black, pistols in hand. Jessica was nowhere in sight. As Bird stepped through the threshold and into the crumbling apartment he looked the crew over before speaking to them. They were obviously disorganized and unsure about which of them was in charge.

"Where's the money?" the largest of them said with a deep voice.

Bird patted the bag he had draped over his shoulder. "Where's Jessica?" Bird asked.

"She's in the area . . . safe." the large one said slowly. "Hand the money over and we'll tell you where you can find her."

The whole exchange sounded like bullshit to Bird. The meeting wasn't an exchange but an ambush. Bird slowly motioned as if he was taking the bag off of his shoulder, using the bag to mask his hand pulling his trusty Glock from his waistband again. As the strap cleared his shoulder he heard four shorts and felt the force of the bullets hitting his back, knocking him to the floor. As he lay on the floor playing possum a slender figure stepped over him with his gun still smoking in the glow of the street lights, snatching the bag off of the floor and tossing it to the large man. Just as the figure walked between the two parties enough to obscure his cohort's line of sight, Bird rolled onto his back and opened fire, landing two shots before taking aim on the others. As the slim figure melted to the floor the smallest of the three let out a glass shattering shriek. The scream registered as that of a woman, stunning Bird for a moment.

He managed to take cover behind a mangled couch. One of the shots he'd let off had found a home in the third man's lower chest, as he took on heavy fire from the other man and woman. Bird dropped the empty magazine and popped in another, waiting for their weapons to go empty. With each muzzle flash the room illuminated like a fireworks display indoors. When the hail of bullets stopped the cloud of gun smoke was thick enough to choke on, Bird tried to rush to his feet. But he collapsed back to one knee from a wound to his calf. Unable to see clearly he squeezed in the direction of the silhouettes the smoke accentuated. The large man grabbed the bag of money and drug the woman out the back of the apartment with him. The third was slumped against the wall near the walkway from his puncture wound. Bird painfully gathered himself to his feet and slowly moved over to him.

"Take the fucking mask off!" Bird demanded with his gun aimed squarely between the man's eyes.

He slowly tilted his head back and looked directly into Bird's eyes as he heaved each breath. The moment Bird saw his eyes he knew they had a personal connection. He reached down and yanked the mask from the man's face and exposed his identity. He couldn't believe his eyes as he did. It was Lynx.

Bird spazzed out and began pacing back and forth in circles. "What the fuck?!" Bird screamed. "Lynx!? Why nigga!?"

"What you mean what the fuck, nigga!?" Lynx said slowly with tears in his eyes. "You left me B. You ain't even come see me once. You let me rot for twelve fuckin' years, man. If you would've broke that bread I coulda been out in seven like Tuff!"

Bird was awe stricken. "Nigga I gave Mz. Tami the money she asked for!" Bird screamed. "Twenty-five racks!"

He could tell from the look in Lynx's face that it was his first time hearing of the money. They both had been played. He explained to Bird that Tuffy had gotten out five years earlier and taken up residence in Cincinnati, hustling with guys he'd met while locked up. "I listened for seven years about how scandalous you are." Lynx explained. "Him and Sheena been writing each other damn near the whole time we was down."

The whole picture had become clear. The large man. The woman's scream. Bird instantly put the story together in his mind. But who was the fourth member? Bird fell to his hands and knees and crawled over to the other body. With his heart racing he prayed that his premonition was wrong before he removed the mask, but to his despair it was dead on. There in front of him barely breathing, clinging on to life was Jace.

"God please." Bird pleaded over and over as he tried to figure out what to do.

The sound of sirens could be heard in the distance. "Bird." Lynx called back out to him. "You gotta GO before they get here!"

"I can't leave him!" he yelled back.

"Bird!" he struggled to scream. "You can't help him or your girl if you're locked up for murder. We was watching the news too."

Bird had all but forgotten about Jessica once he saw Jace. He knew that Lynx was right, staying there meant definite incarceration. "Where is she?" he asked Lynx.

"At She-She's." Lynx said. "She knew you'd never come there and check."

Bird climbed to his feet and gave his son one last glance as the siren's got closer. Then he turned to Lynx. His breathing was now shallow and his eyes glazed over. Looking at his one-time best friend dying in front of him, he didn't see the cocky jail-bred brut but the little black kid he ran the city streets with getting into mischief. Bird knelt beside him as he again spoke.

"B." he whispered. "You still hold on to them guns like Flex taught you?"

Bird looked at the gun he clutched in his palm before answering.

"You can't teach old dog new tricks, right?" He replied.

Lynx mustered his remaining strength to pull off his glove and take Bird's gun from his hand. "I'm sorry B." he gasped. He told Bird to take the keys from his pocket. The three had split the take from the warehouse and were all poised to go their separate ways. He had his in the trunk of a car parked down Eddy Rd.

Lynx's gestures touched him to his core. He picked up the 9mm Taurus that Lynx had dropped on the floor and rushed out. Regardless of what they had been through he couldn't bear to see him take his last breaths. He hobbled down the stairs of the building and to the car—the flashing lights turning the corner of the street just as he was exiting at the opposite end. Bird made it to Eddy Rd. but didn't know the make or model of the car. His only option was to cruise down the street pressing the trunk release on the key fob in hopes that it would trigger the trunk. As he approached St. Clair an Impala's light lit up and the trunk flew open. Bird pulled into the driveway behind the car, transferred its goods to his backseat and sped off to the freeway.

He got on the ramp and headed east to Sheena's. As the nights events sank in he wanted nothing more than to put a bullet in her head. He wanted to stomp the gas to get to her quicker but couldn't with the parcel in his backseat. The sun was peaking over the horizon as he pulled into Sheena's driveway. She wasn't there but Bird hoped that was a good thing for Jessica. He kicked in the side door and raced to the basement but no one was there, just the remnants of her imprisonment. Bird glanced around at the setting at the makeshift cot they likely had Jessica tied up on. The whole basement looked like it had been ransacked. There was no telling what sadistic things Sheena had done to her. Looking closer, the edge of a picture caught his eye from underneath the rubble.

It was the picture of him, Jessica and Jace from his first Christmas. It also was the very same picture that he lost when his apartment was violated and his safe taken over a decade ago. He never would have imagined that Sheena was the culprit. Feeling like a complete fool after learning he had been betrayed by his first love—the mother of his son, the intricate plot to destroy him was almost beyond his comprehension. Sifting the trash on the floor with his foot turned up a cell phone as well.

Bird picked it up and powered it on. A picture of a youthful Tyco and Laura appeared as the wallpaper. It was Lil' Tyco's. He desperately scrolled through his text messages and found what he had been looking for. The location of the car he had parked. The airport was southwest but the perfect distance from Natalie's. Bird didn't want to head into the traffic going I-90 W into the rush hour traffic but he needed to get out of city limits before Blake put out and APB and dragnet to catch him. The freeway going west was particularly more backed up than usually prompting Bird to turn the radio on for the traffic report. They described a high speed chase and accident involving an Audi. The passenger had been ejected after a collision at Dead Man's Curve and taken into custody by the authorities. Somehow the driver managed to escape in the damaged vehicle. Bird was certain that they were talking about Sheena and Tuffy. In his undying spite, he would place everything on Bird if questioned. He'd even go as far as to manufacturing a story to whatever Blake's heart desired if need be.

With that in mind Bird chose to take the long way around to the airport Park 'N' Ride, hoping to avoid the swell of law enforcement that was likely policing the area. Abiding by the traffic laws, he made it without incident and quickly found the car in the sea of vehicles. He opened the fuel door, removed the spare key he had stashed in it and opened the trunk. Seeing all the lost funds recovered was a liberating sight. He transferred the duffle bags from the trunk into his as a curious security guard looked on. But before the rent-a-cop could react Bird was in the wind headed to Natalie's.

He had never showed up unannounced to Natalie's but the circumstances warranted it. After driving thirty minutes he was pulling into the driveway of her home. She heard the car pulling into her drive and came running out. She couldn't believe it was Bird in front of her in tattered bloodstained clothes. Natalie begged Bird to come inside so she could treat his wounds properly but conscience his time was limited he declined. After a little prodding he agreed and she sat him in a chair in her kitchen to give it a look.

From what she could tell nothing was broken and that the bullet had gone through clean, as she sanitized the area and bandaged it up. Her advice was still to get medical attention for a round of antibiotics to stave off infection. Bird watched her every move as she cared for him. Everything that mattered to him most was lost. Except for her. But that still could change with Carlos and his Uncle likely to seek retribution. With everything in a tail spin the words of Lynx and Sauce reverberated in his mind, "You gotta go!"

Bird lifted Natalie's face up by the chin. Tears were already filling her eyes in anticipation of the moment he would tell her goodbye.

"I gotta go Nat." he said softly.

"But . . . you need to get a shower and clean up . . ." She replied in hopes for just a few more moments together.

Bird stared in her face as the tears began to stream. If he could stay he would have but there was no way things would turn out right if he did. He still owed everyone and didn't have enough money or drugs to fulfill his obligations. With Blake still coming full throttle he couldn't hustle what he had and wasn't in financial condition to fend off the ensuing legal battle with the FED's. And with Diego unpaid everyone was still in danger as long as he was around. As they spoke the authorities were likely circulating a warrant for his arrest in the crimes. Bird knew his window of escape was closing faster each second he wasted.

Bird kissed Natalie one last time and thanked her for being there. Without explaining himself any further she knew what his decision was. She helped him up from his seat and out to the car, hugging him tightly before he got inside. She turned to walk away, not wanting to say goodbye or see him leave. Bird stumbled out of the car and called her back. He opened the backseat and tossed the duffle bags in her driveway.

"Take this." he said giving her all of the money. "Half a millions for you . . . the money you gave me. Give Penelope a half and the rest to Carlos, that should keep them off you. I'll work the rest out. I just need time."

"How are you going to survive?" she asked.

"I'll be okay." he responded. "Just check your emails. I'm done with these phones til' I get settled somewhere. I'll be back though."

Natalie nodded and watched as the car pulled from her drive. Bird watched her back through the rear view mirror. He didn't know if he'd ever be able to come back, but couldn't leave without offering some sense of hope. He didn't know exactly where he was heading, but since he was so far west already he figured he'd continue that way until a location found him. One thing was certain, and that's the fact that he would make the most of his cargo where ever he landed. Hustling is all that he knew. Whether legit or illegal he treated them both the same, applying the same passion.

You get to learn a lot about a person on lengthy car trips and this one was no different. After five hours of continuous driving, Bird learned more about himself. The replay of his life and the events of the last two days settled on his mind. He took an inventory of his past transgressions and mistakes, wondering if he'd done too much for God to even forgive him. He pulled the picture of Jace's first Christmas from his pocket and traced his face with his weary eyes. It was the catalyst that finally toppled the barriers that held his emotions hostage for so long. For the first time since he could remember tears flowed from his eyes and continued for forty-five minutes.

As they dried he craved nothing more than to see a familiar face or a friendly smile. Just then he happened to look around and notice a stretch of highway he'd been on before. Bird exited and took the scenic route through the city. "For as much as things had changed they were still the same." he thought to himself as he rode up Madison Avenue past the United Center. The change of atmosphere gave his fatigued frame just enough energy to make it to his destination. He pulled into the alley behind the Westside building and drug himself through the gangway to the door, knocking several times. A minute past and he gave the door several more raps before it flung open. On the other side of it was a look of shock.

"I know I shoulda called Ben . . . but . . ." Bird said before he got cut off.

"Nigga we family!" Benji said as he rushed to catch Bird with his good arm before he collapsed from exhaustion. "Laura called me and told me what was goin' on."

He pulled Bird inside and sat him on the couch. The look of shock had protracted into a concerned smile. "Don't worry B. You're at home here."

"I know Ben." Bird said as he stretched out with his eyes closed. "But I gotta get right and straighten shit out. I gotta go back."

"No doubt. But that shit you left is gon' be there whenever you do. Real hustlers always bounce back." Benji reassured. "I'ma make sure of it! Just take your time. First you gotta get healthy though."

His words were the much need vote of confidence Bird needed as he slowly succumb to his fatigue. His body settled, preparing for the dreaded blankness that would surely come when his eyes closed.

"A hustler always bounces back." he sleepily repeated as he dozed off. "I'll be back . . . I can't leave it like this."

Acknowledgements

First, I have to thank GOD for giving me the ability to undergo a project like this, and the patience to actually complete it. I have to admit it was one of the most time and energy consuming things I've ever done—but also one of the most gratifying.

To my wife; thank you for having the patience to deal with a person that's as layered and complex as me. For the late nights up with me, and the early mornings with the kids, my thanks alone could never suffice. I love you.

To my Princess's; your successes in life are my supreme reason for being. My love for you both is my driving force, and I'm more than thankful for being your Dad. In return hope that I'll be able to instill the many underlying contexts of this into you both—aiding you both in the lessons of life.

Special thanks to my family (my parents, grandmother, mother-in-law, aunt's, cousin's and siblings) and loved ones for continuous support. Much love to those friends who believed and encourage me to keep driving forward. Thank you to my editor, Rod Hinson of HHB, for thoroughly sifting through my project. My sincerest, most heartfelt thanks to those who never believed—without the fuel from you all I don't know if it would have been possible.

Last but certainly not least, thanks to Clarence "Bird" Carter, for teaching me how to see things as clearly as possible, and to follow my own direction no matter what—a lesson still serving me well to this day. This one's for you!